THE UNDEAD

James Dickie is Lecturer in Islamic Studies at Lancaster University. A graduate in Arabic of Glasgow and Barcelona Universities, he took his doctorate in Arabic Literature at Granada in 1967, whereafter he has worked in several British universities, contributing irregularly to the 'learned' journals in the field of his speciality. Although the author of two books on the poetry of the Arabs in Spain, he dislikes all narrowly based academic specialists and prefers to be known as a dilettante after the eighteenth century manner rather than as a scholar.

Who's Who lists his recreations as 'flagellation and ecclesiology', and such time as the pleasures of the rod and the study of church furniture leave over in the academic vacations he uses for travelling the Middle East in pursuit of mosques and excitement in an area prolific of both. A bachelor temperamentally averse to any ties, he travels widely in Asia and Africa. This leaves him free to espouse the cause of the Radical Right and other attitudes untypical of the academic moron.

THE UNDEAD

Edited by JAMES DICKIE

In tombs of gold and lapis lazuli
Bodies of holy men and women exude
Miraculous oil, odour of violet.

But under heavy loads of trampled clay
Lie bodies of vampires full of blood;
Their shrouds are bloody and their lips are wet.

– Yeats

UNABRIDGED

PAN BOOKS LTD : LONDON

First published in Great Britain 1971 by
Neville Spearman Ltd
This edition published 1973 by Pan Books Ltd,
33 Tothill Street, London SW1

ISBN 0 330 23797 7

Printed and bound in England by
Hazell Watson & Viney Ltd
Aylesbury, Bucks

CONTENTS

ACKNOWLEDGEMENTS

Acknowledgements are made to the following for permission to reprint:

The Undead from *The Beautiful Changes*. Richard Wilbur. 1954. Faber and Faber Ltd.

The Tomb of Sarah from the *Pall Mall Magazine*. F. G. Loring. 1900

Dracula's Guest from *Dracula's Guest and Other Weird Stories*. Bram Stoker. 1914. Routledge.

For the Blood is the Life from *Uncanny Tales*. F. Marion Crawford. 1911. Unwin.

The Old Man's Story from *Raggle Taggle*. Walter Starkie. 1933. John Murray.

The Room in the Tower from *The Room in the Tower and Other Stories*. E. F. Benson. 1912. Mills and Boon.

The End of the Story and *The Death of Ilalotha* from *Weird Tales*. Clark Ashton Smith. 1930, 1937. Popular Fiction Publishing Co.

The Canal from *Weird Tales*. Everil Worrell. 1927. Popular Fiction Publishing Co.

Revelations in Black from *Weird Tales*. Carl Jacobi. 1933. Popular Fiction Publishing Co.

The Hound from *Weird Tales*. H. P. Lovecraft. 1924. Popular Fiction Publishing Co.

The Death of Halpin Frayser from *Can Such Things Be?* Ambrose Bierce. 1893. Cape.

When it was Moonlight from *Unknown Worlds*. Manly Wade Wellman. 1940. Wellman.

The True Story of a Vampire from *Studies of Death*. Eric, Count Stenbock. 1894. David Nutt.

The editor also wishes to record his gratitude to Mr Ian Miller, Dr Peter Moore, Miss Sheena MacQueen, Mr Lawrence Blair, Mrs Sally Sharpe, Mrs Mary Williams, Mrs Helen Parkin, Mr Jeffrey Somers and Mr Anthony Carreras who have all contributed with their time or advice to the present volume.

THE UNDEAD
by
Richard Wilbur

Even as children they were late sleepers,
Preferring their dreams, even when quick with monsters,
    To the world with all its breakable toys,
        Its compacts with the dying;

From the stretched arms of withered trees
They turned, fearing contagion of the mortal,
    And even under the plums of summer
        Drifted like winter moons.

Secret, unfriendly, pale, possessed
Of the one wish, the thirst for mere survival,
    They came, as all extremists do
        In time, to a sort of grandeur:

Now, to their Balkan battlements
Above the vulgar town of their first lives,
    They rise at the moon's rising. Strange
        That their utter self-concern

Should, in the end, have left them selfless:
Mirrors fail to perceive them as they float
    Through the great hall and up the staircase:
        Nor are the cobwebs broken.

Into the pallid night emerging,
Wrapped in their flapping capes, routinely maddened
    By a wolf's cry, they stand for a moment
        Stoking the mind's eye

With lewd thoughts of the pressed flowers
And bric-a-brac of rooms with something to lose, –
    Of love-dismembered dolls, and children
       Buried in quilted sleep.

Then they are off in a negative frenzy,
Their black shapes cropped into sudden bats
    That swarm, burst, and are gone. Thinking
       Of a thrush cold in the leaves

Who has sung his few summers truly,
Or an old scholar resting his eyes at last,
    We cannot be much impressed with vampires,
       Colourful though they are:

Nevertheless, their pain is real,
And requires our pity. Think how sad it must be
    To thirst always for a scorned elixir,
       The salt quotidian blood

Which, if mistrusted, has no savour;
To pray on life forever and not possess it,
    As rock-hollows, tide after tide,
       Glassily strand the sea.

INTRODUCTION

It is not often that the genesis of a literary genre can be dated with any accuracy, but the inception, or rather conception, of two genres on one and the same day must surely be unique in the history of literature. Though the origins of the supernatural thriller are to be sought in the cult of the Gothic novel, two identifiable species of horror fiction, the monster tale and the vampire tale, may be said to owe their conception to the boredom of a June evening on the shores of Lake Geneva. At the Maison Chapuis on the night of June 18th, 1816, Byron was reciprocating one of the visits which the Shelley *ménage* was in the habit of paying him at the Villa Diodati. Several such evenings had already been spent at both places reading aloud German ghost stories in the French; yet this was to be no ordinary evening but one which would witness before its close a quite extraordinary demonstration of Shelley's eccentricity of manner. Instead of reading they turned to recounting experiences of the supernatural, and all went thrillingly until, at one point in his spectral narrative Byron felt impelled to quote from *Christabel*:

> Behold! her bosom and half her side –
> A sight to dream of, not to tell!

Upon nerves so delicately wrought as those of Shelley this sudden evocation of the lamia had a quite predictable impact. He leapt to his feet and, seizing a candlestick, fled from the room. After he had been brought to his senses with cold water and a dose of ether the company prevailed upon him to relate what had happened. It transpired that Coleridge's ghastly image had so affected him that, as he looked at Mary, it seemed that he could see her with eyes in place of the nipples of her breasts: unreasoning terror and panic supervened. Clearly, a paroxysm of fear on a scale like this demanded expression in literary form, and before the company broke up it was agreed that all present should try their hands at a tale of horror. But fate had settled that it was to be the day of the minor writers. The Muses yielded neither to the importunities of Byron nor of Shelley, who both gave up after several false starts, but chose to lavish their favours upon Shelley's mistress, Mary, and Byron's physician, Polidori (whose sister was to be the mother of Dante Gabriel and Christina Rossetti).

Such were the origins of *Frankenstein* (1818), which has withstood the acid test of time and survived all Hollywood's efforts to discredit it, and of *The Vampyre* (1819) which failed the test but established the genre. A perusal of *The Vampyre*, with its sad prolixity and ill-constructed plot, creaking piteously at every badly oiled hinge, suffices to dispel any doubts the reader may have entertained as to the wisdom of Polidori's decision to commit suicide. This he brought off, with the aid of poison, several years afterward, exasperated at not having attained literary fame. But the tale, attributed first to Byron, to whom indeed is due the credit for the idea, and with its central character, Lord Ruthven, evidently drawn from life (the poet himself), achieved a notoriety in excess of its merits.

The late entry of the vampire theme into the Gothic cult, whose high noon was already past, may account for its surviving the eclipse of the Gothic novel. Certainly, the theme now lay to hand, awaiting the notice of the French romantics; and the vampire, later to be typed in the person of Count Dracula, lent itself *par excellence* to romantic treatment. According to the sex of the vampire it could feature either the Byronic hero – aloof, aristocratic, disdainful and misanthropic – or the *femme fatale*. Both were stock types and were to compete with each other for domination of the romantic scene, victory falling in the end to the *femme fatale*, in the slowly expiring, messily deliquescent romanticism of the *fin de siècle*; when woman stood revealed as an emotional vampire feasting on men's admiration and finally destroying them with sadistic relish. The vampiress never came to haunt the imagination of the Decadence with the same terrible intensity as the figure of Salome, but to a mind so diseased as Baudelaire's her appeal could not but be fatal. The sensation of being sucked opened up fresh vistas of perversity, and in *Les Métamorphoses du Vampire* the poet pictures himself in ecstasy under her teeth. If Polidori's inept narrative sought to portray the Byronic hero at his most sinisterly irresistible, Gautier's beautiful and poetic *La Morte Amoureuse* (1836) so exploited the potential of the *femme fatale* that we are left wondering how any subsequent writer ever had the temerity to attempt the same approach. In its parallelisms between dreaming and waking states of consciousness the work has an involuted, convoluted structure that anticipates the even more daring structural technique that Flaubert intended to apply in *La Spirale*, the novel he projected but never finished.

That the approach was similar but not identical may account for the success of what is incomparably the most powerful treatment of the theme in English, Sheridan le Fanu's *Carmilla* (1871). Ignoring the Gothic stage properties – dilapidated castle, ruined church, aristocratic milieu – and by concentrating on essentials, namely the emotional interaction between the two protagonists, a connexion with *Christabel* becomes explicit once the reader recognizes the Lesbian drives which make this particular *femme fatale* fatal not exclusively but preferably to a member of her own sex. The first person narrative allows a degree of psychological morbidity placed beside which the sensational horrors of *Dracula* seem wan and limpid. Few exponents of vampirology have risked committing themselves to a description of what it feels like when one is being vampirized. The sensations, it would seem, are not destitute of pleasure: 'The prevailing one was of that pleasant, peculiar cold thrill which we feel in bathing when we move against the current of a river ... Sometimes it was as if warm lips kissed me, and longer and more lovingly as they reached my throat, but there the caress fixed itself. My heart beat faster, my breathing rose and fell rapidly and full-drawn; a sobbing, that rose into a sense of strangulation, supervened, and turned into a dreadful convulsion in which my senses left me, and I became unconscious.' In Carmilla's courtship of the heroine it is not fanciful to discern the methods of seduction by which Geraldine might, in the end, have won Christabel : 'In the rapture of my enormous humiliation I live in your warm life, and you shall die – die, sweetly die – into mine. I cannot help it; as I draw near to others, and learn the rapture of that cruelty, which yet is love; so, for a while seek to know no more of me and mine, but trust me with all your loving spirit.' The 'sweet dying' was to be, in the heroine's case, a protracted process, proving that the vampiress found sado-masochistic satisfaction in prolonging her own pleasure by refusing to abbreviate the agony of her victim. And the closing phrases of the story hint that the victim reciprocated some of the affection which the vampiress had felt for her. Reluctantly, we have excluded *Carmilla* from this collection to prevent overlapping with Roger Vadim's *The Vampire* (Pan, 1965). The story has inspired several films which, with one exception, stray from the plot. This is Roy Ward Baker's *The Vampire Lovers* (Hammer-AI, 1970) in which the role of Carmilla was brilliantly interpreted by Ingrid Pitt.

After spasms so voluptuous as these it is not a little difficult at first to account for the popularity of *Dracula* (1897). In its sensationalism and maudlin sentiment Bram Stoker's exploration of the myth relates more to the Victorian penny-dreadful *Varney the Vampire* (1847) than to the subtle psychological analyses of the Dublin recluse whose morbid imagination had resurrected Countess Mircalla from her grave in the church at Karnstein. But Stoker was conscious of his indebtedness to more than the travel books on Transylvania he had perused in the British Museum. That the incident was too reminiscent of Carmilla was doubtless the reason for the excision from the final draft of *Dracula* of the chapter which opens the book which the reader has in front of him. Found among Stoker's papers after his death,

Dracula's Guest was published by his widow. This attempt by the author to conceal his debt to le Fanu has had the result of obscuring the deeper level on which *Dracula* sometimes communicates, that of symbols and archetypes. The difficulties in the way of conveying this visually may explain why no film version has ever even remotely succeeded in capturing the horror of the book with all its chillingly effective detail: for, in places, Stoker was writing far more deeply than he knew. The reader or director in pursuit of sensation may be relied upon to miss the point of passages such as that where Harker confides to his journal how three vampiresses came to rape him in his sleep. 'Two were dark ... The other was fair ... I seemed somehow to know her face, and to know it in connection with some dreamy fear, but I could not recollect at the moment how or where.' Indeed it would have been strange if he had! The vampires and not Nina, the insipid little English miss, was the woman of his dreams. She produced a vague sense of familiarity precisely because she corresponded with the archetype within his own subconscious: the woman who initiates man and then destroys. *Dracula's Guest*, the omitted episode, is in no wise inferior to the rest of the novel. A wealth of atmospheric detail (for instance, cypress and yew – both death symbols) brilliantly anticipates the castle perched atop a precipice in the Carpathians where Harker's fate awaits him. But in spite of literary feats on this scale the subject was far from exhausted. Montague Summers's researches were to establish how the undead behave in fact as distinct from fiction; and the vampire tale is at its most effective when it draws on the established lore of the vampire tradition and eschews the fashionable habiliments of space-fiction, psychoanalysis (the 'psychic sponge') or modern medicine (blood transfusions). The sheer hideousness of the subject, so evident from the revolting instances laboriously catalogued by Summers in *The Vampire in Europe*, is not amenable to facetious treatment any more than it lends itself to the mock seriousness of imaginary biology in descriptions of vampiric organisms.

It is the conventional approach as exhibited in an acquaintance with ecclesiology so accurate as to invite comparison with the exquisite pedantry of M. R. James, incongruously linked to the sailor's gift for telling a yarn, which won Commander Loring's *The Tomb of Sarah* (1900) a place in this anthology alongside better known practitioners of the macabre like E. F. Benson. The latter author's *Room in the Tower* (1912) stands out from among his three or four other incursions into the realm of the vampire by virtue of its clever use of psychic phenomenon like apports – blood on the hands, the movements of the sinister portrait – and the predictive dream. *For the Blood is the Life* (1911) returns to the lyrical mood of Gautier but manages to petrify the reader with its extraordinary image of an elastic vampire.

A wider range of cultural reference is found in some of the stories. In H. P. Lovecraft's miniature masterpiece (1924) the hero is a *calque* of Des Esseintes, and, were it not for a certain hint of parody, the narrative would not be unworthy of Huysmans's pen. Two morbid conditions, thanatophilia and haematophilia, are shown in conflict. The haematophilia of the vampire who seeks to live again through the agency of blood enables the two heroes to realize their subconscious desire to die themselves, which till the vampire's advent had sought vicarious expression in grave robbing. Though unfashionable at the moment, thanatophilia in other centuries was reckoned nothing strange. Charles V, we may be sure, felt no embarrassment at rehearsing his own funeral at Yuste. And the famous cardinal, Erard de la Mark, bishop of Liège in the sixteenth century, was so impatient for his demise that he regularly rehearsed his own obsequies, following the empty coffin to the tomb he had erected for himself in the cathedral. Louis XV too had tastes not dissimilar. Bierce, the other Transatlantic misanthrope to be featured in the present collection, gives the Oedipus complex a new twist in *The Death of Halpin Frayser* (1893); and we are left wondering whether the dead woman mistook the identity of her visitor, vampirizing her own son instead of her murderer, or whether some oedipal magnetism brought about the encounter.

Jacobi's *Revelations in Black* (1933) is a clever, suspenseful story, which skilfully effects a transference of vampiric activity from its centre of power in the Old World to the New. The failure of the vampiress to show up on a photographic plate makes sense in terms of the mirror legend. Without becoming expatriates like Henry James or Eliot, writers such as Lovecraft and Clark Ashton Smith so contrived to ignore the vulgarity of their environment that in the isolation of the study they recaptured in their style the elegance of another age. Lovecraft's prose, admittedly, is redolent of excessive use of the midnight oil, and the reek of the charred wick is never far from any one paragraph; but Smith's style, though not free of affectation, has a lyrical fervour, than which no medium could be more apt for the depiction of the haunted glades of the Forest of Averoigne. Inspired by Philostratus's life of Apollonius by way of Burton (*The Anatomy of Melancholy*) and Keats (*Lamia*), Smith's *The End of the Story* (1930) is nothing less than the quintessence of the Gothick. Hellenism, the Middle Ages and the eighteenth century achieve symbiosis through the alchemy of Smith's prose, and in so enchanted an atmosphere the echoes of Gérard de Nerval find an added resonance. The window opening on the past in *The End of the Story*, gives way in *The Death of Ilalotha* (1937) to direct portrayal of classical conditions. Smith's verbal craftsmanship is seen here at its best; a phrase like, 'Hovering from tree to tree, the moon accompanied her like a worm-hollowed visage' makes it clear that what we are reading is nothing less than a prose poem. For sheer saturated horror the climax of *Ilalotha* would be difficult to surpass.

Everil Worrell's story operates on a different level altogether. Set like Jacobi's *Revelations* in the midst of the industrial squalors of the New World, *The Canal* (1927) had perforce to dispense with many of the conventions of the genre. The indecisive ending which leaves the reader in doubt as to the outcome seems to look forward to contemporary drama, where a continuation of the action is implied, beyond the moment of its visible termination on the stage.

Vampire and lamia shade off into one another, and the stories selected illustrate by their diversity how varied are the species and sub-genera of the *genus vampiricus*. In the case of *When it was Moonlight* (1940) the species particularized, a vampire afraid of the dark, is wholly imaginary. Contrasted with the visibly putrescent writing of Clark Ashton Smith is the controlled understatement of Wellman, which yet achieves a comparable degree of horror in ultimate effect. Particularly ingenious is the author's idea of casting the story in the form of a fictitious episode in the life of Poe.

The Old Man's Story (1933) is the title given to the tale which ends this collection, and with it our book returns to the point from which it set out, for Starkie's story purports to be not fiction but fact. The obvious embellishments detract from such evidential value as the narrative might have rejoiced in had it not been so unfortunate as to find for narrator one of the twentieth century's most incorrigible romantics. One quality which the folklorist's vampire shares with the novelist's is the dramatic; and so imbued with drama is this story that, in it, the two are for once reconciled.

The True Story of a Vampire (1894) achieves its effect by the unaffected simplicity of the pathos with which it is told. Its author, Count Stenbock, an eccentric homosexual, typifies the nineties in a way that writers like Yeats, who outgrew the period, cannot. The story is from his *Studies of Death* than which no more appropriate title could be imagined for a book by an author who was wont to dine seated in his own coffin with his familiar in the shape of a toad squatting on his shoulder.

As in *Carmilla* Styria provides the *mise en scène* for Count Stenbock's story, and this question of vampire geography raises the cognate issue of the source of inspiration of these tales. An uncommon number of them have for setting Transylvania, Styria or Moldavia, and the former provinces of the Habsburg Empire furnish the most part of what is known about the habits as well as the habitat of the vampire. Harker's journal records that he had 'read that every known superstition in the world is gathered into the horseshoe of the Carpathians, as it were the centre of some sort of imaginative whirlpool . . .' Although the locale of the vampire's operation is by no means confined to Europe, Roger Vadim may be correct in thinking that the vampire legend in the Balkans springs from half-submerged memories of the subjugation of the region by some conquering race – an interesting point because the fictional vampire frequently rejoices in the fact of gentle birth – having their origins in some esoteric community in Palestine who had preserved amongst themselves for the secret of Jesus's resurrection. The former group nourishing themselves on the blood of their subjects: the latter employing blood in their secret rituals. Certainly, in both the Jewish and Moslem faiths blood has paramount importance as the vehicle of life and is in consequence taboo.

None the less, it seems more likely that the vampire of fiction is indebted for his aristocratic traits to that stock figure of Continental pornography, the depraved English nobleman, and owes little or nothing to the grim reality of the peasant *vampyr* or *vrykolokas*. Even in Hungary or Slovakia at the height of the epidemic of vampirism in the eighteenth century proven vampires like Peter Ploglojowitz and Arnot Paole were men of humble origin, remote indeed from the conventional image of a sinister count keeping solitary state amidst the cobwebbed splendours of the condal castle. Most mysterious and intriguing of all occult phenomena, the vampire, whatever his social status in life, becomes in death the expression of sadistic erotomania at its intensest. He is the hyphen between life and death; through his agency death poaches on the reproductive function peculiar to the living. All the evidence amassed to prove the existence of the vampire contributes not an iota to his understanding, for in spite of all efforts he remains an undecipherable hieroglyphic in the language of the Unseen.

The eighteenth century, so ineptly styled the Age of Reason, might more fitly have been termed the Age of Unreason, since few recorded centuries bear more marks of obsession with the supernatural and the rationally inexplicable. Neither the spiritualist cult of the nineteenth nor the witchcraft of the seventeenth enables these centuries to compete in morbidity with the multifaceted brilliance of the eighteenth; the age of Cagliostro and the Hell-Fire Clubs, it was pre-eminently the era of charlatanry, mesmerism, satanism, black magic and sexual deviancy. On no subsequent occasion in fact have the British ever been able to devise a national export that could vie with *la vice anglaise* in popularity. The misconstruction placed upon this period by literary and social historians incontinently conforming with one another's presuppositions entails a surprise in store for the newcomer to the subject, who is never less than astonished when he learns that not the 'monkish darkness' of the Middle Ages but the late seventeenth and early eighteenth century witnessed the peak of vampiric activity in Europe.

The ancillary phenomenon of manducation in the grave associated, inexplicably, with plague outbreaks belongs rather to the mid seventeenth century and seems, in retrospect, to have been preparing the way for the more terrible epidemics that were to follow.

This relative proximity to our own times yields several advantages to the occult researcher not the least of which is ease of access to important documents. Several instances of vampirism were well attested, sometimes even by Imperial commissions from Belgrade sent to investigate the matter. Thus the data are recorded reasonably free from legendary admixture, and we are acquainted not in outline but in detail with all the symptoms of vampiric infestation. Prominent among them is the condition of the grave. More, the Cambridge Platonist, reports the state of affairs obtaining in the case of Johannes Cuntius (the Silesian vampire), who had been buried at the Epistle side of the high altar of the church at Pentsch: 'His gravestone was turned of one side, shelving, and there were several holes in the earth, about the bigness of mouseholes, that went down to his very

Coffin, which however they were filled up with earth over night, yet they would be sure to be laid open the next morning.' Normally the uneven lay of the slab would be accounted for by natural subsidence, but how explain the holes? A vampire's grave commonly exhibits four or five holes as though the soil had been pierced with a pencil or the finger, and it is not rash to conjecture that these are the channels by which the grave's contents issue forth ectoplasmically upon the upper world. Of the various hypotheses advanced to explain how the undead maintain their amphibious existence the closest to the truth would appear to be that dematerialization takes place inside the grave to be followed by rematerialization outside. Quite evidently some sort of 'double' must be built up by the ectoplasmic leakage. This double then proceeds to attack the living, its presence being announced by certain 'signals' which accompany the manifestation of a vampire. His element is mist, but unnaturally suspended dust can also be an indication of his impending appearance, for among the vampire's other endearing traits is the ability to metamorphose into any one of a variety of shapes at will. Associated phenomena are the presence, seen or heard, of bats and wolves.

The most effective prophylactic is garlic, although in its absence dog roses may be resorted to as an alternative. If no prophylactic be present to hinder his advance the vampire, like the serpent, paralyses the victim with his glance, which operates as though it were a narcotic or anaesthetic. Without wasting time on preliminaries the vampire makes straight for his objective, namely the jugular vein, and fastening on it, draws forth the blood from the body with hideous great gusts. By the time he is sated his chosen victim is so drained of blood as to be as pale as asparagus; alternatively, the vampire may stop short of satiety and return to assuage his thirst more than once at the same source. The languor and emaciation induced by repeated attacks beggar all description. Unless fortunate enough to be protected in some such manner as indicated the object of the vampire's attentions is sure to perish of anaemia, because no mortal force can resist the supernatural suction his attacker commands. Add to which the inoculation of the subject with the vampire virus, which ends in his joining the legions of the undead. No other virus can approach this one in virulence, by virtue of whose mere infection the soul is placed in jeopardy. The immobilization of the subject is a phenomenon frequent in the annals of psychic research, as the dead often succeed in manifesting precisely by harnessing the energy of the living. This is the reason why someone who has seen a ghost may be heard to remark: 'I went cold all over and couldn't stir a limb, because all the energy seemed to drain out of me.'

Such a repast leaves the vampire satiated for a while, and the body, when exhumed by day, is found to be, in virtue of the night's excesses, extraordinarily florid and even tumescent. More's description of the disinterment of the Pentsch vampire referred to illustrates the point to perfection: 'To be short therefore, finding no rest nor being able to excogitate any better remedy, they dig up *Cuntius* his body ... His skin was tender and florid, his Joynts not at all stiff but limber and movable ... His eyes also of themselves would be one time open, and another time shut; they opened a vein in his leg, and the blood sprang out as fresh as in the living ...' But no single instance excels Summers's graphic account of the appearance the body exhibits on exhumation: 'Sometimes the eyes are closed; more frequently open, glazed, fixed and glaring fiercely. The lips which will be markedly full and red are drawn back from the teeth which gleam long, sharp as razors and ivory white. Often the gaping mouth is stained and foul with great slab gouts of blood, which trickles down from the corners on to the lawn shroudings and linen cerements, the offal of the last night's feast. In the case of an epidemic of vampirism it is recorded that whole graves have been discovered soaked and saturated with squelching blood, which the horrid inhabitant has gorged until he is replete and vomited forth in great quantities like some swollen leech discharges when thrown into brine.' Disposal of the vampire is effected by transfixing the heart with a hawthorn stake, although whitethorn may also be used. Decapitation is recommended as an additional precaution.

Only symptoms such as those which the Rev Montague Summers describes with ill-concealed relish qualify for identification of the grave as that of a vampire. Miraculous preservation which has resulted in many an innocuous body receiving, in Greece, the treatment normally reserved for the undead elsewhere, is altogether insufficient to serve as decisive evidence. Indeed the all too frequent profanation of innocent graves in that country illustrates the contrasting attitudes of the Latin and Greek churches towards incorruption. Failure to decompose to the Catholic (or to the Moslem) is, under circumstances where the opposite may have been expected, evidence (but not proof) of sanctity. In the Orthodox Church exactly the reverse applies: absence of decomposition is thought to be a consequence of excommunication. The ignorance and superstitition of the Greek peasantry must be held responsible for the hyperbolic exaggeration of vampiric activity in south-east Europe.

Although probably no country in the world is wholly devoid of vampirism in one form or another it seems most characteristic of the Balkans; and in this country instances of its occurrence are very rare. Recently the best-known case on record, that of the Croglin Grange (properly Croglin Low Hall) vampire, has been scientifically examined by Clive-Ross in *Tomorrow* (Spring 1963), where the evidence given to him as later to the present writer by Mrs Helen Parkin (of Slack Cottage, Ainstable) points toward a date full two centuries earlier than that implied by Augustus Hare, who was the first to commit the Croglin case to writing, in his *Story of my Life*.

Just prior to the time of writing a perfectly normal case of haunting in Highgate gave rise to rumours of vampirism. A correspondent, Mr David Farrant, in the columns of the *Hampstead and Highgate Express*, reported having sighted a grey spectre moving about behind the cemetery gates at the head of Swains Lane. The vampire, if such it were, was in good company, for, but a few yards from this spot, in St Michael's church, the author of *Christabel* reposes beneath a slate slab. Vampirism was not to begin with suspected, however; not, in fact, until after a number of letters from other witnesses had been received. Mr Sean Manchester (of the British Occult Society) on 27 February 1970, advanced the claim that 'the King Vampire of the Undead', originally a Wallachian nobleman of the Middle Ages who dabbled in black magic, was abroad, 'His followers eventually brought him to England in a coffin at the beginning of the eighteenth century and bought a house for him in the West End. His unholy resting-place became Highgate cemetery.

'When parts of Britain were plagued by vampirism centuries ago, the Highgate area was the centre of a lot of activity. It has been ever since.

'And now that there is so much desecration of graves by satanism, I'm convinced that this has been happening in Highgate cemetery in an attempt by a body of satanists to resurrect the King Vampire.'

This would appear pure conjecture without other support than the unexplained death of several foxes in the cemetery, whose bodies nevertheless bore no evidence of having suffered attack by one of the undead; and on March 20th a member of an amateur ciné group disclosed that five weeks previously Highgate cemetery had been used by them as a stage-setting for a vampire film. The publicity given by the Press and television to the possibility of a vampire in an area so rich in Bram Stoker associations made it inevitable that the police should be called in to control the crowd, totalling over a hundred, who scaled the walls and rattled the gates, clamouring to be vouchsafed a glimpse of the vampire. But only disappointment was in store for voluntary victims. No ghost, much less a vampire, chose to manifest. It would stand to reason that Highgate, like any other graveyard, has its fair share of apparitions, but that is no warrant for leaping to conclusions about vampires, although subsequent discovery (1st August) of the corpse of a woman, buried in 1926, with the head missing and the shroud charred certainly reeks of vampirism. Notwithstanding, it would be safer to conclude that a corpse had been laid under contribution for the purpose of some satanic rite.

Of far greater interest, almost unknown and previously unpublished, is a report of vampirism in Yorkshire. If authentic, this is the only surviving vampire grave in Britain. The vampire was male, and his staking affords a most striking instance of the use of sympathetic magic. He was staked down with a metal spike driven through memorial stone and coffin, whilst inside, on the chancel steps of the church, a ceremony was performed in which an animal (said to be a lizard but almost certainly a bat) was transfixed through the heart with a pin. The villagers therefore took the added precaution of laying the vampire by means of sympathetic magic, presumably because they were too frightened to raise the coffin and stake down the subject properly and so resorted to the expedient of simultaneously transfixing a bat. The village of Dent is one of the most picturesque in the West Riding and richer in folklore than most. On the gravestone the following inscription is perfectly legible: 'Here lyes the body of George Hodgson who depart[ed] this life June ye 4th 1715 aged 94.' The stone cracked across about half a century ago, and what most surprises is the legibility of the letters given that George Hodgson died 250 years ago. Our informant, Mrs Mary Williams, assures us that the stone is not in its original position, having been moved from the north-east corner of the south porch to a position outside where it serves now as one of the three flagstones forming the approach to the porch. This could account for the well-preserved quality of the characters as also for the stone's odd orientation at right angles to the church. Axial burial in Christianity requires that the feet point east in the case of a layman and here, if the stone indicate the attitude of the body, they point south. Archaeologically, the evidence for the staking is insignificant: immediately below the inscription there is a small rectangular matrix such as would have held a latten plate, a not uncommon feature. In the middle of this rectangle is a hole filled with metal, which would appear to be no more than the lead plug by which the brass was secured to the stone. Or is this the top of the metal stake? This simple plug, observable in hundreds of cathedrals and churches wherever matrices survive, may have formed a nucleus around which tales of vampirism clustered. Only exhumation can show, and over this as over the Croglin case hangs a question mark. Were there ever vampires in Britain?

DRACULA'S GUEST

by

Bram Stoker

When we started for our drive the sun was shining brightly on Munich, and the air was full of the joyousness of early summer. Just as we were about to depart, Herr Delbrück (the maître d'hôtel of the Quatre Saisons,* where I was staying) came down, bareheaded, to the carriage and, after wishing me a pleasant drive, said to the coachman, still holding his hand on the handle of the carriage door:

'Remember you are back by nightfall. The sky looks bright but there is a shiver in the north wind that says there may be a sudden storm. But I am sure you will not be late.' Here he smiled, and added, 'for you know what night it is.'

Johann answered with an emphatic, 'ja, mein Herr,' and, touching his hat, drove off quickly. When we had cleared the town, I said, after signalling to him to stop:

'Tell me, Johann, what is tonight?'

He crossed himself, as he answered laconically:

'Walpurgis Nacht.' Then he took out his watch, a great, old-fashioned German silver thing as big as a turnip, and looked at it, with his eyebrows gathered together and a little impatient shrug of his shoulders. I realized that this was his way of respectfully protesting against this unnecessary delay, and sank back into the carriage, merely motioning him to proceed. He started off rapidly, as if to make up for lost time. Every now and then the horses seemed to throw up their heads and sniff the air suspiciously. On such occasions I often looked round in alarm. The road was pretty bleak, for we were traversing a sort of high, wind-swept plateau. As we drove, I saw a road that looked but little used, and which seemed to dip through a little, winding valley. It looked so inviting that, even at the risk of offending him, I called Johann to stop – and when he had pulled up, I told him I would like to drive down that road. He made all sorts of excuses, and frequently crossed himself as he spoke. This somewhat piqued my curiosity, so I asked him various questions. He answered fencingly, and repeatedly looked at his watch in protest. Finally I said :

'Well, Johann, I want to go down this road. I shall not ask you to come unless you like; but tell me why you do not like to go, that is all I ask.' For answer he seemed to throw himself off the box, so quickly did he reach the ground. Then he stretched out his hands appealingly to me, and implored me not to go. There was just enough of English mixed with the German for me to understand the drift of his talk. He seemed always just about to tell me something – the very idea of which evidently frightened him – but each time he pulled himself up, saying, as he crossed himself :

'Walpurgis Nacht!'

I tried to argue with him, but it was difficult to argue with a man when I did not know his language. The advantage certainly rested with him, for although he began to speak in English, of a very crude and broken kind, he always got excited and broke into his native tongue – and every time he did so, he looked at his watch. Then the horses became restless and sniffed the air. At this he grew very pale, and, looking around in a frightened way, he suddenly jumped forward, took them by the bridles and led them on some twenty feet. I followed, and asked why he had done this. For answer he crossed himself, pointed to the spot we had left and drew his carriage in the direction of the other road, indicating a cross, and said, first in German, then in English : 'Buried him – him what killed themselves.'

I remembered the old custom of burying suicides at crossroads : 'Ah! I see, a suicide. How interesting!' But for the life of me I could not make out why the horses were frightened.

Whilst we were talking, we heard a sort of sound between

a yelp and a bark. It was far away; but the horses got very
restless, and it took Johann all his time to quiet them. He
was pale, and said: 'It sounds like a wolf – but yet there are
no wolves here now.'

'No?' I said, questioning him; 'isn't it long since the
wolves were so near the city?'

'Long, long,' he answered, 'in the spring and summer;
but with the snow the wolves have been here not so long.'

Whilst he was petting the horses and trying to quiet them,
dark clouds drifted rapidly across the sky. The sunshine
passed away, and a breath of cold wind seemed to drift past
us. It was only a breath, however, and more in the nature
of a warning than a fact, for the sun came out brightly
again. Johann looked under his lifted hand at the horizon
and said:

'The storm of snow, he comes before long time.'

Then he looked at his watch again, and, straightaway holding his reins firmly – for the horses were still pawing the
ground restlessly and shaking their heads – he climbed to his
box as though the time had come for proceeding on our
journey.

I felt a little obstinate and did not at once get into the
carriage.

'Tell me,' I said, 'about this place where the road leads,'
and I pointed down.

Again he crossed himself and mumbled a prayer, before
he answered: 'It is unholy.'

'What is unholy?' I inquired.

'The village.'

'Then there is a village.'

'No, no. No one lives there hundreds of years.'

My curiosity was piqued: 'But you said there was a village.'

'There was.'

'Where is it now?'

Whereupon he burst out into a long story in German and
English, so mixed up that I could not quite understand
exactly what he said, but roughly I gathered that long ago,

hundreds of years, men had died there and been buried in
their graves; and sounds were heard under the clay, and
when the graves were opened, men and women were found
rosy with life, and their mouths red with blood. And so, in
haste to save their lives (aye, and their souls! – and here he
crossed himself) those who were left fled away to other
places, where the living lived, and the dead were dead and
not – not something. He was evidently afraid to speak the
last words. As he proceeded with his narration, he grew
more and more excited. It seemed as if his imagination had
got hold of him, and he ended in a perfect paroxysm of
fear – white-faced, perspiring, trembling and looking round
him, as if expecting that some dreadful presence would
manifest itself there in the bright sunshine on the open plain.
Finally, in an agony of desperation, he cried:

'Walpurgis Nacht!' and pointed to the carriage for me to
get in. All my English blood rose at this, and, standing back,
I said:

'You are afraid, Johann – you are afraid. Go home; I
shall return alone; the walk will do me good.' The carriage
door was open. I took from the seat my oak walking-stick –
which I always carry on my holiday excursions – and closed
the door, pointing back to Munich, and said, 'Go home,
Johann – Walpurgis Nacht doesn't concern Englishmen.'

The horses were now more restive than ever, and Johann
was trying to hold them in, while excitedly imploring me
not to do anything so foolish. I pitied the poor fellow, he
was so deeply in earnest; but all the same I could not help
laughing. His English was quite gone now. In his anxiety he
had forgotten that his only means of making me understand was to talk my language, so he jabbered away in his
native German. It began to be a little tedious. After giving
the direction, 'Home!' I turned to go down the crossroad
into the valley.

With a despairing gesture, Johann turned his horses towards Munich. I leaned on my stick and looked after him.
He went slowly along the road for a while : then there came
over the crest of the hill a man tall and thin. I could see so

much in the distance. When he drew near the horses, they began to jump and kick about, then to scream with terror. Johann could not hold them in; they bolted down the road, running away madly. I watched them out of sight, then looked for the stranger, but I found that he, too, was gone.

With a light heart I turned down the side road through the deepening valley to which Johann had objected. There was not the slightest reason, that I could see, for his objection; and I daresay I tramped for a couple of hours without thinking of time or distance, and certainly without seeing a person or a house. So far as the place was concerned, it was desolation itself. But I did not notice this particularly till, on turning a bend in the road, I came upon a scattered fringe of wood; then I recognized that I had been impressed unconsciously by the desolation of the region through which I had passed.

I sat down to rest myself, and began to look around. It struck me that it was considerably colder than it had been at the commencement of my walk – a sort of sighing sound seemed to be around me, with, now and then, high overhead, a sort of muffled roar. Looking upwards I noticed that great thick clouds were drifting rapidly across the sky from North to South at a great height. There were signs of coming storm in some lofty stratum of air. I was a little chilly, and, thinking that it was the sitting still after the exercise of walking, I resumed my journey.

The ground I passed over was now much more picturesque. There were no striking objects that the eye might single out; but in all there was a charm of beauty. I took little heed of time and it was only when the deepening twilight forced itself upon me that I began to think of how I should find my way home. The brightness of the day had gone. The air was cold, and the drifting of clouds high overhead was more marked. They were accompanied by a sort of far-away rushing sound, through which seemed to come at intervals that mysterious cry which the driver had said came from a wolf. For a while I hesitated. I had said I would see the deserted village, so on I went, and presently came on a wide stretch of open country, shut in by hills all around. Their sides were covered with trees which spread down to the plain, dotting, in clumps, the gentler slopes and hollows which showed here and there. I followed with my eye the winding of the road, and saw that it curved close to one of the densest of these clumps and was lost behind it.

As I looked there came a cold shiver in the air, and the snow began to fall. I thought of the miles and miles of bleak country I had passed, and then hurried on to seek the shelter of the wood in front. Darker and darker grew the sky, and faster and heavier fell the snow, till the earth before and around me was a glistening white carpet the further edge of which was lost in misty vagueness. The road was here but crude, and when on the level its boundaries were not so marked as when it passed through the cuttings, and in a little while I found that I must have strayed from it, for I missed underfoot the hard surface, and my feet sank deeper in the grass and moss. Then the wind grew stronger and blew with ever increasing force, till I was fain to run before it. The air became icy cold, and in spite of my exercise I began to suffer. The snow was now falling so thickly and whirling around me in such rapid eddies that I could hardly keep my eyes open. Every now and then the heavens were torn asunder by vivid lightning, and in the flashes I could see ahead of me a great mass of trees, chiefly yew and cypress and heavily coated with snow.

I was soon amongst the shelter of the trees, and there, in comparative silence, I could hear the rush of the wind high overhead. Presently the blackness of the storm had become merged in the darkness of the night. By-and-by the storm seemed to be passing away: it now only came in fierce puffs or blasts. At such moments the weird sound of the wolf appeared to be echoed by many similar sounds around me.

Now and again, through the black mass of drifting cloud, came a straggling ray of moonlight, which lit up the expanse, and showed me that I was at the edge of a dense mass of cypress and yew trees. As the snow had ceased to fall, I walked out from the shelter and began to investigate more closely. It appeared to me that, amongst so many old foundations as I had passed, there might be still standing a house in which, though in ruins, I could find some sort of shelter for a while. As I skirted the edge of the copse, I found that a low wall encircled it and following this I presently found an opening. Here the cypresses formed an alley leading up to a square mass of some kind of building. Just as I caught sight of this, however, the drifting clouds obscured the moon, and I passed up the path in darkness. The wind must have grown colder, for I felt myself shiver as I walked; but there was hope of shelter, and I groped my way blindly on.

I stopped, for there was a sudden stillness. The storm had passed; and in sympathy with nature's silence, my heart seemed to cease to beat. But this was only momentarily; for suddenly the moonlight broke through the clouds, showing me that I was in a graveyard, and that the square object before me was a great massive tomb of marble, as white as the snow that lay on and all round it. With the moonlight there came a fierce sigh of the storm, which appeared to resume its course with a long, low howl, as of many dogs or wolves. I was awed and shocked, and felt the cold perceptibly grow upon me till it seemed to grip me by the heart. Then while the flood of moonlight still fell on the marble tomb, the storm gave further evidence of renewing, as though it was returning on its track. Impelled by some sort of fascination, I approached the sepulchre to see what it was, and why such a thing stood alone in such a place. I walked around it, and read, over the Doric door, in German –

COUNTESS DOLINGEN OF GRATZ
IN STYRIA
SOUGHT AND FOUND DEATH
1801

On the top of the tomb, seemingly driven through the solid marble – for the structure was composed of a few vast blocks of stone – was a great iron spike or stake. On going to the back I saw, graven in great Russian letters:

'The dead travel fast.'

There was something so weird and uncanny about the whole thing that it gave me a turn and made me feel quite faint. I began to wish, for the first time, that I had taken Johann's advice. Here a thought struck me, which came under almost mysterious circumstances and with a terrible shock. This was Walpurgis Night!

Walpurgis Night, when, according to the belief of millions of people, the devil was abroad – when the graves were opened and the dead came forth and walked. When all evil things of earth and air and water held revel. This very place the driver had specially shunned. This was the depopulated village of centuries ago. This was where the suicide lay; and this was the place where I was alone – unmanned, shivering with cold in a shroud of snow with a wild storm gathering again upon me! It took all my philosophy, all the religion I had been taught, all my courage, not to collapse in a paroxysm of fright.

And now a perfect tornado burst upon me. The ground shook as though thousands of horses thundered across it; and this time the storm bore on its icy wings, not snow, but great hailstones which drove with such violence that they might have come from the thongs of Balearic slingers – hailstones that beat down leaf and branch and made the shelter of the cypresses of no more avail than though their stems were standing corn. At the first I had rushed to the nearest tree; but I was soon fain to leave it and seek the only spot that seemed to afford refuge, the deep Doric doorway of the marble tomb. There, crouching against the massive bronze door, I gained a certain amount of protection from the beating of the hailstones, for now they only drove against me as they ricocheted from the ground and the side of the marble.

As I leaned against the door, it moved slightly and opened inwards. The shelter of even a tomb was welcome in that pitiless tempest, and I was about to enter it when there came a flash of forked lightning that lit up the whole expanse of the heavens. In the instant, as I am a living man, I saw, as my eyes were turned into the darkness of the tomb, a beautiful woman, with rounded cheeks and red lips, seemingly sleeping on a bier. As the thunder broke overhead, I was grasped as by the hand of a giant and hurled out into the storm. The whole thing was so sudden that, before I could realize the shock, moral as well as physical, I found the hailstones beating me down. At the same time I had a strange dominating feeling that I was not alone. I looked towards the tomb. Just then there came another blinding flash which seemed to strike the iron stake that surmounted the tomb and to pour through to the earth, blasting and crumbling the marble, as in a burst of flame. The dead woman rose for a moment of agony, while she was lapped in the flame, and her bitter scream of pain was drowned in the thundercrash. The last thing I heard was this mingling of dreadful sound, as again I was seized in the giant-grasp and dragged away, while the hailstones beat on me, and the air around seemed reverberant with the howling of wolves. The last sight that I remembered was a vague, white, moving mass, as if all the graves around me had sent out the phantoms of their sheeted dead, and that they were closing in on me through the white cloudiness of the driving hail.

Gradually there came a sort of vague beginning of consciousness; then a sense of weariness that was dreadful. For a time I remembered nothing; but slowly my senses returned. My feet seemed positively racked with pain, yet I could not move them. They seemed to be numbed. There was an icy feeling at the back of my neck and all down my spine, and my ears, like my feet, were dead, yet in torment; but there was in my breast a sense of warmth which was, by comparison, delicious. It was as a nightmare – a physical nightmare, if one may use such an expression; for some heavy weight on my chest made it difficult for me to breathe.

This period of semi-lethargy seemed to remain a long time, and as it faded away I must have slept or swooned. Then came a sort of loathing, like the first stage of sea-sickness, and a wild desire to be free from something – I knew not what. A vast stillness enveloped me, as though all the world were asleep or dead – only broken by the low panting as of some animal close to me. I felt a warm rasp-ing at my throat, then came a consciousness of the awful truth, which chilled me to the heart and sent the blood surg-ing up through my brain. Some great animal was lying on me and now licking my throat. I feared to stir, for some instinct of prudence bade me lie still; but the brute seemed to realize that there was now some change in me, for it raised its head. Through my eyelashes I saw above me the two great flaming eyes of a gigantic wolf. Its sharp white teeth gleamed in the gaping red mouth, and I could feel its hot breath fierce and acrid upon me.

For another spell of time I remembered no more. Then I became conscious of a low growl, followed by a yelp, re-newed again and again. Then seemingly very far away, I heard a 'Holloa! holloa!' as of many voices calling in uni-son. Cautiously I raised my head and looked in the direc-tion whence the sound came; but the cemetery blocked my view. The wolf still continued to yelp in a strange way, and a red glare began to move round the grove of cypresses, as though following the sound. As the voices drew closer, the wolf yelped faster and louder. I feared to make either sound or motion. Nearer came the red glow, over the while pall which stretched into the darkness around me. Then all at once from beyond the trees there came at a trot a troop of horsemen bearing torches. The wolf rose from my breast and made for the cemetery. I saw one of the horsemen (soldiers by the caps and their long military cloaks) raise his carbine and take aim. A companion knocked up his arm, and I heard the ball whizz over my head. He had evidently taken my body for that of the wolf. Another sighted the animal as it slunk away, and a shot followed. Then, at a gallop, the troop rode forward – some towards me, others following the wolf as it disappeared amongst the snow-clad cypresses.

As they drew nearer I tried to move, but was powerless, although I could see and hear all that went on around me. Two or three of the soldiers jumped from their horses and knelt beside me. One of them raised my head, and placed his hand over my heart.

'Good news, comrades!' he cried. 'His heart still beats!'

Then some brandy was poured down my throat; it put vigour into me, and I was able to open my eyes and look around. Lights and shadows were moving among the trees, and I heard men call to one another. They drew together, uttering frightened exclamations; and the lights flashed as the others came pouring out of the cemetery pell-mell, like men possessed. When the further ones came close to us, those who were around me asked them eagerly:

'Well, have you found him?'

The reply rang out hurriedly:

'No! no! Come away quick – quick! This is no place to stay, and on this of all nights!'

'What was it?' was the question, asked in all manner of keys. The answer came variously and all indefinitely as though the men were moved by some common impulse to speak, yet were restrained by some common fear from giving their thoughts.

'It-it-indeed!' gibbered one, whose wits had plainly given out for the moment.

'A wolf – and yet not a wolf!' another put in shudderingly.

'No use trying for him without the sacred bullet,' a third remarked in a more ordinary manner.

'Serve us right for coming out on this night! Truly we have earned our thousand marks!' were the ejaculations of a fourth.

'There was blood on the broken marble,' another said after a pause – 'the lightning never brought that there. And for him – is he safe? Look at his throat! See, comrades, the wolf has been lying on him and keeping his blood warm.'

The officer looked at my throat and replied:

'He is all right; the skin is not pierced. What does it all mean? We should never have found him but for the yelping of the wolf.'

'What became of it?' asked the man who was holding up my head, and who seemed the least panic-stricken of the party, for his hands were steady and without tremor. On his sleeve was the chevron of a petty officer.

'It went to its home,' answered the man, whose long face was pallid, and who actually shook with terror as he glanced around him fearfully. 'There are graves enough there in which it may lie. Come, comrades – come quickly! Let us leave this cursed spot.'

The officer raised me to a sitting posture, as he uttered a word of command; then several men placed me upon a horse. He sprang to the saddle behind me, took me in his arms, gave the word to advance; and, turning our faces away from the cypresses, we rode away in swift, military order.

As yet my tongue refused its office, and I was perforce silent. I must have fallen asleep; for the next thing I remember was finding myself standing up, supported by a soldier on each side of me. It was almost broad daylight, and to the north a red streak of sunlight was reflected, like a path of blood, over the waste of snow. The officer was telling the men to say nothing of what they had seen, except that they found an English stranger, guarded by a large dog.

'Dog! That was no dog,' cut in the man who had exhibited such fear. 'I think I know a wolf when I see one.'

The young officer answered calmly: 'I said a dog.'

'Dog!' reiterated the other ironically. It was evident that his courage was rising with the sun; and, pointing to me, he said, 'Look at his throat. Is that the work of a dog, master?'

Instinctively I raised my hand to my throat, and as I touched it I cried out in pain. The men crowded round to look, some stooping down from their saddles; and again there came the calm voice of the young officer:

'A dog, as I said. If aught else were said we should only be laughed at.'

I was then mounted behind a trooper, and we rode on

into the suburbs of Munich. Here we came across a stray carriage, into which I was lifted, and it was driven off to the Quatre Saisons – the young officer accompanying me, whilst a trooper followed with his horse, and the others rode off to their barracks.

When we arrived, Herr Delbrück rushed so quickly down the steps to meet me, that it was apparent he had been watching within. Taking me by both hands he solicitously led me in. The officer saluted me and was turning to withdraw, when I recognized his purpose, and insisted that he should come to my rooms. Over a glass of wine I warmly thanked him and his brave comrades for saving me. He replied simply that he was more than glad, and that Herr Delbrück had at the first taken steps to make all the searching party pleased; at which ambiguous utterance the maître d'hôtel smiled, while the officer pleaded duty and withdrew.

'But Herr Delbrück,' I inquired, 'how and why was it that the soldiers searched for me?'

He shrugged his shoulders, as if in depreciation of his own deed, as he replied:

'I was so fortunate as to obtain leave from the commander of the regiment in which I served, to ask for volunteers.'

'But how did you know I was lost?' I asked.

'The driver came hither with the remains of his carriage, which had been upset when the horses ran away.'

'But surely you would not send a search party of soldiers merely on this account?'

'Oh, no!' he answered; 'but even before your coachman arrived, I had this telegram from the Boyar whose guest you are,' and he took from his pocket a telegram which he handed to me, and I read:

BISTRITZ.

'Be careful of my guest – his safety is most precious to me. Should aught happen to him, or if he be missed, spare nothing to find him and ensure his safety. He is English and therefore adventurous. There are often dangers from

snow and wolves at night. Lose not a moment if you suspect harm to him. I answer your zeal with my fortune. –
Dracula.'

As I held the telegram in my hand, the room seemed to
whirl around me; and, if the attentive maître d'hôtel had not
caught me, I think I should have fallen. There was something so strange in all this, something so weird and impossible to imagine, that there grew on me a sense of my being
in some way the sport of opposite forces – the mere vague
idea of which seemed in a way to paralyse me. I was certainly under some form of mysterious protection. From a
distant country had come, in the very nick of time, a mes-
sage that took me out of the danger of the snow-sleep and
the jaws of the wolf.

* This is not fictional detail. The Hotel Vier Jahreszeiten existed,
and still exists, in Munich (Ed).

FOR THE BLOOD IS THE LIFE

by

F. Marion Crawford

We had dined at sunset on the broad roof of the old tower, because it was cooler there during the great heat of summer. Besides, the little kitchen was built at one corner of the great square platform, which made it more convenient than if the dishes had to be carried down the steep stone steps broken in places and everywhere worn with age. The tower was one of those built all down the west coast of Calabria by the Emperor Charles V early in the sixteenth century, to keep off the Barbary pirates, when the unbelievers were allied with Francis I against the Emperor and the Church. They have gone to ruin, a few still stand intact, and mine is one of the largest. How it came into my possession ten years ago, and why I spend a part of each year in it, are matters which do not concern this tale. The tower stands in one of the loneliest spots in Southern Italy, at the extremity of a curving, rocky promontory, which forms a small but safe natural harbour at the southern extremity of the Gulf of Policastro, and just north of Cape Scalea, the birthplace of Judas Iscariot, according to the old local legend. The tower stands alone on this hooked spur of the rock, and there is not a house to be seen within three miles of it. When I go there I take a couple of sailors, one of whom is a fair cook, and when I am away it is in charge of a gnome-like little being who was once a miner and who attached himself to me long ago.

My friend, who sometimes visits me in my summer solitude, is an artist by profession, a Scandinavian by birth, and a cosmopolitan by force of circumstances.

We had dined at sunset; the sunset glow had reddened and faded again, and the evening purple steeped the vast chain of the mountains that embrace the deep gulf to eastward and rear themselves higher and higher towards the south. It was hot, and we sat at the landward corner of the platform, waiting for the night breeze to come down from the lower hills. The colour sank out of the air, there was a little interval of deep-grey twilight, and a lamp sent a yellow streak from the open door of the kitchen, where the men were getting their supper.

Then the moon rose suddenly above the crest of the promontory, flooding the platform and lighting up every little spur of rock and knoll of grass below us, down to the edge of the motionless water. My friend lighted his pipe and sat looking at a spot on the hillside. I knew that he was looking at it, and for a long time past I had wondered whether he would ever see anything there that would fix his attention. I knew that spot well. It was clear that he was interested at last, though it was a long time before he spoke. Like most painters, he trusts to his own eyesight, as a lion trusts his strength and a stag his speed, and he is always disturbed when he cannot reconcile what he sees with what he believes that he ought to see.

'It's strange,' he said. 'Do you see that little mound just on this side of the boulder?'

'Yes,' I said, and I guessed what was coming.

'It looks like a grave,' observed Holger.

'Very true. It does look like a grave.'

'Yes,' continued my friend, his eyes still fixed on the spot. 'But the strange thing is that I see the body lying on the top of it. Of course,' continued Holger, turning his head on one side as artists do, 'it must be an effect of light. In the first place, it is not a grave at all. Secondly, if it were, the body would be inside and not outside. Therefore, it's an effect of the moonlight. Don't you see it?'

'Perfectly; I always see it on moonlight nights.'

'It doesn't seem to interest you much,' said Holger.

'On the contrary, it does interest me, though I am used to

it. You're not so far wrong, either. The mound is really a grave.'

'Nonsense!' cried Holger incredulously. 'I suppose you'll tell me that what I see lying on it is really a corpse!'

'No,' I answered, 'it's not. I know, because I have taken the trouble to go down and see.'

'Then what is it?' asked Holger.

'It's nothing.'

'You mean that it's an effect of light, I suppose?'

'Perhaps it is. But the inexplicable part of the matter is that it makes no difference whether the moon is rising or setting, or waxing or waning. If there's any moonlight at all, from east or west or overhead, so long as it shines on the grave you can see the outline of the body on top.'

Holger stirred up his pipe with the point of his knife, and then used his finger for a stopper. When the tobacco burned well he rose from his chair.

'If you don't mind,' he said, 'I'll go down and take a look at it.'

He left me, crossed the roof, and disappeared down the dark steps. I did not move, but sat looking down until he came out of the tower below. I heard him humming an old Danish song as he crossed the open space in the bright moonlight, going straight to the mysterious mound. When he was ten paces from it, Holger stopped short, made two steps forward, and then three or four backward, and then stopped again. I know what that meant. He had reached the spot where the Thing ceased to be visible – where, as he would have said, the effect of light changed.

Then he went on till he reached the mound and stood upon it. I could see the Thing still, but it was no longer lying down; it was on its knees now, winding its white arms round Holger's body and looking up into his face. A cool breeze stirred my hair at that moment, as the night wind began to come down from the hills, but it felt like a breath from another world.

The Thing seemed to be trying to climb to its feet helping itself up by Holger's body while he stood upright, quite unconscious of it and apparently looking towards the tower, which is very picturesque when the moonlight falls upon it on that side.

'Come along!' I shouted. 'Don't stay there all night!'

It seemed to me that he moved reluctantly as he stepped from the mound, or else with difficulty. That was it. The Thing's arms were still round his waist, but its feet could not leave the grave. As he came slowly forward it was drawn and lengthened like a wreath of mist, thin and white, till I saw distinctly that Holger shook himself, as a man does who feels a chill. At the same instant a little wail of pain came to me on the breeze – it might have been the cry of the small owl that lives among the rocks – and the misty presence floated swiftly back from Holger's advancing figure and lay once more at its length upon the mound.

Again I felt the cool breeze in my hair, and this time an icy thrill of dread ran down my spine. I remembered very well that I had once gone down there alone in the moonlight; that presently, being near, I had seen nothing; that, like Holger, I had gone and had stood upon the mound; and I remembered how when I came back, sure that there was nothing there, I had felt the sudden conviction that there was something after all if I would only look behind me. I remembered the strong temptation to look back, a temptation I had resisted as unworthy of a man of sense, until, to get rid of it, I had shaken myself just as Holger did.

And now I knew that those white, misty arms had been round me, too; I knew it in a flash, and I shuddered as I remembered that I had heard the night owl then, too. But it had not been the night owl. It was the cry of the Thing.

I refilled my pipe and poured out a cup of strong southern wine; in less than a minute Holger was seated beside me again.

'Of course there's nothing there,' he said, 'but it's creepy, all the same. Do you know, when I was coming back I was so sure that there was something behind me that I wanted to turn round and look? It was an effort not to.'

He laughed a little, knocked the ashes out of his pipe, and

poured himself out some wine. For a while neither of us spoke, and the moon rose higher and we both looked at the Thing that lay on the mound.

'You might make a story about that,' said Holger after a long time.

'There is one,' I answered. 'If you're not sleepy, I'll tell it to you.'

'Go ahead,' said Holger, who likes stories.

Old Alario was dying up there in the village behind the hill. You remember him, I have no doubt. They say that he made his money by selling sham jewellery in South America, and escaped with his gains when he was found out. Like all those fellows, if they bring anything back with them, he at once set to work to enlarge his house, and as there are no masons here, he sent all the way to Paola for two workmen. They were a rough-looking pair of scoundrels – a Neapolitan who had lost one eye and a Sicilian with an old scar half an inch deep across his left cheek. I often saw them, for on Sundays they used to come down here and fish off the rocks. When Alario caught the fever that killed him the masons were still at work. As he had agreed that part of their pay should be their board and lodgings, he made them sleep in the house. His wife was dead, and he had an only son called Angelo, who was a much better sort than himself. Angelo was to marry the daughter of the richest man in the village, and, strange to say, though the marriage was arranged by their parents, the young people were said to be in love with each other.

For that matter, the whole village was in love with Angelo, and among the rest a wild, good-looking creature called Cristina, who was more like a gipsy than any girl I ever saw about here. She had very red lips and very black eyes, she was built like a greyhound, and had the tongue of the devil. But Angelo did not care a straw for her. He was rather a simple-minded fellow, quite different from his old scoundrel of a father, and under what I should call normal circumstances I really believe that he would never have looked at any girl except the nice plump little creature, with a fat dowry, whom his father meant him to marry. But things turned up which were neither normal nor natural.

On the other hand, a very handsome young shepherd from the hills above Maratea was in love with Cristina, who seems to have been quite indifferent to him. Cristina had no regular means of subsistence, but she was a good girl and willing to do any work or go on errands to any distance for the sake of a loaf of bread or a mess of beans, and permission to sleep under cover. She was especially glad when she could get something to do about the house of Angelo's father. There is no doctor in the village, and when the neighbours saw that old Alario was dying they sent Cristina to Scalea to fetch one. That was late in the afternoon, and if they had waited so long it was because the dying miser refused to allow any such extravagance while he was able to speak. But while Cristina was gone matters grew rapidly worse, the priest was brought to the bedside, and when he had done what he could he gave it as his opinion to the bystanders that the old man was dead, and left the house.

You know these people. They have a physical horror of death. Until the priest spoke, the room had been full of people. The words were hardly out of his mouth before it was empty. It was night now. They hurried down the dark steps and out into the street.

Angelo, as I have said, was away. Cristina had not come back – the simple woman-servant who had nursed the sick man fled with the rest, and the body was left alone in the flickering light of the earthen oil lamp.

Five minutes later two men looked in cautiously and crept forward towards the bed. They were the one-eyed Neapolitan mason and his Sicilian companion. They knew what they wanted. In a moment they had dragged from under the bed a small but heavy iron-bound box, and long before anyone thought of coming back to the dead man they had left the house and the village under cover of the darkness. It was easy enough, for Alario's house is the last towards the gorge which leads down here, and the thieves merely went out by the back door, got over the stone wall, and had nothing to risk after that except the possibility of meeting some belated countryman, which was very small indeed, since few of the people use that path. They had a mattock and shovel, and they made their way without accident.

I am telling you this story as it must have happened, for, of course, there were no witnesses to this part of it. The men brought the box down by the gorge, intending to bury it until they should be able to come back and take it away in a boat. They must have been clever enough to guess that some of the money would be in paper notes, for they would otherwise have buried it on the beach in the wet sand, where it would have been much safer. But the paper would have rotted if they had been obliged to leave it there long, so they dug their hole down there, close to that boulder. Yes, just where the mound is now.

Cristina did not find the doctor in Scalea, for he had been sent for from a place up the valley, halfway to San Domenico. If she had found him he would have come on his mule by the upper road, which is smoother but much longer. But Cristina took the short cut by the rocks, which passes about fifty feet above the mound, and goes round that corner. The men were digging when she passed, and she heard them at work. It would not have been like her to go by without finding out what the noise was, for she was never afraid of anything in her life, and, besides, the fishermen sometimes come ashore here at night to get a stone for an anchor or to gather sticks to make a little fire. The night was dark and Cristina probably came close to the two men before she could see what they were doing. She knew them, of course, and they knew her, and understood instantly that they were in her power. There was only one thing to be done for their safety, and they did it. They knocked her on the head, they dug the hole deep, and they buried her quickly with the iron-bound chest. They must have understood that their only chance of escaping suspicion lay in getting back to the village before their absence was noticed, for they returned immediately, and were found half an hour later gossiping quietly with the man who was making Alario's coffin. He was a crony of theirs, and had been working at the repairs in the old man's house. So far as I have been able to make out, the only persons who were supposed to know where Alario kept his treasure were Angelo and the one woman-servant I have mentioned. Angelo was away; it was the woman who discovered the theft.

It is easy enough to understand why no one else knew where the money was. The old man kept his door locked and the key in his pocket when he was out, and did not let the women enter to clean the place unless he was there himself. The whole village knew that he had money somewhere, however, and the masons had probably discovered the whereabouts of the chest by climbing in at the window in his absence. If the old man had not been delirious until he lost consciousness he would have been in frightful agony of mind for his riches. The faithful woman-servant forgot their existence only for a few moments when she fled with the rest, overcome by the horror of death. Twenty minutes had not passed before she returned with the two hideous old hags who were always called in to prepare the dead for burial. Even then she had not at first the courage to go near the bed with them, but she made a pretence of dropping something, went down on her knees as if to find it, and looked under the bedstead. The walls of the room were newly white-washed down to the floor, and she saw at a glance that the chest was gone. It had been there in the afternoon, it had therefore been stolen in the short interval since she had left the room.

There are no carabineers stationed in the village; there is not so much as a municipal watchman, for there is no municipality. There never was such a place, I believe. Scalea is supposed to look after it in some mysterious way, and it takes a couple of hours to get anybody from there. As the old woman had lived in the village all her life, it did not even occur to her to apply to any civil authority for help. She simply set up a howl and ran through the village in the dark, screaming out that her dead master's house had been robbed. Many of the people looked out, but at first no one seemed inclined to help her. Most of them, judging her by themselves, whispered to each other that she had probably stolen the money herself. The first man to move was the father of the girl whom Angelo was to marry; having collected his household, all of whom felt a personal interest in the wealth which was to have come into the family, he declared it to be his opinion that the chest had been stolen by the two journeymen masons who lodged in the house. He headed a search for them, which naturally began in Alario's house and ended in the carpenter's workshop, where the thieves were found discussing a measure of wine with the carpenter over the half-finished coffin, by the light of one earthen lamp filled with oil and tallow. The search party at once accused the delinquents of the crime, and threatened to lock them up in the cellar till the carabineers could be fetched from Scalea. The two men looked at each other for one moment, and then without the slightest hesitation they put out the single light, seized the unfinished coffin between them, and using it as a sort of battering ram, dashed upon their assailants in the dark. In a few moments they were beyond pursuit.

That is the end of the first part of the story. The treasure had disappeared, and as no trace of it could be found the people naturally supposed that the thieves had succeeded in carrying it off. The old man was buried, and when Angelo came back at last he had to borrow money to pay for the miserable funeral, and had some difficulty in doing so. He hardly needed to be told that in losing his inheritance he had lost his bride. In this part of the world marriages are made on strictly business principles, and if the promised cash is not forthcoming on the appointed day, the bride or the bridegroom whose parents have failed to produce it may as well take themselves off, for there will be no wedding. Poor Angelo knew that well enough. His father had been possessed of hardly any land, and now that the hard cash which he had brought from South America was gone, there was nothing left but debts for the building materials that were to have been used for enlarging and improving the old house. Angelo was beggared, and the nice plump little creature who was to have been his, turned up her nose at him in the most approved fashion. As for Cristina, it was several days before she was missed, for no one remembered that she had been sent to Scalea for the doctor, who had never come. She often disappeared in the same way for days together, when she could find a little work here and there at the distant farms among the hills. But when she did not come back at all, people began to wonder, and at last made up their minds that she had connived with the masons and had escaped with them.

I paused and emptied my glass.

'*That sort of thing could not happen anywhere else,*' observed Holger, *filling his everlasting pipe again.* '*It is wonderful what a natural charm there is about murder and sudden death in a romantic country like this. Deeds that would be simply brutal and disgusting anywhere else become dramatic and mysterious because this is Italy, and we are living in a genuine tower of Charles V built against genuine Barbary pirates.*'

'*There's something in that,*' *I admitted. Holger is the most romantic man in the world inside of himself, but he always thinks it necessary to explain why he feels anything.*

'*I suppose they found the poor girl's body with the box,*' *he said presently.*

'*As it seems to interest you,*' *I answered,* '*I'll tell you the rest of the story.*'

The moon had risen high by this time; the outline of the Thing on the mound was clearer to our eyes than before.

The village very soon settled down to its small dull life. No one missed old Alario, who had been away so much on his voyages to South America that he had never been a familiar figure in his native place. Angelo lived in the half-finished house, and because he had no money to pay the old woman-servant, she would not stay with him, but once in a long time she would come and wash a shirt for him for old acquaintance' sake. Besides the house, he had inherited a small patch of ground at some distance from the village; he tried to cultivate it, but he had no heart in the work, for he knew he could never pay the taxes on it and on the house, which would certainly be confiscated by the Government, or seized for the debt of the building material, which the man who had supplied it refused to take back.

Angelo was very unhappy. So long as his father had been alive and rich, every girl in the village had been in love with him; but that was all changed now. It had been pleasant to be admired and courted, and invited to drink wine by fathers who had girls to marry. It was hard to be stared at coldly, and sometimes laughed at because he had been robbed of his inheritance. He cooked his miserable meals for himself, and from being sad became melancholy and morose.

At twilight, when the day's work was done, instead of hanging about in the open space before the church with young fellows of his own age, he took to wandering in lonely places on the outskirts of the village till it was quite dark. Then he slunk home and went to bed to save the expense of a light. But in those lonely twilight hours he began to have strange waking dreams. He was not always alone, for often when he sat on the stump of a tree, where the narrow path turns down the gorge, he was sure that a woman came up noiselessly over the rough stones, as if her feet were bare; and she stood under a clump of chestnut trees only half a dozen yards down the path, and beckoned to him without speaking. Though she was in the shadow he knew that her lips were red, and that when they parted a little and smiled at him she showed two small sharp teeth. He knew this at first rather than saw it, and he knew that it was Cristina, and that she was dead. Yet he was not afraid; he only wondered whether it was a dream, for he thought that if he had been awake he should have been frightened.

Besides, the dead woman had red lips, and that could only happen in a dream. Whenever he went near the gorge after sunset she was already there waiting for him, or else she very soon appeared, and he began to be sure that she came a little nearer to him every day. At first he had only been sure of her blood-red mouth, but now each feature grew distinct, and the pale face looked at him with deep and hungry eyes.

It was the eyes that grew dim. Little by little he came to know that someday the dream would not end when he turned away to go home, but would lead him down the gorge out of which the vision rose. She was nearer now when she beckoned to him. Her cheeks were not livid like those of the dead, but pale with starvation, with the furious and un-appeased physical hunger of her eyes that devoured him. They feasted on his soul and cast a spell over him, and at last they were close to his own and held him. He could not tell whether her breath was as hot as fire, or as cold as ice; he could not tell whether her red lips burned his or froze them, or whether her five fingers on his wrists seared scorching scars or bit his flesh like frost; he could not tell whether he was awake or asleep, whether she was alive or dead, but he knew that she loved him, she alone of all creatures, earthly or unearthly, and her spell had power over him.

When the moon rose high that night the shadow of that Thing was not alone down there upon the mound.

Angelo awoke in the cool dawn, drenched with dew and chilled through flesh, and blood, and bone. He opened his eyes to the faint grey light, and saw the stars still shining overhead. He was very weak, and his heart was beating so slowly that he was almost like a man fainting. Slowly he turned his head on the mound, as on a pillow, but the other face was not there. Fear seized him suddenly, a fear un-speakable and unknown; he sprang to his feet and fled up the gorge, and he never looked behind him until he reached the door of the house on the outskirts of the village. Drearily he went to his work that day, and wearily the hours dragged themselves after the sun, till at last it touched the sea and sank, and the great sharp hills above Maratea turned purple against the dove-coloured eastern sky.

Angelo shouldered his heavy hoe and left the field. He felt less tired now than in the morning when he had begun to work, but he promised himself that he would go home without lingering by the gorge, and eat the best supper he could get himself, and sleep all night in his bed like a Christian man. Not again would he be tempted down the narrow way by a shadow with red lips and icy breath; not again would he dream that dream of terror and delight. He was near the village now; it was half an hour since the sun had set, and the cracked church bell sent little discordant echoes across the rocks and ravines to tell all good people that the day was done. Angelo stood still a moment where the path forked, where it led towards the village on the left, and down to the gorge on the right, where a clump of chestnut trees overhung the narrow way. He stood still a minute, lifting his battered hat from his head and gazing at the fast-fading sea westward, and his lips moved as he silently repeated the familiar evening prayer. His lips moved, but the words that followed them in his brain lost their meaning and turned into others, and ended in a name that he spoke aloud – Cristina! With the name, the tension of his will relaxed suddenly, reality went out and the dream took him again, and bore him on swiftly and surely like a man walking in his sleep, down, down, by the steep path in the gathering darkness. And as she glided beside him, Cristina whispered strange, sweet things in his ear, which somehow, if he had been awake, he knew that he could not quite have understood; but now they were the most wonderful words he had ever heard in his life. And she kissed him also, but not upon his mouth. He felt her sharp kisses upon his white throat, and he knew that her lips were red. So the wild dream sped on through twilight and darkness and moonrise, and all the glory of the summer's night. But in the chilly dawn he lay as one half dead upon the mound down there, recalling and not recalling, drained of his blood, yet strangely longing to give those red lips more. Then came the fear, the awful nameless panic, the mortal horror that guards the confines of the world we see not, neither know of as we know of other things, but which we feel when its icy chill freezes our bones and stirs our hair with the touch of a ghostly hand. Once more Angelo sprang from the mound and fled up the gorge in the breaking day, but his step was less sure this time, and he panted for breath as he ran; and when he came to the bright spring of water that rises halfway up the hillside, he dropped upon his knees and hands and plunged his whole face in and drank as he had never drunk before – for it was the thirst of the wounded man who has lain all night long upon the battle-field.

She had him fast now, and he could not escape her, but would come to her every evening at dusk until she had drained him of his last drop of blood. It was in vain that when the day was done he tried to take another turning and to go home by a path that did not lead near the gorge. It was in vain that he made promises to himself each morning at dawn when he climbed the lonely way up from the shore to the village. It was all in vain, for when the sun sank burning into the sea, and the coolness of the evening stole out as from a hiding-place to delight the weary world, his feet turned towards the old way, and she was waiting for him in the shadow under the chestnut trees; and then all happened as before, and she fell to kissing his white throat even as she flitted lightly down the way, winding one arm about him. And as his blood failed, she grew more hungry and more thirsty every day, and every day when he awoke in the early dawn it was harder to rouse himself to the effort of climbing the steep path to the village; and when he went to his work his feet dragged painfully, and there was hardly strength in his arms to wield the heavy hoe. He scarcely spoke to any-one now, but the people said he was 'consuming himself' for love of the girl he was to have married when he lost his in-heritance; and they laughed heartily at the thought, for this is not a very romantic country. At this time Antonio, the man who stays here to look after the tower, returned from a visit to his people, who live near Salerno. He had been away all the time since before Alario's death and knew nothing of what had happened. He has told me that he came back late in the afternoon and shut himself up in the tower to eat and sleep, for he was very tired. It was past midnight when he awoke, and when he looked out the waning moon was rising over the shoulder of the hill. He looked out towards the mound, and he saw something, and he did not sleep again that night. When he went out again in the morning it was broad daylight, and there was nothing to be seen on the mound but loose stones and driven sand. Yet he did not go very near it; he went straight up the path to the village and directly to the house of the old priest.

'I have seen an evil thing this night,' he said; 'I have seen how the dead drink the blood of the living. And the blood is the life.'

'Tell me what you have seen,' said the priest in reply.

Antonio told him everything he had seen.

'You must bring your book and your holy water tonight,' he added. 'I will be here before sunset to go down with you, and if it pleases your reverence to sup with me while we wait, I will make ready.'

'I will come,' the priest answered, 'for I have read in old books of these strange beings which are neither quick nor dead, and which lie ever fresh in their graves, stealing out in the dusk to taste life and blood.'

Antonio cannot read, but he was glad to see that the priest understood the business; for, of course, the books must have instructed him as to the best means of quieting the half-living Thing for ever.

So Antonio went away to his work, which consists largely in sitting on the shady side of the tower, when he is not perched upon a rock with a fishing-line catching nothing. But on that day he went twice to look at the mound in the bright sunlight, and he searched round and round it for some hole through which the being might get in and out; but he found none. When the sun began to sink and the air was cooler in the shadows, he went up to fetch the old priest, carrying a little wicker basket with him; and in this they placed a bottle of holy water, and the basin, and sprinkler, and the stole which the priest would need; and they came down and waited in the door of the tower till it should be dark. But while the light still lingered very grey and faint, they saw something moving, just there, two figures, a man's that walked, and a woman's that flitted beside him, and while her head lay on his shoulder she kissed his throat. The priest has told me that, too, and that his teeth chattered and he grasped Antonio's arm. The vision passed and disappeared into the shadow. Then Antonio got the leathern flask of strong liquor, which he kept for great occasions, and poured such a draught as made the old man feel almost young again; and gave the priest his stole to put on and the holy water to carry, and they went out together towards the spot where the work was to be done. Antonio says that in spite of the rum his own knees shook together, and the priest stumbled over his Latin. For when they were yet a few yards from the mound the flickering light of the lantern fell upon Angelo's white face, unconscious as if in sleep, and on his upturned throat, over which a very thin red line of blood trickled down into his collar; and the flickering light of the lantern played upon another face that looked up from the feast, upon two deep, dead eyes that saw in spite of death – upon parted lips, redder than life itself – upon two gleaming teeth on which glistened a rosy drop. Then the priest, good old man, shut his eyes tight and showered holy water before him, and his cracked voice rose almost to a scream; and then Antonio, who is no coward after all, raised his pick in one hand and the lantern in the other, as he sprang forward, not knowing what the end should be; and then he swears that he heard a woman's cry, and the Thing was gone, and Angelo lay alone on the mound unconscious, with the red line on his throat and the beads of deathly sweat on his cold forehead. They lifted him, half-dead as he was, and laid him on the ground close by; then Antonio went to work, and the priest helped him, though he was old and could not do much; and they dug deep, and at last Antonio, standing in the grave, stooped down with his lantern to see what he might see.

His hair used to be dark brown, with grizzled streaks about the temples; in less than a month from that day he was as grey as a badger. He was a miner when he was young, and most of these fellows have seen ugly sights now and then, when accidents have happened, but he had never seen what he saw that night – that Thing which is neither alive nor dead, that Thing that will abide neither above ground nor in the grave. Antonio had brought something with him which the priest had not noticed. He had made it that afternoon – a sharp stake shaped from a piece of tough old driftwood. He had it with him now, and he had his heavy pick, and he had taken the lantern down into the grave. I don't think any power on earth could make him speak of what happened then, and the old priest was too frightened to look in. He says he heard Antonio breathing like a wild beast, and moving as if he were fighting with something almost as strong as himself; and he heard an evil sound also, with blows, as of something violently driven through flesh and bone; and then, the most awful sound of all – a woman's shriek, the unearthly scream of a woman neither dead nor alive, but buried deep for many days. And he, the poor old priest, could only rock himself as he knelt there in the sand, crying aloud his prayers and exorcisms to drown those dreadful sounds. Then suddenly a small iron-bound chest was thrown up and rolled over against the old man's knee, and in a moment more Antonio was beside him, his face as white as tallow in the flickering light of the lantern, shovelling the sand and pebbles into the grave with furious haste, and looking over the edge till the pit was half full; and the priest said that there was much fresh blood on Antonio's hands and on his clothes.

I had come to the end of my story. Holger finished his wine and leaned back in his chair.

'So Angelo got his own again,' he said. 'Did he marry the prim and plump young person to whom he had been betrothed?'

'No; he had been badly frightened. He went to South America, and has not been heard of since.'

'And that poor thing's body is there still, I suppose,' said Holger. 'Is it quite dead yet, I wonder?'

I wonder, too. But whether it be dead or alive, I should hardly care to see it, even in broad daylight. Antonio is as grey as a badger, and he has never been quite the same man since that night.

THE END OF THE STORY

by

Clark Ashton Smith

The following narrative was found among the papers of
Christophe Morand, a young law student of Tours, after his
unaccountable disappearance during a visit at his father's
home near Moulins, in November, 1789:

A sinister brownish-purple autumn twilight, made premature by the imminence of a sudden thunderstorm, had filled
the forest of Averoigne. The trees along my road were already blurred to ebon masses, and the road itself, pale and
spectral before me in the thickening gloom, seemed to waver
and quiver slightly, as with the tremor of some mysterious
earthquake. I spurred my horse, who was woefully tired with
a journey begun at dawn, and had fallen hours ago to a protesting and reluctant trot, and we galloped adown the darkening road between enormous oaks that seemed to lean
towards us with boughs like clutching fingers as we passed.

With dreadful rapidity, the night was upon us, the blackness became a tangible clinging veil; a nightmare confusion
and desperation drove me to spur my mount again with a
more cruel rigour; and now, as we went, the first far-off
mutter of the storm mingled with the clatter of my horse's
hoofs, and the first lightning flashes illumed our way, which
to my amazement (since I believed myself on the main highway through Averoigne), had inexplicably narrowed to a
well-trodden footpath. Feeling sure that I had gone astray,
but not caring to retrace my steps in the teeth of darkness
and the towering clouds of the tempest, I hurried on, hoping, as seemed reasonable, that a path so plainly worn would
lead eventually to some house or château where I could find
refuge for the night. My hope was well-founded, for within

a few minutes I descried a glimmering light through the forest-boughs, and came suddenly to an open glade, where, on a gentle eminence, a large building loomed, with several litten windows in the lower storey, and a top that was well-nigh indistinguishable against the bulks of driven cloud.

'Doubtless a monastery,' I thought, as I drew rein, and descending from my exhausted mount, lifted the heavy brazen knocker in the form of a dog's head and let it fall on the oaken door. The sound was unexpectedly loud and sonorous, with a reverberation almost sepulchral, and I shivered involuntarily, with a sense of startlement, of un-wonted dismay. This, a moment later, was wholly dissipated when the door was thrown open and a tall, ruddy-featured monk stood before me in the cheerful glow of the cressets that illumed a capacious hallway.

'I bid you welcome to the abbey of Perigon,' he said, in a suave rumble, and even as he spoke, another robed and hooded figure appeared and took my horse in charge. As I murmured my thanks and acknowledgements, the storm broke and tremendous gusts of rain, accompanied by ever-nearing peals of thunder, drove with demoniac fury on the door that had closed behind me.

'It is fortunate that you found us when you did,' observed my host. ' 'Twere ill for man and beast to be abroad in such a hell-brew.'

Divining without question that I was hungry as well as tired, he led me to the refectory and set before me a bounti-ful meal of mutton, brown bread, lentils, and a strong excel-lent red wine.

He sat opposite me at the refectory table while I ate, and, with my hunger a little mollified, I took occasion to scan him more attentively. He was both tall and stoutly built, and his features, where the brow was no less broad than the power-ful jaw, betokened intellect as well as a love for good living. A certain delicacy and refinement, an air of scholarship, of good taste and good breeding, emanated from him, and I thought to myself: 'This monk is probably a connoisseur of books as well as of wines.' Doubtless my expression betrayed the quickening of my curiosity, for he said, as if in answer:

'I am Hilaire, the abbot of Perigon. We are a Benedictine order, who live in amity with God and with all men, and we do not hold that the spirit is to be enriched by the mortification or impoverishment of the body. We have in our butteries an abundance of wholesome fare, in our cellars the best and oldest vintage of the district of Averoigne. And, if such things interest you, as mayhap they do, we have a library that is stocked with rare tomes, with precious manuscripts, with the finest works of heathendom and christendom, even to certain unique writings that survived the holocaust of Alexandria.'

'I appreciate your hospitality,' I said bowing. 'I am Christophe Morand, a law student, on my way home from Tours to my father's estate near Moulins. I, too, am a lover of books, and nothing would delight me more than the privilege of inspecting a library so rich and curious as the one whereof you speak.'

Forthwith, while I finished my meal, we fell to discussing the classics, and to quoting and capping passages from Latin, Greek, or Christian authors. My host, I soon discovered, was a scholar of uncommon attainments, with an erudition, a ready familiarity with both ancient and modern literature that made my own seem as that of the merest beginner by comparison. He, on his part, was so good as to commend my far from perfect Latin, and by the time I had emptied my bottle of red wine we were chatting familiarly like old friends.

All my fatigue had now flown, to be succeeded by a rare sense of well-being, of physical comfort combined with mental alertness and keenness. So, when the abbot suggested that we pay a visit to the library, I assented with alacrity.

He led me down a long corridor, on each side of which were cells belonging to the brothers of the order, and unlocked, with a large brazen key that depended from his girdle, the door of a great room with lofty ceiling and several deepset windows. Truly, he had not exaggerated the resources of the library, for the long shelves were over-crowded with books, and many volumes were piled high on the tables or stacked in corners. There were rolls of papyrus, of parchment, of vellum; there were strange Byzantine or Coptic bibles; there were old Arabic and Persian manuscripts with floriated or jewel-studded covers; there were scores of incunabula from the first printing presses; there were innumerable monkish copies of antique authors, bound in wood or ivory, with rich illuminations and lettering that was often in itself a work of art.

With a care that was both loving and meticulous, the abbot Hilaire brought out volume after volume for my inspection. Many of them I had never seen before; some were unknown to me even by fame or rumour. My excited interest, my unfeigned enthusiasm, evidently pleased him, for at length he pressed a hidden spring in one of the library tables and drew out a long drawer, in which, he told me, were certain treasures that he did not care to bring forth for the edification or delectation of many, and whose very existence was undreamed of by the monks.

'Here,' he continued, 'are three odes by Catullus which you will not find in any published edition of his works. Here, also, is an original manuscript of Sappho – a complete copy of a poem otherwise extant only in brief fragments; here are two of the lost tales of Miletus, a letter of Pericles to Aspasia, an unknown dialogue of Plato, and an old Arabian work on astronomy, by some anonymous author, in which the theories of Copernicus are anticipated. And, lastly, here is the somewhat infamous *Histoire d'Amour*, by Bernard de Vaillantcoeur, which was destroyed immediately on publication, and of which only one other copy is known to exist.'

As I gazed with mingled awe and curiosity on the unique, unheard-of treasures he displayed, I saw in one corner of the drawer what appeared to be a thin volume with plain un-titled binding of dark leather. I ventured to pick it up, and found that it contained a few sheets of closely written manuscript in old French.

'And this?' I queried, turning to look at Hilaire, whose

face, to my amazement, had suddenly assumed a melancholy and troubled expression.

'It were better not to ask, my son.' He crossed himself as he spoke, and his voice was no longer mellow, but harsh, agitated, full of sorrowful perturbation. 'There is a curse on the pages that you hold in your hand: an evil spell, a malign power is attached to them, and he who would venture to peruse them is henceforward in dire peril both of body and soul.' He took the little volume from me as he spoke, and returned it to the drawer, again crossing himself as he did so.

'But father,' I dared to expostulate, 'how can such things be? How can there be danger in a few written sheets of parchment?'

'Christophe, there are things beyond your understanding, things that it were not well for you to know. The might of Satan is manifestable in devious modes, in diverse manners; there are other temptations than those of the world and the flesh, there are evils no less subtle than irresistible, there are hidden heresies, and necromancies other than those which sorcerers practise.'

'With what, then, are these pages concerned, that such occult peril, such unholy power, lurks within them?'

'I forbid you to ask.' His tone was one of great rigour, with a finality that dissuaded me from further questioning.

'For you, my son,' he went on, 'the danger would be doubly great, because you are young, ardent, full of desires and curiosities. Believe me, it is better to forget that you have even seen this manuscript.' He closed the hidden drawer, and as he did so, the melancholy troubled look was replaced by his former benignity.

'Now,' he said, as he turned to one of the bookshelves, 'I will show you the copy of Ovid that was owned by the poet Petrarch.' He was again the mellow scholar, the kindly, jovial host, and it was evident that the mysterious manuscript was not to be referred to again. But his odd perturbation, the dark and awful hints he had let fall, the vague terrific terms of his proscription, had all served to awaken my wildest curiosity, and, though I felt the obsession to be unreasonable, I was quite unable to think of anything else for the rest of the evening. All manner of speculations, fantastic, absurd, outrageous, ludicrous, terrible, defiled through my brain as I duly admired the incunabula which Hilaire took down so tenderly from the shelves for my delectation.

At last, towards midnight, he led me to my room – a room especially reserved for visitors, and with more of comfort, of actual luxury in its hangings, carpets and deeply quilted bed than was allowable in the cells of the monks or of the abbot himself. Even when Hilaire had withdrawn, and I had proved for my satisfaction the softness of the bed allotted me, my brain still whirled with questions concerning the forbidden manuscript. Though the storm had now ceased, it was long before I fell asleep; but slumber, when it finally came, was dreamless and profound.

When I awoke, a river of sunshine clear as molten gold was pouring through my window. The storm had wholly vanished, and no lightest tatter of cloud was visible anywhere in the pale-blue October heavens. I ran to the window and peered out on a world of autumnal forest and fields all a-sparkle with the diamonds of rain. All was beautiful, all was idyllic to a degree that could be fully appreciated only by one who had lived for a long time, as I had, within the walls of a city, with towered buildings in lieu of trees and cobbled pavements where grass should be. But, charming as it was, the foreground held my gaze only for a few moments; then, beyond the tops of the trees, I saw a hill, not more than a mile distant, on whose summit there stood the ruins of some old château, the crumbling, broken-down condition of whose walls and towers was plainly visible. It drew my gaze irresistibly, with an overpowering sense of romantic attraction which somehow seemed so natural, so inevitable, that I did not pause to analyse or wonder; and once having seen it, I could not take my eyes away, but lingered at the window for how long I knew not, scrutinizing as closely as I could the details of each time-shaken turret and bastion. Some undefinable fascination was inherent in the very form, the extent, the disposition of the pile – some fascination not dissimilar to that exerted by a strain of music, by a magical combination of words in poetry, by the features of a beloved face. Gazing, I lost myself in reveries that I could not recall afterwards, but which left behind them the same tantalizing sense of innominable delight which forgotten nocturnal dreams may sometimes leave.

I was recalled to the actualities of life by a gentle knock at my door, and realized that I had forgotten to dress myself. It was the abbot, who came to inquire how I had passed the night, and to tell me that breakfast was ready whenever I should care to arise. For some reason, I felt a little embarrassed, even shamefaced, to have been caught day-dreaming; and, though this was doubtless unnecessary, I apologized for my dilatoriness. Hilaire, I thought, gave me a keen, inquiring look, which was quickly withdrawn, as, with the suave courtesy of a good host, he assured me that there was nothing whatever for which I need apologize.

When I had breakfasted, I told Hilaire, with many expressions of gratitude for his hospitality, that it was time for me to resume my journey. But his regret at the announcement of my departure was so unfeigned, his invitation to tarry for at least another night was so genuinely hearty, so sincerely urgent, that I consented to remain. In truth, I required no great amount of solicitation, for, apart from the real liking I had taken to Hilaire, the mystery of the forbidden manuscript had entirely enslaved my imagination, and I was loth to leave without having learned more concerning it. Also, for a youth with scholastic leanings, the freedom of the abbot's library was a rare privilege, a precious opportunity not to be passed over.

'I should like,' I said, 'to pursue certain studies while I am here, with the aid of your incomparable collection.'

'My son, you are more than welcome to remain for any length of time, and you can have access to my books whenever it suits your need or inclination.' So saying, Hilaire detached the key of the library from his girdle and gave it to me. 'There are duties,' he went on, 'which will call me away from the monastery for a few hours today, and doubtless you will desire to study in my absence.'

A little later, he excused himself and departed. With inward felicitations on the longed-for opportunity that had fallen so readily into my hands, I hastened to the library, with no thought save to read the proscribed manuscript. Giving scarcely a glance at the laden shelves, I sought the table with the secret drawer, and fumbled for the spring. After a little anxious delay, I pressed the proper spot and drew forth the drawer. An impulse that had become a veritable obsession, a fever of curiosity that bordered upon actual madness, drove me, and if the safety of my soul had really depended upon it, I could not have denied the desire which forced me to take from the drawer the thin volume with plain unlettered binding.

Seating myself in a chair near one of the windows, I began to peruse the pages, which were only six in number. The writing was peculiar, with letter-forms of a fantasticality I had never met before, and the French was not only old but well-nigh barbarous in its quaint singularity. Notwithstanding the difficulty I found in deciphering them, a mad, unaccountable thrill ran through me at the first words, and I read on with all the sensations of a man who has been bewitched or who has drunken a philtre of bewildering potency.

There was no title, no date, and the writing was a narrative which began almost as abruptly as it ended. It concerned one Gérard, Comte de Venteillon, who, on the eve of his marriage to the renowned and beautiful demoiselle, Eleanor des Lys, had met in the forest near his château a strange, half-human creature with hoofs and horns. Now Gérard, as the narrative explained, was a knightly youth of indisputably proven valour, as well as a true Christian; so, in the name of our Saviour, Jesus Christ, he bade the creature stand and give an account of itself.

Laughing wildly in the twilight, the bizarre being capered before him, and cried:

'I am a satyr, and your Christ is less to me than the weeds that grow on your kitchen-middens.'

Appalled by such blasphemy, Gerard would have drawn his sword to slay the creature, but again it cried, saying:

'Stay, Gérard de Venteillon, and I will tell you a secret, knowing which, you will forget the worship of Christ, and forget your beautiful bride of tomorrow, and turn your back on the world and on the very sun itself with no reluctance and no regret.'

Now, albeit unwillingly, Gerard lent the satyr an ear and it came closer and whispered to him. And that which it whispered is not known; but before it vanished amid the blackening shadows of the forest, the satyr spoke aloud once more, and said:

'The power of Christ has prevailed like a black frost on all the woods, the fields, the rivers, the mountains, where abode in their felicity the glad, immortal goddesses and nymphs of yore. But still, in the cryptic caverns of earth, in places far underground, like the hell your priests have fabled, there dwells the pagan loveliness, there cry pagan ecstasies.' And with the last words, the creature laughed again its wild unhuman laugh, and disappeared among the darkening boles of the twilight trees.

From that moment, a change was upon Gérard de Venteillon. He returned to his château with downcast mien, speaking no cheery or kindly word to his retainers, as was his wont, but sitting or pacing always in silence, and scarcely heeding the food that was set before him. Nor did he go that evening to visit his betrothed, as he had promised, but, towards midnight, when a waning moon had arisen red as from a bath of blood, he went forth clandestinely by the postern door of the château, and following an old, half-obliterated trail through the woods, found his way to the ruins of the Château des Faussesflammes, which stands on a hill opposite the Benedictine abbey of Perigon.

Now these ruins (said the manuscript) are very old, and have long been avoided by the people of the district; for a legendry of immemorial evil clings about them, and it is said that they are the dwelling-place of foul spirits, the rendezvous of sorcerers and succubi. But Gérard, as if oblivious or fearless of their ill-renown, plunged like one who is devil-driven into the shadow of the crumbling walls, and went, with the careful groping of a man who follows some given direction, to the northern end of the courtyard. There, directly between and below the two centremost windows, which, it may be, looked forth from the chamber of forgotten chatelaines, he pressed with his right foot on a flagstone differing from those about it in being of a triangular form. And the flagstone moved and tilted beneath his foot revealing a flight of granite steps that went down into the earth.

Then, lighting a taper he had brought with him, Gérard descended the steps, and the flagstone swung into place behind him.

On the morrow, his betrothed, Eleanor des Lys, and all her bridal train, waited vainly for him at the cathedral of Vyones, the principal town of Averoigne, where the wedding had been set. And from that time his face was beheld by no man, and no vaguest rumour of Gérard de Venteillon or of the fate that befell him has ever passed among the living . . .

Such was the substance of the forbidden manuscript, and thus it ended. As I have said before, there was no date, nor was there anything to indicate by whom it had been written or how the knowledge of the happenings related had come into the writer's possession. But, oddly enough, it did not occur to me to doubt their veridity for a moment; and the curiosity I had felt concerning the contents of al the manuscript was now replaced by a burning desire, a thousandfold more powerfull, more obsessive, to know the ending of the story and to learn what Gérard de Venteillon had found when he descended the hidden steps.

In reading the tale, it had of course occurred to me that the ruins of the Château des Faussesflammes, described therein, were the very same ruins I had seen that morning from my chamber window; and pondering this, I became more and more possessed by an insane fever, by a frenetic, unholy excitement. Returning the manuscript to the secret drawer, I left the library and wandered for awhile in an aimless fashion about the corridors of the monastery. Chancing to meet there the same monk who had taken my horse in charge the previous evening, I ventured to question him, as discreetly as I could, regarding the ruins which were visible from the abbey windows.

He crossed himself, and a frightened look came over his broad, placid face at my query.

'The ruins are those of the Château des Faussesflammes,' he replied. 'For untold years, men say, they have been the haunt of unholy spirits, of witches and demons; and festivals not to be described or even named are held within their walls. No weapon known to man, no exorcism or holy water, has ever prevailed against these demons; many brave cavaliers and monks have disappeared amid the shadows of Faussesflammes, never to return; and once, it is told, an abbot of Perigon went thither to make war on the powers of evil; but what befell him at the hands of the succubi is not known or conjectured. Some say that the demons are abominable hags whose bodies terminate in serpentine coils; others, that they are women of more than mortal beauty, whose kisses are diabolic delight that consumes the flesh of men with the fierceness of hell-fire ... As for me, I know not whether such tales are true; but I should not care to venture within the walls of Faussesflammes.'

Before he had finished speaking, a resolve had sprung to life full-born in my mind; I felt that I must go to the Château des Faussesflammes and learn for myself, if possible, all that could be learned. The impulse was immediate, overwhelming, ineluctable; and even if I had so desired, I could no more have fought against it than if I had been the victim of some sorcerer's invultuation. The proscription of the abbot Hilaire, the strange unfinished tale in the old manuscript, the evil legendry at which the monk had now hinted – all these, it would seem, should have served to frighten and deter me from such a resolve; but, on the contrary, by some bizarre inversion of thought, they seemed to conceal some delectable mystery, to denote a hidden world of ineffable things, of vague undreamable pleasures that set my brain on fire and made my pulses throb deliriously. I did not know, I could not conceive, of what these pleasures would consist; but in some mystical manner I was as sure of their ultimate reality as the abbot Hilaire was sure of heaven.

I determined to go that very afternoon, in the absence of Hilaire, who, I felt instinctively, might be suspicious of any such intention on my part and would surely be inimical towards its fulfilment.

My preparations were very simple: I put in my pockets a small taper from my room and the heel of a loaf of bread from the refectory; and making sure that a little dagger which I always carried was in its sheath, I left the monastery forthwith. Meeting two of the brothers in the courtyard, I told them I was going for a short walk in the neighbouring woods. They gave me a jovial '*pax vobiscum*' and went upon their way in the spirit of their words.

Heading as directly as I could for Faussesflammes, whose turrets were often lost behind the high and interlacing boughs, I entered the forest. There were no paths, and often I was compelled to brief detours and divagations by the thickness of the underbrush. In my feverous hurry to reach the ruins, it seemed hours before I came to the top of the hill which Faussesflammes surmounted, but probably it was little more than thirty minutes. Climbing the last declivity of the boulderstrewn slope, I came suddenly within view of the château, standing close at hand in the centre of the level table which formed the summit. Trees had taken root in its broken-down walls, and the ruinous gateway that gave on the courtyard was half-choked by bushes, brambles and nettle-plants. Forcing my way through, not without difficulty, and with clothing that had suffered from the bramblethorns, I went, like Gerard de Venteillon in the old manuscript, to the northern end of the court. Enormous evil-looking weeds were rooted between the flagstones, rearing their thick and fleshy leaves that had turned to dull sinister maroons and purples with the onset of autumn. But I soon found the triangular flagstone indicated in the tale, and without the slightest delay or hesitation I pressed upon it with my right foot.

A mad shiver, a thrill of adventurous triumph that was mingled with something of trepidation, leaped through me when the great flagstone tilted easily beneath my foot, disclosing dark steps of granite, even as in the story. Now, for a moment, the vaguely hinted horrors of the monkish legends became imminently real in my imagination, and I paused before the black opening that was to engulf me, wondering if some satanic spell had not drawn me thither to perils of unknown terror and inconceivable gravity.

Only for a few instants, however, did I hesitate. Then the sense of peril faded, the monkish horrors became a fantastic dream, and the charm of things unformulable, but ever closer at hand, always more readily attainable, tightened about me like the embrace of amorous arms. I lit my taper, I descended the stair, and even as behind Gérard de Venteillon, the triangular block of stone silently resumed its place in the paving of the court above me. Doubtless it was moved by some mechanism operable by a man's weight on one of the steps; but I did not pause to consider its *modus operandi*, or to wonder if there were any way by which it could be worked from beneath to permit my return.

There were perhaps a dozen steps, terminating in a low, narrow, musty vault that was void of anything more substantial than ancient, dust-encumbered cobwebs. At the end, a small doorway admitted me to a second vault that differed from the first only in being larger and dustier. I passed through several such vaults, and then found myself in a long passage or tunnel, half blocked in places by boulders or heaps of rubble that had fallen from the crumbling sides. It was very damp, and full of the noisome odour of stagnant waters and subterranean mould. My feet splashed more than once in little pools, and drops fell upon me from above, fetid and foul as if they had oozed from a charnel. Beyond the wavering circle of light that my taper maintained, it seemed to me that the coils of dim and shadowy serpents slithered away in the darkness at my approach; but I could not be sure whether they really were serpents, or only the troubled and retreating shadows, seen by an eye that was still unaccustomed to the gloom of the vaults.

Rounding a sudden turn in the passage, I saw the last thing I had dreamt of seeing – the gleam of sunlight at what was apparently the tunnel's end. I scarcely know what I had expected to find, but such an eventuation was somehow altogether unanticipated. I hurried on, in some confusion of thought, and stumbled through the opening, to find myself blinking in the full rays of the sun.

Even before I had sufficiently recovered my wits and my eyesight to take note of the landscape before me, I was struck by a strange circumstance. Though it had been early afternoon when I entered the vaults, and though my passage through them could have been a matter of no more than a few minutes, the sun was now nearing the horizon. There was also a difference in its light, which was both brighter and mellower than the sun I had seen above Averoigne; and the sky itself was intensely blue, with no hint of autumnal pallor.

Now, with ever-increasing stupefaction, I stared about me and could find nothing familiar or even credible in the scene upon which I had emerged. Contrary to all reasonable expectation, there was no semblance of the hill upon which Faussesflammes stood, or of the adjoining country; but around me was a placid land of rolling meadows, through which a golden-gleaming river meandered towards a sea of deepest azure that was visible beyond the tops of laurel-trees ... But there are no laurel-trees in Averoigne, and the sea is hundreds of miles away: judge, then, my complete confusion and dumbfoundment.

It was a scene of such loveliness as I have never before beheld. The meadow-grass at my feet was softer and more lustrous than emerald velvet, and was full of violets and many-coloured asphodels. The dark green of ilex-trees was mirrored in the golden river, and far away I saw the pale gleam of a marble acropolis on a low summit above the plain. All things bore the aspect of a mild and clement spring that was verging upon an opulent summer. I felt as if I had stepped into a land of classic myth, of Grecian legend; and moment by moment, all surprise, all wonder as to how I could have come there, was drowned in a sense of ever-growing ecstasy before the utter, ineffable beauty of the landscape.

Near by, in a laurel-grove, a white roof shone in the late rays of the sun. I was drawn towards it by the same allurement, only far more potent and urgent, which I had felt on seeing the forbidden manuscript and the ruins of Fausses-flammes. Here, I knew with an esoteric certainty, was the culmination of my quest, the reward of all my mad and perhaps impious curiosity.

As I entered the grove, I heard laughter among the trees, blending harmoniously with the low murmur of their leaves in a soft, balmy wind. I thought I saw vague forms that melted among the boles at my approach; and once a shaggy, goat-like creature with human head and body ran across my path, as if in pursuit of a flying nymph. In the heart of the grove, I found a marble palace with a portico of Doric columns. As I neared it, I was greeted by two women in the costume of ancient slaves; and though my Greek is of the meagrest, I found no difficulty whatever in comprehending their speech, which was of Attic purity.

'Our mistress, Nycea, awaits you,' they told me. I could no longer marvel at anything, but accepted my situation without question or surmise, like one who resigns himself to the progress of some delightful dream. Probably, I thought, it was a dream, and I was still lying in my bed at the monastery; but never before had I been favoured by nocturnal visions of such clarity and surpassing loveliness.

The interior of the palace was full of a luxury that verged upon the barbaric, and which evidently belonged to the period of Greek decadence, with its intermingling of Oriental influences. I was led through a hallway gleaming with onyx and polished porphyry, into an opulently furnished room, where, on a couch of gorgeous fabrics, there reclined a woman of goddess-like beauty.

At sight of her, I trembled from head to foot with the violence of a strange emotion. I had heard of the sudden mad loves by which men are seized on beholding for the first time a certain face and form; but never before had I experienced a passion of such intensity, such all-consuming ardour, as the one I conceived immediately for this woman. Indeed, it seemed as if I had loved her for a long time, without knowing that it was she whom I loved, and without being able to identify the nature of my emotion or to orient the feeling in any manner.

She was not tall, but was formed with exquisite voluptuous purity of line and contour. Her eyes were of a dark sapphire blue, with molten depths into which the soul was fain to plunge as into the soft abysses of a summer ocean. The curve of her lips was enigmatic, a little mournful, and gravely tender as the lips of an antique Venus. Her hair, brownish rather than blonde, fell over her neck and ears and forehead in delicious ripples confined by a plain fillet of silver. In her expression, there was a mixture of pride and voluptuousness, of regal imperiousness and feminine yielding. Her movements were all as effortless and graceful as those of a serpent.

'I knew you would come,' she murmured in the same soft-vowelled Greek I had heard from the lips of her servants. 'I have waited for you long; but when you sought refuge from the storm in the abbey of Perigon, and saw the manuscript in the secret drawer, I knew that the hour of your arrival was at hand. Ah! you did not dream that the spell which drew you so irresistibly, with such unaccountable potency, was the spell of my beauty, the magical allurement of my love!'

'Who are you?' I queried. I spoke readily in Greek, which would have surprised me greatly an hour before. But now, I was prepared to accept anything whatever, no matter how fantastic or preposterous, as part of the miraculous fortune, the unbelievable adventure which had befallen me.

'I am Nycea,' she replied to my question. 'I love you, and the hospitality of my palace and of my arms is at your disposal. Need you know anything more?'

The slaves had disappeared. I flung myself beside the couch and kissed the hand she offered me, pouring out protestations that were no doubt incoherent, but were nevertheless full of an ardour that made her smile tenderly.

Her hand was cool to my lips, but the touch of it fired my passion. I ventured to seat myself beside her on the couch, and she did not deny my familiarity. While a soft purple twilight began to fill the corners of the chamber, we conversed happily, saying over and over again all the sweet absurd litanies, all the felicitous nothings that come instinctively to the lips of lovers. She was incredibly soft in my arms, and it seemed almost as if the completeness of her yielding was unhindered by the presence of bones in her lovely body.

The servants entered noiselessly, lighting rich lamps of intricately carven gold, and setting before us a meal of spicy meats, of unknown savorous fruits and potent wines. But I could eat little, and while I drank, I thirsted for the sweeter wine of Nycea's mouth.

I do not know when we fell asleep; but the evening had flown like an enchanted moment. Heavy with felicity, I drifted off on a silken tide of drowsiness, and the golden lamps and the face of Nycea blurred in a blissful mist and were seen no more.

Suddenly, from the depths of a slumber beyond all dreams, I found myself compelled into full wakefulness. For an instant, I did not even realize where I was, still less what had aroused me. Then I heard a footfall in the open doorway of the room, and peering across the sleeping head of Nycea, saw in the lamplight the abbot Hilaire, who had paused on the threshold. A look of absolute horror was imprinted upon his face, and as he caught sight of me, he began to gibber in Latin, in tones where something of fear was blended with fanatical abhorrence and hatred. I saw that he carried in his hands a large bottle and an aspergillum. I felt sure that the bottle was full of holy water, and of course divined the use for which it was intended.

Looking at Nycea, I saw that she too was awake, and knew that she was aware of the abbot's presence. She gave me a strange smile, in which I read an affectionate pity, mingled with the reassurance that a woman offers a frightened child.

'Do not fear for me,' she whispered.

'Foul vampire! Accursed Lamia! She-serpent of hell!' thundered the abbot suddenly, as he crossed the threshold of the room, raising the aspergillum aloft. At the same moment, Nycea glided from the couch, with an unbelievable swiftness of motion, and vanished through an outer door that gave upon the forest of laurels. Her voice hovered in my ear, seeming to come from an immense distance

'Farewell for awhile, Christophe. But have no fear. You shall find me again if you are brave and patient.'

As the words ended, the holy water from the aspergillum fell on the floor of the chamber and on the couch where Nycea had lain beside me. There was a crash as of many thunders, and the golden lamps went out in a darkness that seemed full of falling dust, of raining fragments. I lost all consciousness, and when I recovered, I found myself lying on a heap of rubble in one of the vaults I had traversed earlier in the day. With a taper in his hand, and an expression of great solicitude, of infinite pity upon his face, Hilaire was stooping over me. Beside him lay the bottle and the dripping aspergillum.

'I thank God, my son, that I found you in good time,' he said. 'When I returned to the abbey this evening and learned that you were gone, I surmised all that had happened. I knew you had read the accursed manuscript in my absence, and had fallen under its baleful spell, as have so many others, even to a certain reverend abbot, one of my predecessors. All of them, alas! beginning hundreds of years ago with Gérard de Venteillon, have fallen victims to the lamia who dwells in these vaults.'

'The lamia?' I questioned, hardly comprehending his words.

'Yes, my son, the beautiful Nycea who lay in your arms this night is a lamia, an ancient vampire, who maintains in these noisome vaults her palace of beatific illusions. How she came to take up her abode at Faussesflammes is not known, for her coming antedates the memory of men. She is as old as paganism: the Greeks knew her; she was exorcised by Apollonius of Tyana; and if you could behold her as she really is, you would see, in lieu of her voluptuous body, the folds of a foul and monstrous serpent. All those whom she loves and admits to her hospitality, she devours in the end, after she has drained them of life and vigour with the diabolic delight of her kisses. The laurel-wooded plain you saw, the ilex-bordered river, the marble palace and all the luxury therein, were no more than a satanic delusion, a lovely bubble that arose from the dust and mould of immemorial death, of ancient corruption. They crumbled at the kiss of the holy water I brought with me when I followed you. But Nycea, alas! has escaped, and I fear she will still survive, to build again her palace of demoniacal enchantments, to commit again and again the unspeakable abomination of her sins.'

Still in a sort of stupor at the ruin of my new-found happiness, at the singular revelations made by the abbot, I followed him obediently as he led the way through the vaults of Faussesflammes. He mounted the stairway by which I had descended, and as he neared the top and was forced to stoop a little, the great flagstone swung upward, letting in a stream of chill moonlight. We emerged, and I permitted him to take me back to the monastery.

As my brain began to clear, and the confusion into which I had been thrown resolved itself, a feeling of resentment grew apace – a keen anger at the interference of Hilaire. Unheedful whether or not he had rescued me from dire physical and spiritual perils, I lamented the beautiful dream of which he had deprived me. The kisses of Nycea burned softly in my memory, and I knew that whatever she was, woman or demon or serpent, there was no one in all the world who could ever arouse in me the same love and the same delight. I took care, however, to conceal my feelings from Hilaire, realizing that a betrayal of such emotions would merely lead him to look upon me as a soul that was lost beyond redemption.

On the morrow, pleading the urgency of my return home, I departed from Perigon. Now, in the library of my father's house near Moulins, I write this account of my adventures. The memory of Nycea is magically clear, ineffably dear as if she were still beside me, and still I see the rich draperies of a midnight chamber illumed by lamps of curiously carven gold, and still I hear the words of her farewell:

'Have no fear. You shall find me again if you are brave and patient.'

Soon I shall return, to visit again the ruins of the Château des Fausseflammes, and redescend into the vaults below the triangular flagstone. But, in spite of the nearness of Perigon to Faussesflammes, in spite of my esteem for the abbot, my gratitude for his hospitality, and my admiration for his incomparable library, I shall not care to revisit my friend Hilaire.

THE DEATH OF ILALOTHA

by

Clark Ashton Smith

Black Lord of bale and fear, master of all confusion!
By thee, thy prophet saith,
New power is given to wizards after death,
And witches in corruption draw forbidden breath,
And weave such wild enchantment and illusion
As none but lamiae may use;
And through thy grace the charnelled corpses lose
Their horror, and nefandous loves are lighted
In noisome vaults long nighted
And vampires make their sacrifice to thee –
Disgorging blood as if great urns had poured
Their bright vermilion hoard
About the washed and weltering sarcophagi.
                    – Ludar's Litany to Thasaidon.

According to the custom in old Tasuun, the obsequies of Ilalotha, lady-in-waiting to the self-widowed Queen Xantlicha, had formed an occasion of much merry-making and prolonged festivity. For three days, on a bier of diverse-coloured silks from the Orient, under a rose-hued canopy that might well have domed some nuptial couch, she had lain clad with gala garments amid the great feasting hall of the royal palace in Miraab. About her, from morning dusk to sunset, from cool even to torridly glaring dawn, the feverish tide of the funeral orgies had surged and eddied without slackening. Nobles, court officials, guardsmen, scullions, astrologers, eunuchs, and all the high ladies, waiting women and female slaves of Xantlicha had taken part in that prodigal debauchery which was believed to honour most fitly the deceased. Mad songs and obscene ditties were sung, and dancers whirled in vertiginous frenzy to the lascivious pleading of untirable lutes. Wines and liquors were poured torrentially from monstrous amphoras; the tables fumed with spicy meats piled in huge hummocks and forever replenished. The drinkers offered libation to Ilathola, till the fabrics of her bier were stained to darker hues by the spilt vintages. On all sides around her, in attitudes of disorder or prone abandonment, lay those who had yielded to amorous licence or the fullness of their potations. With half-shut eyes and lips slightly parted, in the rosy shadow cast by the catafalque, she bore no aspect of death but seemed a sleeping empress who ruled impartially over the living and the dead. This appearance, together with a strange heightening of her natural beauty, was remarked by many: and some said that she seemed to await a lover's kiss rather than the kisses of the worm.

On the third evening, when the many-tongued brazen lamps were lit and the rites drew to their end, there returned to court the Lord Thulos, acknowledged lover of Queen Xantlicha, who had gone a week previous to visit his domain on the western border and had heard nothing of Ilalotha's death. Still unaware, he came into the hall at that hour when the saturnalia began to flag and the fallen revellers to outnumber those who still moved and drank and made riot.

He viewed the disordered hall with little surprise, for such scenes were familiar to him from childhood. Then, approaching the bier, he recognized its occupant with a certain startlement. Among the numerous ladies of Miraab who had drawn his libertine affections, Ilalotha had held sway longer than most; and, it was said, she had grieved more passionately over his defection than any other. She had been superseded a month before by Xantlicha, who had shown favour to Thulos in no ambiguous manner; and Thulos, perhaps, had abandoned her not without regret: for the role of lover to the queen, though advantageous and not wholly disagreeable, was somewhat precarious. Xantlicha, it was universally believed, had rid herself of the late King Archain by means of a tomb-discovered vial of poison that owed its peculiar subtlety and virulence to the art of ancient sorcerers. Following this act of disposal, she had taken many lovers, and those who failed to please her came invariably to ends no less violent than that of Archain. She was exigent, exorbitant, demanding a strict fidelity somewhat irksome to Thulos; who, pleading urgent affairs on his remote estate, had been glad enough of a week away from court.

Now, as he stood beside the dead woman, Thulos forgot the queen and bethought him of certain summer nights that had been honeyed by the fragrance of jasmine and the jasmine-white beauty of Ilalotha. Even less than the others could he believe her dead: for her present aspect differed in no wise from that which she had often assumed during their old intercourse. To please his whim, she had feigned the inertness and complaisance of slumber or death; and at such times he had loved her with an ardour undismayed by the pantherine vehemence with which, at other whiles, she was wont to reciprocate or invite his caresses.

Moment by moment, as if through the working of some powerful necromancy, there grew upon him a curious hallucination, and it seemed that he was again the lover of those lost nights, and had entered that bower in the palace gardens where Ilalotha waited him on a couch strewn with overblown petals, lying with bosom quiet as her face and hands. No longer was he aware of the crowded hall: the high-flaring lights, the wine-flushed faces had become a moon-bright parterre of drowsily nodding blossoms, and the voices of the courtiers were no more than a faint suspiration of wind amid cypress and jasmine. The warm, aphrodisiac perfumes of the June night welled about him; and again, as of old, it seemed that they arose from the person of Ilalotha no less than from the flowers. Prompted by intense desire, he stooped over and felt her cool arm stir involuntarily beneath his kiss.

Then, with the bewilderment of a sleepwalker awakened

rudely, he heard a voice that hissed in his ear with soft venom: 'Hast forgotten thyself, my Lord Thulos? Indeed, I wonder little, for many of my bawcocks deem that she is fairer in death than in life.' And, turning from Ilalotha, while the weird spell dissolved from his senses, he found Xantlicha at his side. Her garments were disarrayed, her hair was unbound and dishevelled, and she reeled slightly, clutching him by the shoulder with sharp-nailed fingers. Her full, poppy-crimson lips were curled by a vixenish fury, and in her long-lidded yellow eyes there blazed the jealousy of an amorous cat.

Thulos, overwhelmed by a strange confusion, remembered but partially the enchantment to which he had succumbed; and he was unsure whether or not he had actually kissed Ilalotha and had felt her flesh quiver to his mouth. Verily, he thought, this thing could not have been, and a waking dream had momentarily seized him. But he was troubled by the words of Xantlicha and her anger, and by the half-furtive drunken laughters and ribald whispers that he heard passing among the people about the hall.

'Beware, my Thulos,' the queen murmured, her strange anger seeming to subside; 'for men say that she was a witch . . .'

'How did she die?' queried Thulos.

'From no other fever than that of love, it is rumoured.'

'Then, surely, she was no witch,' Thulos argued with a lightness that was far from his thoughts and feelings: 'for true sorcery should have found the cure.'

'It was from love of thee,' said Xantlicha darkly; 'and, as all women know, thy heart is blacker and harder than black adamant. No witchcraft, however potent, could prevail thereon.' Her mood, as she spoke, appeared to soften suddenly. 'Thy absence has been over-long, my lord. Come to me at midnight: I will wait for thee in the south pavilion.' Then, eyeing him sultrily for an instant from under drooped lids, and pinching his arm in such manner that her nails pierced through cloth and skin like a cat's talons, she turned from Thulos to hail certain of the harem eunuchs.

Thulos, when the queen's attention was disengaged from him, ventured to look again at Ilalotha; pondering, meanwhile, the curious remarks of Xantlicha. He knew that Ilalotha, like many of the court ladies, had dabbled in spells and philtres; but her witchcraft had never concerned him, since he felt no interest in other charms or enchantments than those with which nature had endowed the bodies of women. And it was quite impossible for him to believe that Ilalotha had died from a fatal passion : since, in his experience, passion was never fatal.

Indeed, as he regarded her with confused emotions, he was again beset by the impression that she had not died at all. There was no repetition of the weird, half-remembered hallucination of other time and place; but it seemed to him that she had stirred from her former position on the wine-stained bier, turning her face towards him a little, as a woman turns to an expected lover; that the arm he had kissed (either in dream or reality) was outstretched a little farther from her side.

Thulos bent nearer, fascinated by the mystery and drawn by a stronger attraction that he could not have named. Again, surely, he had dreamt or had been mistaken. But even as the doubt grew, it seemed that the bosom of Ilalotha stirred in faint respiration and he heard an almost inaudible but thrilling whisper: 'Come to me at midnight. I will wait for thee . . . in the tomb.'

At this instant there appeared beside the catafalque certain people in the sober and rusty raiment of sextons, who had entered the hall silently, unperceived by Thulos or by any of the company. They carried among them a thin-walled sarcophagus of newly welded and burnished bronze. It was their office to remove the dead woman and bear her to the sepulchral vaults of her family, which were situated in the old necropolis lying somewhat to northward of the palace gardens.

Thulos would have cried out to restrain them from their purpose; but his tongue clove tightly; nor could he move any of his members. Not knowing whether he slept or woke, he watched the people of the cemetery as they placed Ilalotha in the sarcophagus and bore her quickly from the hall, unfollowed and still unheeded by the drowsy bacchanalians. Only when the sombre cortège had departed was he able to stir from his position by the empty bier. His thoughts were sluggish, and full of darkness and indecision. Smitten by an immense fatigue that was not unnatural after his daylong journey, he withdrew to his apartments and fell instantly into death-deep slumber.

Freeing itself gradually from the cypress-boughs, as if from the long, stretched fingers of witches, a waning and misshapen moon glared horizontally through the eastern window when Thulos awoke. By this token, he knew that the hour drew towards midnight, and recalled the assignation which Queen Xantlicha had made with him: an assignation which he could hardly break without incurring the queen's deadly displeasure. Also, with singular clearness, he recalled another rendezvous ... at the same time but in a different place. Those incidents and impressions of Ilalotha's funeral, which, at the time, had seemed so dubitable and dreamlike, returned to him with a profound conviction of reality, as if etched on his mind by some mordant chemistry of sleep ... or the strengthening of some sorcerous charm. He felt that Ilalotha had indeed stirred on her bier and spoken to him; that the sextons had borne her still living to the tomb. Perhaps her supposed demise had been merely a sort of catalepsy; or else she had deliberately feigned death in a last effort to revive his passion. These thoughts awoke within him a raging fever of curiosity and desire; and he saw before him her pale, inert, luxurious beauty, presented as if by enchantment.

Direly distraught, he went down by the lampless stairs and hallways to the moonlit labyrinth of the gardens. He cursed the untimely exigence of Xantlicha. However, as he told himself, it was more than likely that the queen, continuing to imbibe the liquors of Tasuun, had long since reached a condition in which she would neither keep nor recall her appointment. This thought reassured him: in his queerly bemused mind, it soon became a certainty; and he did not hasten towards the south pavilion but strolled vaguely amid the wan and sombre boscage.

More and more it seemed unlikely that any but himself was abroad: for the long unlit wings of the palace sprawled as in vacant stupor; and in the gardens there were only dead shadows, and pools of still fragrance in which the winds had drowned. And over all, like a pale, monstrous poppy, the moon distilled her death-white slumber.

Thulos, no longer mindful of his rendezvous with Xantlicha, yielded without further reluctation to the urgence that drove him towards another goal. Truly, it was no less than obligatory that he should visit the vaults and learn whether or not he had been deceived in his belief concerning Ilalotha. Perhaps, if he did not go, she would stifle in the shut sarcophagus, and her pretended death would quickly become an actuality. Again, as if spoken in the moonlight before him, he heard the words she had whispered, or seemed to whisper, from the bier: 'Come to me at midnight ... I will wait for thee ... in the tomb.'

With the quickening steps and pulses of one who fares to the warm, petal-sweet couch of an adored mistress, he left the palace grounds by an unguarded northern postern and crossed the weedy common between the royal gardens and the old cemetery. Unchilled and undismayed, he entered those always-open portals of death, where ghoulheaded monsters of black marble, glaring with hideously pitted eyes, maintained their charnel postures before the crumbling pylons.

The very stillness of the low-bosomed graves, the rigour and pallor of the tall shafts, the deepness of bedded cypress shadows, the inviolacy of death by which all things were invested, served to heighten the singular excitement that had fired Thulos' blood. It was as if he had drunk a philtre spiced with mummia. All around him the mortuary silence seemed to burn and quiver with a thousand memories of Ilalotha, together with those expectations to which he had given as yet no formal image ...

Once, with Ilalotha, he had visited the subterranean tomb of her ancestors; and recalling its situation clearly, he came without indirection to the low-arched and cedar-darkened entrance. Rank nettles and fetid fumitories, growing thickly about the seldom-used adit, were crushed down by the tread of those who had entered there before Thulos; and the rusty, iron-wrought door sagged heavily inward on its loose hinges. At his feet there lay an extinguished flambeau, dropped, no doubt, by one of the departing sextons. Seeing it, he realized that he had brought with him neither candle nor lanthorn for the exploration of the vaults, and found in that providential torch an auspicious omen.

Bearing the lit flambeau, he began his investigation. He gave no heed to the piled and dusty sarcophagi in the first reaches of the subterrane: for during their past visit, Ilalotha had shown to him a niche at the innermost extreme, where, in due time, she herself would find sepulture among the members of that decaying line. Strangely, insidiously, like the breath of some vernal garden, the languid and luscious odour of jasmine swam to meet him through the musty air, amid the tiered presence of the dead; and it drew him to the sarcophagus that stood open between others tightly lidded. There he beheld Ilalotha, lying in the gay garments of her funeral, with half-shut eyes and half-parted lips; and upon her was the same weird and radiant beauty, the same voluptuous pallor and stillness, that had drawn Thulos with a necromantic charm.

'I knew that thou wouldst come, O Thulos,' she murmured, stirring a little, as if involuntarily, beneath the deepening ardour of his kisses that passed quickly from throat to bosom . . .

The torch that had fallen from Thulos' hand expired in the thick dust . . .

Xantlicha, retiring to her chamber betimes, had slept illy. Perhaps she had drunk too much or too little of the dark ardent vintages; perhaps her blood was fevered by the return of Thulos, and her jealousy still troubled by the hot kiss which he had laid on Ilalotha's arm during the obsequies. A restlessness was upon her; and she rose well before the hour of her meeting with Thulos, and stood at her chamber window seeking such coolness as the night air might afford.

The air, however, seemed heated as by the burning of hidden furnaces; her heart appeared to swell in her bosom and stifle her; and her unrest and agitation were increased rather than diminished by the spectacle of the moon-lulled gardens. She would have hurried forth to the tryst in the pavilion; but despite her impatience, she thought it well to keep Thulos waiting. Leaning thus from her sill, she beheld Thulos when he passed amid the parterres and arbors below. She was struck by the unusual haste and intentness of his steps; and she wondered at their direction, which could only bring him to places remote from the rendezvous she had named. He disappeared from her sight in the cypress-lined alley that led to the north garden gate; and her wonderment was soon mingled with alarm and anger when he did not return.

It was incomprehensible to Xantlicha that Thulos, or any man, would dare to forget the tryst in his normal senses; and seeking an explanation, she surmised that the working of some baleful and potent sorcery was probably involved. Nor, in the light of certain incidents that she had observed, and much else that had been rumoured, was it hard for her to identify the sorceress. Ilalotha, the queen knew, had loved Thulos to the point of frenzy, and had grieved inconsolably after his desertion for her. People said that she had wrought various ineffectual spells to bring him back; that she had vainly invoked demons and sacrificed to them, and had made futile invultuations and death-charms against Xantlicha. In the end, she had died of sheer chagrin and despair, or perhaps had slain herself with some undetected poison ... But, as was commonly believed in Tasuun, a witch dying thus, with unslaked desires and frustrate cantrips, could turn herself into a lamia or vampire and procure thereby the consummation of all her sorceries ...

The queen shuddered, remembering these things; and remembering also the hideous and malign transformation that was said to accompany the achievement of such ends: for those who used in this manner the power of hell must take on the very character and the actual semblance of infernal beings. Too well she surmised the destination of Thulos, and the danger to which he had gone forth if her suspicions were true. And, knowing that she might face an equal danger, Xantlicha determined to follow him.

She made little preparation, for there was no time to waste; but took from beneath her silken bedcushions a small, straight-bladed dagger that she kept always within reach. The dagger had been anointed from point to hilt with such venom as was believed efficacious against either the living or the dead. Bearing it in her right hand, and carrying in the other a slot-eyed lanthorn that she might require later, Xantlicha stole swiftly from the palace.

The last lees of the evening's wine ebbed wholly from her brain, and dim, ghastly fears awoke, warning her like the voices of ancestral phantoms. But, firm in her determination, she followed the path taken by Thulos; the path taken earlier by those sextons who had borne Ilalotha to her place of sepulture. Hovering from tree to tree, the moon accompanied her like a worm-hollowed visage. The soft, quick patter of her cothurns, breaking the white silence, seemed to tear the filmy cobweb pall that withheld from her a world of spectral abominations. And more and more she recalled of those legendries that concerned such beings as Ilalotha; and her heart was shaken within her: for she knew that she would meet no mortal woman but a thing raised up and inspirited by the seventh hell. But amid the chill of these horrors, the thought of Thulos in the lamia's arms was like a red brand that seared her bosom.

Now the necropolis yawned before Xantlicha, and her path entered the cavernous gloom of far-vaulted funeral trees, as if passing into monstrous and shadowy mouths that were tusked with white monuments. The air grew dank and noisome, as if filled with the breathings of open crypts. Here

the queen faltered, for it seemed that black, unseen caco-
demons rose all about her from the graveyard ground, towering higher than the shafts and boles, and standing in
readiness to assail her if she went farther. Nevertheless, she
came anon to the dark adit that she sought. Tremulously
she lit the wick of the slot-eyed lanthorn; and, piercing the
gross underground darkness before her with its bladed beam,
she passed with ill-subdued terror and repugnance into that
abode of the dead ... and perchance of the Undead.

However, as she followed the first turnings of the cata-
comb, it seemed that she was to encounter nothing more abhorrent than charnel mould and century-sifted dust; nothing
more formidable than the serried sarcophagi that lined the
deeply hewn shelves of stone: sarcophagi that had stood
silent and undisturbed ever since the time of their deposition.
Here, surely, the slumber of all the dead was unbroken, and
the nullity of death was inviolate.

Almost the queen doubted that Thulos had preceded her
there; till, turning her light on the ground, she discerned the
print of his poulaines, long-tipped and slender in the deep
dust amid those footmarks left by the rudely shod sextons.
And she saw that the footprints of Thulos pointed only in
one direction, while those of the others plainly went and
returned.

Then, at an undetermined distance in the shadows ahead,
Xantlicha heard a sound in which the sick moaning of some
amorous woman was blent with a snarling as of jackals
over the meat. Her blood returned frozen upon her heart as
she went onward step by slow step, clutching her dagger in
a hand drawn sharply back, and holding the light high in
advance. The sound grew louder and more distinct; and
there came to her now a perfume as of flowers in some warm
June night; but, as she still advanced, the perfume was
mixed with more and more of a smothering foulness such as
she had never heretofore known, and was touched with the
hot reeking of blood.

A few paces more, and Xantlicha stood as if a demon's

arm had arrested her: for her lanthorn's light had found the
inverted face and upper body of Thulos, hanging from the
end of a burnished, new-wrought sarcophagus that occupied
a scant interval between others green with rust. One of
Thulos' hands clutched rigidly the rim of the sarcophagus,
while the other hand, moving feebly, seemed to caress a
dim shape that leaned above him with arms showing jasmine-
white in the narrow beam, and dark fingers plunging into
his bosom. His head and body seemed but an empty hull,
and his hand hung skeleton-thin on the bronze rim, and his
whole aspect was vein-drawn, as if he had lost more blood
than was evident on his torn throat and face, and in his sod-
den raiment and dripping hair.

From the thing stooping above Thulos, there came cease-
lessly that sound which was half moan and half snarl. And
as Xantlicha stood in petrific fear and loathing, she seemed
to hear from Thulos' lips an indistinct murmur, more of
ecstasy than pain. The murmur ceased, and his head hung
slacklier than before, so that the queen deemed him verily
dead. At this she found such wrathful courage as enabled
her to step nearer and raise the lanthorn higher: for, even
amid her extreme panic, it came to her that by means of the
wizard-poisoned dagger she might still haply slay the thing
that had slain Thulos.

Waveringly the light crept aloft, disclosing inch by inch
that infamy which Thulos had caressed in the darkness.

... It crept even to the crimson-smeared wattles, and the
fanged and ruddled orifice that was half mouth and half
beak ... till Xantlicha knew why the body of Thulos was a
mere shrunken hull ... In what the queen saw, there remained nothing of Ilalotha except the white, voluptuous
arms, and a vague outline of human breasts melting mo-
mently into breasts that were not human, like clay moulded
by a demon sculptor. The arms too began to change and
darken; and, as they changed, the dying hand of Thulos
stirred again and fumbled with a caressing movement towards the horror. And the thing seemed to heed him not
but withdrew its fingers from his bosom, and reached across

him with members stretching enormously, as if to claw the queen or fondle her with its dribbling talons.

It was then that Xantlicha let fall the lanthorn and the dagger, and ran with shrill, endless shriekings and laughters of immitigable madness from the vault.

THE TOMB OF SARAH

by

F. G. Loring

My father was the head of a celebrated firm of church restorers and decorators about sixty years ago. He took a keen interest in his work, and made an especial study of any old legends or family histories that came under his observation. He was necessarily very well read and thoroughly well posted in all questions of folk-lore and medieval legend. As he kept a careful record of every case he investigated the manuscripts he left at his death have a special interest. From amongst them I have selected the following, as being a particularly weird and extraordinary experience. In presenting it to the public I feel it is superfluous to apologize for its supernatural character.

MY FATHER'S DIARY

1841, *17th June*. Received a commission from my old friend, Peter Grant, to enlarge and restore the chancel of his church at Hagarstone, in the wilds of the west country.

5th July. Went down to Hagarstone with my head man, Somers. A very long and tiring journey.

7th July. Got the work well started. The old church is one of special interest to the antiquarian, and I shall endeavour while restoring it to alter the existing arrangements as little as possible. One large tomb, however, must be moved bodily ten feet at least to the southward. Curiously enough there is a somewhat forbidding inscription upon it in Latin, and I am sorry that this particular tomb should have to be moved. It stands amongst the graves of the Kenyons, an old family which has been extinct in these parts for centuries. The inscription on it runs thus:

SARAH
1630
For the sake of the dead and the welfare of the
living, let this sepulchre remain untouched
and its occupant undisturbed until
the Coming of Christ.
In the name of the Father, the Son
and the Holy Ghost.

8th July. Took counsel with Grant concerning the 'Sarah
Tomb'. We are both very loth to disturb it, but the ground
has sunk so beneath it that the safety of the church is in
danger; thus we have no choice. However, the work shall
be done as reverently as possible under our own direction.

Grant says there is a legend in the neighbourhood that it
is the tomb of the last of the Kenyons, the evil Countess
Sarah, who was murdered in 1630. She lived quite alone in
the old castle, whose ruins still stand three miles from here
on the road to Bristol. Her reputation was an evil one even
for those days. She was a witch or were-woman, the only
companion of her solitude being a familiar in the shape of a
huge Asiatic wolf. This creature was reputed to seize upon
children, or failing these, sheep and other small animals, and
convey them to the castle, where the countess used to suck
their blood. It was popularly supposed that she could never
be killed. This, however, proved a fallacy, since she was
strangled one day by a mad peasant woman who had lost
two children, she declaring that they had both been seized
and carried off by the countess's familiar. This is a very
interesting story, since it points to a local superstition very
similar to that of the vampire, existing in Slavonic and Hungarian Europe.

The tomb is built of black marble, surmounted by an
enormous slab of the same material. On the slab is a magnificent group of figures. A young and handsome woman re-
clines upon a couch; round her neck is a piece of rope, the
end of which she holds in her hand. At her side is a gigantic dog with bared fangs and lolling tongue. The face of the

reclining figure is a cruel one; the corners of the mouth are curiously lifted, showing the sharp points of long canine or dog teeth. The whole group, though magnificently executed, leaves a most unpleasant sensation.

If we move the tomb it will have to be done in two pieces, the covering slab first and then the tomb proper. We have decided to remove the covering slab tomorrow.

9th July 6 PM. A very strange day.

By noon everything was ready for lifting off the covering stone, and after the men's dinner we started the jacks and pulleys. The slab lifted easily enough, though it fitted closely into its seat and was further secured by some sort of mortar or putty, which must have kept the interior perfectly airtight.

None of us was prepared for the horrible rush of foul, mouldy air that escaped as the cover lifted clear of its seating. And the contents that gradually came into view were more startling still. There lay the fully dressed body of a woman, wizened and shrunk and ghastly pale as if from starvation. Round her neck was a loose cord, and, judging by the scars still visible, the story of death by strangulation was true enough.

The most horrible part, however, was the extraordinary freshness of the body. Except for the appearance of starvation, life might have been only just extinct. The flesh was soft and white, the eyes were wide open and seemed to stare at us with a fearful understanding in them. The body itself lay on mould, without any pretence to coffin or shell.

For several moments we gazed with horrible curiosity, and then it became too much for my workmen, who implored us to replace the covering slab. That, of course, we would not do; but I set the carpenters to work at once to make a temporary cover while we moved the tomb to its new position. This is a long job, and will take two or three days at least.

9 PM. Just at sunset we were startled by the howling of, seemingly, every dog in the village. It lasted for ten minutes

or a quarter of an hour, and then ceased as suddenly as it began. This, and a curious mist that has risen round the church, makes me feel rather anxious about the 'Sarah Tomb'. According to the best established traditions of the vampire-haunted countries, the disturbance of dogs or wolves at sunset is supposed to indicate the presence of one of these fiends, and local fog is always considered to be a certain sign. The vampire has the power of producing it for the purpose of concealing its movements near its hiding-place at any time.

I dare not mention or even hint my fears to the rector, for he is, not unnaturally perhaps, a rank disbeliever in many things that I know, from experience, are not only possible but even probable. I must work this out alone at first, and get his aid without his knowing in what direction he is helping me. I shall now watch till midnight at least.

10.15 PM. As I feared and half expected. Just before ten there was another outburst of the hideous howling. It was commenced most distinctly by a particularly horrible and blood-curdling wail from the vicinity of the churchyard. The chorus lasted only a few minutes, however, and at the end of it I saw a large dark shape, like a huge dog, emerge from the fog and lope away at a rapid canter towards the open country. Assuming this to be what I fear, I shall see it return soon after midnight.

12.30 PM. I was right. Almost as midnight struck I saw the beast returning. It stopped at the spot where the fog seemed to commence, and, lifting up its head, gave tongue to that particularly long-drawn wail that I had noticed as preceding the outburst earlier in the evening.

Tomorrow I shall tell the rector what I have seen; and if, as I expect, we hear of some neighbouring sheepfold having been raided, I shall get him to watch with me for this nocturnal marauder. I shall also examine the 'Sarah Tomb' for something which he may notice without any previous hint from me.

10th July. I found the workmen this morning much disturbed in mind about the howling of the dogs. 'We doan't like it, zur,' one of them said to me – 'we doan't like it; there was summat abroad last night that was unholy.' They were still more uncomfortable when the news came round that a large dog had made a raid upon a flock of sheep, scattering them far and wide, and leaving three of them dead with torn throats in the field.

When I told the rector of what I had seen and what was being said in the village, he immediately decided that we must try and catch or at least identify the beast I had seen. 'Of course,' said he, 'it is some dog lately imported into the neighbourhood, for I know of nothing about here nearly as large as the animal you describe, though its size may be due to the deceptive moonlight.'

This afternoon I asked the rector, as a favour, to assist me in lifting the temporary cover that was on the tomb, giving as an excuse the reason that I wished to obtain a portion of the curious mortar with which it had been sealed. After a slight demur he consented, and we raised the lid. If the sight that met our eyes gave me a shock, at least it appalled Grant.

'Great God!' he exclaimed; 'the woman is alive!'

And so it seemed for a moment. The corpse had lost much of its starved appearance and looked hideously fresh and alive. It was still wrinkled and shrunken, but the lips were firm, and of the rich red hue of health. The eyes, if possible, were more appalling than ever, though fixed and staring. At one corner of the mouth I thought I noticed a slight dark-coloured froth, but I said nothing about it then.

'Take your piece of mortar, Harry,' gasped Grant, 'and let us shut the tomb again. God help me! Parson though I am, such dead faces frighten me!'

Nor was I sorry to hide that terrible face again; but I got my bit of mortar, and I have advanced a step towards the solution of the mystery.

This afternoon the tomb was moved several feet towards its new position, but it will be two or three days yet before we shall be ready to replace the slab.

10.15 PM. Again the same howling at sunset, the same

fog enveloping the church, and at ten o'clock the same great beast slipping silently out into the open country. I must get the rector's help and watch for its return. But precautions we must take, for if things are as I believe, we take our lives in our hands when we venture out into the night to waylay the – vampire. Why not admit it at once? For that the beast I have seen is the vampire of that evil thing in the tomb I can have no reasonable doubt.

Not yet come to its full strength, thank Heaven! after the starvation of nearly two centuries, for the present it can only maraud as wolf apparently. But, in a day or two, when full power returns, that dreadful woman in new strength and beauty will be able to leave her refuge. Then it would not be sheep merely that would satisfy her disgusting lust for blood, but victims that would yield their life-blood without a murmur to her caressing touch – victims that, dying of her foul embrace, themselves must become vampires in their turn to prey on others.

Mercifully my knowledge gives me a safeguard; for that little piece of mortar that I rescued today from the tomb contains a portion of the sacred host, and who holds it, humbly and firmly believing in its virtue, may pass safely through such an ordeal as I intended to submit myself and the rector to tonight.

12.30 PM. Our adventure is over for the present, and we are back safe.

After writing the last entry recorded above, I went off to find Grant and tell him that the marauder was out on the prowl again. 'But, Grant,' I said, 'before we start out tonight I must insist that you will let me prosecute this affair in my own way; you must promise to put yourself completely under my orders, without asking any questions as to the why and wherefore.'

After a little demur, and some excusable chaff on his part at the serious view I was taking of what he called a 'dog hunt', he gave me his promise. I then told him that we were to watch tonight and try and track the mysterious beast, but not to interfere with it in any way. I think, in spite of his jests, that I impressed him with the fact that there might be, after all, good reason for my precautions.

It was just after eleven when we stepped out into the still night.

Our first move was to try and penetrate the dense fog round the church, but there was something so chilly about it, and a faint smell so disgustingly rank and loathsome, that neither our nerves nor our stomachs were proof against it. Instead, we stationed ourselves in the dark shadow of a yew-tree that commanded a good view of the wicket entrance to the churchyard.

At midnight the howling of the dogs began again, and in a few minutes we saw a large grey shape, with green eyes shining like lamps, shamble swiftly down the path towards us.

The rector started forward, but I laid a firm hand upon his arm and whispered a warning: 'Remember!' Then we both stood very still and watched as the great beast cantered swiftly by. It was real enough, for we could hear the clicking of its nails on the stone flags. It passed within a few yards of us, and seemed to be nothing more nor less than a great grey wolf, thin and gaunt, with bristling hair and dripping jaws. It stopped where the mist commenced, and turned around. It was truly a horrible sight, and made one's blood run cold. The eyes burnt like fires, the upper lip was snarling and raised, showing the great canine teeth, while round the mouth clung and dripped a dark-coloured froth.

It raised its head and gave tongue to its long wailing howl, which was answered from afar by the village dogs. After standing for a few moments it turned and disappeared into the thickest part of the fog.

Very shortly afterwards the atmosphere began to clear, and within ten minutes the mist was all gone, the dogs in the village were silent, and the night seemed to reassume its normal aspect. We examined the spot where the beast had been standing and found, plainly enough upon the stone flags, dark spots of froth and saliva.

'Well, rector,' I said, 'will you admit now, in view of the

things you have seen today, in consideration of the legend, the woman in the tomb, the fog, the howling dogs, and, last but not least, the mysterious beast you have seen so close, that there is something not quite normal in it all? Will you put yourself unreservedly in my hands and help me, whatever I may do, first to make assurance doubly sure, and finally to take the necessary steps for putting an end to this horror of the night?' I saw that the uncanny influence of the night was strong upon him, and wished to impress it as much as possible.

'Needs must,' he replied, 'when the Devil drives: and in the face of what I have seen I must believe that some unholy forces are at work. Yet, how can they work in the sacred precincts of a church? Shall we not call rather upon Heaven to assist us in our needs?'

'Grant,' I said solemnly, 'that we must do, each in his own way. God helps those who help themselves, and by His help and the light of my knowledge we must fight this battle for Him and the poor lost soul within.'

We then returned to the rectory and to our rooms, though I have sat up to write this account while the scene is fresh in my mind.

11th July. Found the workmen again very much disturbed in their minds, and full of a strange dog that had been seen during the night by several people, who had hunted it. Farmer Stotman, who had been watching his sheep (the same flock that had been raided the night before), had surprised it over a fresh carcass and tried to drive it off, but its size and fierceness so alarmed him that he had beaten a hasty retreat for a gun. When he returned the animal was gone, though he found that three more sheep from his flock were dead and torn.

The 'Sarah Tomb' was moved today to its new position; but it was a long, heavy business, and there was not time to replace the covering slab. For this I was glad, as in the prosaic light of day the rector almost disbelieves the events of the night, and is prepared to think everything to have been magnified and distorted by our imagination.

As, however, I could not possibly proceed with my war of extermination against this foul thing without assistance, and as there is nobody else I can rely upon, I appealed to him for one more night – to convince him that it was no delusion, but a ghastly, horrible truth, which must be fought and conquered for our own sakes, as well as that of all those living in the neighbourhood.

'Put yourself in my hands, rector,' I said, 'for tonight at least. Let us take those precautions which my study of the subject tells me are the right ones. Tonight you and I must watch in the church; and I feel assured that tomorrow you will be as convinced as I am, and be equally prepared to take those awful steps which I know to be proper, and I must warn you that we shall find a more startling change in the body lying there than you noticed yesterday.'

My words came true; for on raising the wooden cover once more the rank stench of a slaughterhouse arose, making us feel positively sick. There lay the vampire, but how changed from the starved and shrunken corpse we saw two days ago for the first time! The wrinkles had almost disappeared, the flesh was firm and full, the crimson lips grinned horribly over the long pointed teeth, and a distinct smear of blood had trickled down one corner of the mouth. We set our teeth, however, and hardened our hearts. Then we replaced the cover and put what we had collected into a safe place in the vestry. Yet even now Grant could not believe that there was any real or pressing danger concealed in that awful tomb, as he raised strenuous objections to any apparent desecration of the body without further proof. This he shall have tonight. God grant that I am not taking too much on myself! If there is any truth in old legends it would be easy enough to destroy the vampire now; but Grant will not have it.

I hope for the best of this night's work, but the danger in waiting is very great.

6 PM. I have prepared everything: the sharp knives, the pointed stake, fresh garlic, and the wild dog-roses. All these

I have taken and concealed in the vestry, where we can get at them when our solemn vigil commences.

If either or both of us die with our fearful task undone, let those reading my record see that this is done. I lay it upon them as a solemn obligation. 'That the vampire be pierced through the heart with the stake, then let the burial service be read over the poor clay at last released from its doom. Thus shall the vampire cease to be, and a lost soul rest.'

12 July. All is over. After the most terrible night of watching and horror, one vampire at least will trouble the world no more. But how thankful should we be to a merciful Providence that that awful tomb was not disturbed by anyone not having the knowledge necessary to deal with its dreadful occupant! I write this with no feelings of self-complacency, but simply with a great gratitude for the years of study I have been able to devote to this subject.

And now to my tale.

Just before sunset last night the rector and I locked ourselves into the church, and took up our position in the pulpit. It was one of those pulpits, to be found in some churches, which is entered from the vestry, the preacher appearing at a good height through an arched opening in the wall. This gave us a sense of security (which we felt we needed), a good view of the interior, and direct access to the implements which I had concealed in the vestry.

The sun set and the twilight gradually deepened and faded. There was, so far, no sign of the usual fog, nor any howling of the dogs. At nine o'clock the moon rose, and her pale light gradually flooded the aisles, and still no sign of any kind from the 'Sarah Tomb.' The rector had asked me several times what he might expect, but I was determined that no words or thought of mine should influence him, and that he should be convinced by his own senses alone.

By half-past ten we were both getting very tired, and I began to think that perhaps after all we should see nothing that night. However, soon after eleven we observed a light mist rising from the 'Sarah Tomb'. It seemed to scintillate and sparkle as it rose, and curled in a sort of pillar or spiral.

I said nothing, but I heard the rector give a sort of gasp as he clutched my arm feverishly. 'Great Heaven!' he whispered, 'it is taking shape.'

And, true enough, in a very few moments we saw standing erect by the tomb the ghastly figure of the Countess Sarah!

She looked thin and haggard still, and her face was deadly white; but the crimson lips looked like a hideous gash in the pale cheeks, and her eyes glared like red coals in the gloom of the church.

It was a fearful thing to watch as she stepped unsteadily down the aisle, staggering a little as if from weakness and exhaustion. This was perhaps natural, as her body must have suffered much physically from her long incarceration, in spite of the unholy forces which kept it fresh and well.

We watched her to the door, and wondered what would happen; but it appeared to present no difficulty, for she melted through it and disappeared.

'Now, Grant,' I said, 'do you believe?'

'Yes,' he replied, 'I must. Everything is in your hands, and I will obey your commands to the letter, if you can only instruct me how to rid my poor people of this unnameable terror.'

'By God's help I will,' said I; 'but you shall be yet more convinced first, for we have a terrible work to do, and much to answer for in the future, before we leave the church again this morning. And now to work, for in its present weak state the vampire will not wander far, but may return at any time, and must not find us unprepared.'

We stepped down from the pulpit, and taking dog-roses and garlic from the vestry, proceeded to the tomb. I arrived first and, throwing off the wooden cover, cried: 'Look! it's empty!' There was nothing there! Nothing except the impress of the body in the loose damp mould!

I took the flowers and laid them in a circle round the tomb, for legend teaches us that vampires will not pass over these particular blossoms if they can avoid it.

Then, eight or ten feet away, I made a circle on the stone pavement, large enough for the rector and myself to stand in, and within the circle I placed the implements that I had brought into the church with me.

'Now,' I said, 'from this circle, which nothing unholy can step across, you shall see the vampire face to face, and see her afraid to cross that other circle of garlic and dog-roses to regain her unholy refuge. But on no account step beyond the holy place you stand in, for the vampire has a fearful strength not her own, and, like a snake, can draw her victim willingly to his own destruction.'

Now so far my work was done, and, calling the rector, we stepped into the holy circle to await the vampire's return.

Nor was this long delayed. Presently a damp, cold odour seemed to pervade the church, which made our hair bristle and flesh creep. And then, down the aisle with noiseless feet, came That which we watched for.

I heard the rector mutter a prayer, and I held him tightly by the arm, for he was shivering violently.

Long before we could distinguish the features we saw the glowing eyes and the crimson sensual mouth. She went straight to her tomb, but stopped short when she encountered my flowers. She walked right round the tomb seeking a place to enter, and as she walked she saw us. A spasm of diabolical hate and fury passed over her face; but it quickly vanished, and a smile of love, more devilish still, took its place. She stretched out her arms towards us. Then we saw that round her mouth gathered a bloody froth and from under her lips long pointed teeth gleamed and champed.

She spoke: a soft soothing voice, a voice that carried a spell with it, and affected us both strangely, particularly the rector. I wished to test as far as possible, without endangering our lives, the vampire's power.

Her voice had a soporific effect, which I resisted easily enough, but which seemed to throw the rector into a sort of trance. More than this: it seemed to compel him to her in spite of his efforts to resist.

'Come!' she said— 'come! I give sleep and peace – sleep and peace – sleep and peace.'

She advanced a little towards us; but not far, for I noted

that the sacred circle seemed to keep her back like an iron hand.

My companion seemed to become demoralized and spell-bound. He tried to step forward and, finding me detain him, whispered: 'Harry, let go! She is calling me! I must! I must! Oh, help me! help me!' And he began to struggle.

It was time to finish.

'Grant!' I cried, in a loud, firm voice, 'in the name of all that you hold sacred, have done and play the man!' He shuddered violently and gasped: 'Where am I?' Then he remembered, and clung to me convulsively for a moment.

At this a look of damnable hate changed the smiling face before us, and with a sort of shriek she staggered back.

'Back!' I cried: 'back to your unholy tomb! No longer shall you molest the suffering world! Your end is near.'

It was fear that now showed itself in her beautiful face (for it was beautiful in spite of its horror) as she shrank back, back and over the circlet of flowers, shivering as she did so. At last, with a low mournful cry, she appeared to melt back again into her tomb.

As she did so the first gleams of the rising sun lit up the world, and I knew all danger was over for the day.

Taking Grant by the arm, I drew him with me out of the circle and led him to the tomb. There lay the vampire once more, still in her living death as we had a moment before seen her in her devilish life. But in the eyes remained that awful expression of hate, and cringing, appalling fear.

Grant was pulling himself together.

'Now,' I said, 'will you dare the last terrible act and rid the world for ever of this horror?'

'By God!' he said solemnly, 'I will. Tell me what to do.'

'Help me to lift her out of her tomb. She can harm us no more,' I replied.

With averted faces we set to our terrible task, and laid her out upon the flags.

'Now,' I said, 'read the burial service over the poor body, and then let us give it its release from this living hell that holds it.'

Reverently the rector read the beautiful words, and reverently I made the necessary responses. When it was over I took the stake and, without giving myself time to think, plunged it with all my strength through the heart.

As though really alive, the body for a moment writhed and kicked convulsively, and an awful heart-rending shriek woke the silent church; then all was still.

Then we lifted the poor body back; and, thank God! the consolation that legend tells is never denied to those who have to do such awful work as ours came at last. Over the face stole a great and solemn peace; the lips lost their crimson hue, the prominent sharp teeth sank back into the mouth, and for a moment we saw before us the calm, pale face of a most beautiful woman, who smiled as she slept. A few minutes more, and she faded away to dust before our eyes as we watched. We set to work and cleaned up every trace of our work, and then departed for the rectory. Most thankful were we to step out of the church, with its horrible associations, into the rosy warmth of the summer morning.

With the above end the notes in my father's diary, though a few days later this further entry occurs.

15th July. Since the 12th everything has been quiet and as usual. We replaced and sealed up the 'Sarah Tomb' this morning. The workmen were surprised to find the body had disappeared, but took it to be the natural result of exposing it to the air.

One odd thing came to my ears today. It appears that the child of one of the villagers strayed from home the night of the 11th inst, and was found asleep in a coppice near the church, very pale and quite exhausted. There were two small marks on her throat, which have since disappeared.

What does this mean? I have, however, kept it to myself, as, now that the vampire is no more, no further danger either to that child or any other is to be apprehended. It is only those who die of the vampire's embrace that become vampires at death in their turn.

REVELATIONS IN BLACK

by

Carl Jacobi

It was a dreary, forlorn establishment way down on Harbor Street. An old sign announced the legend: 'Giovanni Larla – Antiques', and a dingy window revealed a display half masked in dust.

Even as I crossed the threshold that cheerless September afternoon, driven from the sidewalk by a gust of rain and perhaps a fascination for all antiques, the gloominess fell upon me like a material pall. Inside was half darkness, piled boxes and a monstrous tapestry, frayed with the warp showing in worn places. An Italian Renaissance wine cabinet shrank despondently in its corner and seemed to frown at me as I passed.

'Good afternoon, *Signor*. There is something you wish to buy? A picture, a ring, a vase perhaps?'

I peered at the squat, pudgy bulk of the Italian proprietor there in the shadows and hesitated.

'Just looking around,' I said, turning my eyes to the jumble about me. 'Nothing in particular ...'

The man's oily face moved in a smile as though he had heard the remark a thousand times before. He sighed, stood there in thought a moment, the rain drumming and swishing against the outer pane. Then very deliberately he stepped to the shelves and glanced up and down them considering. I moved to his side, letting my eyes sweep across the stacked array of ancient oddities. At length he drew forth an object which I perceived to be a painted chalice.

'An authentic Sixteenth Century Tandart,' he murmured. 'A work of art, *Signor*.'

I shook my head. 'No pottery,' I said. 'Books perhaps, but no pottery.'

He frowned slowly. 'I have books too,' he replied, 'rare books which nobody sells but me, Giovanni Larla. But you must look at my other treasures too.'

There was, I found, no hurrying the man. A quarter of an hour passed, during which I had to see a Glycon cameo brooch, a carved chair of some indeterminate style and period and a muddle of yellowed statuettes, small oils and one or two dreary Portland vases. Several times I glanced at my watch impatiently, wondering how I might break away from this Italian and his gloomy shop. Already the fascination of its dust and shadows had begun to wear off, and I was anxious to reach the street.

But when he had conducted me well towards the rear of the shop, something caught my fancy. I drew then from the shelf the first book of horror. If I had but known the terrible events that were to follow, if I could only have had a foresight into the future that September day, I swear I would have avoided the book like a leprous thing, would have shunned that wretched antique store and the very street it stood on like places accursed. A thousand times I have wished my eyes had never rested on that cover in black. What writhings of the soul, what terrors, what unrest, what madness would have been spared me!

But never dreaming the hideous secret of its pages I fondled it casually and remarked:

'An unusual book. What is it?'

Larla glanced up and scowled.

'That is not for sale,' he said quietly. 'I don't know how it got on these shelves. It was my poor brother's.'

The volume in my hand was indeed unusual in appearance. Measuring but four inches across and five inches in length and bound in black velvet with each outside corner protected with a triangle of ivory, it was the most beautiful piece of bookbinding I had ever seen. In the centre of the cover was mounted a tiny piece of ivory intricately cut in the shape of a skull. But it was the title of the book that excited my interest. Embroidered in gold braid, the title read:

'*Five Unicorns and a Pearl.*'

I looked at Larla. 'How much?' I asked and reached for my wallet.

He shook his head. 'No, it is not for sale. It is . . . it is the last work of my brother. He wrote it just before he died in the institution.'

'The institution?' I queried.

Larla made no reply but stood staring at the book, his mind obviously drifting away in deep thought. A moment of silence dragged by. There was a strange gleam in his eyes when finally he spoke. And I thought I saw his fingers tremble slightly.

'My brother, Alessandro, was a fine man before he wrote that book,' he said slowly. 'He wrote beautifully, *Signor*, and he was strong and healthy. For hours I could sit while he read to me his poems. He was a dreamer, Alessandro; he loved everything beautiful, and the two of us were very happy.

'All . . . until that terrible night. Then he . . . but no . . . a year has passed now. It is best to forget.' He passed his hand before his eyes and drew in his breath sharply.

'What happened?' I asked sympathetically, his words arousing my curiosity.

'Happened, *Signor*? I do not really know. It was all so confusing. He became suddenly ill, ill without reason. The flush of sunny Italy, which was always on his cheek, faded, and he grew white and drawn. His strength left him day by day. Doctors prescribed, gave medicines, but nothing helped. He grew steadily weaker until . . . until that night.'

I looked at him curiously, impressed by his perturbation. 'And then?' I urged.

Hands opening and closing, Larla seemed to sway unsteadily; his liquid eyes opened wide to the brows, and his voice was strained and tense as he continued:

'And then . . . oh, if I could but forget! It was horrible.

Poor Alessandro came home screaming, sobbing, tearing his hair. He was ... he was stark, raving mad!

'They took him to the institution for the insane and said he needed a complete rest, that he had suffered from some terrific mental shock. He ... died three weeks later with the crucifix on his lips.'

For a moment I stood there in silence, staring out at the falling rain. Then I said:

'He wrote this book while confined to the institution?'

Larla nodded absently.

'Three books,' he replied. 'Two others exactly like the one you have in your hand. The bindings he made, of course, when he was quite well. It was his original intention, I believe, to pen in them by hand the verses of Marini. He was very clever at such work. But the wanderings of his mind which filled the pages now, I have never read. Nor do I intend to. I want to keep with me the memory of him when he was happy. This book has come on these shelves by mistake. I shall put it with his other possessions.'

My desire to read the few pages bound in velvet increased a thousandfold when I found they were unobtainable. I have always had an interest in abnormal psychology and have gone through a number of books on the subject. Here was the work of a man confined in the asylum for the insane. Here was the unexpurgated writing of an educated brain gone mad. And unless my intuition failed me, here was a suggestion of some deep mystery. My mind was made up. I must have it.

I turned to Larla and chose my words carefully.

'I can well appreciate your wish to keep the book,' I said, 'and since you refuse to sell, may I ask if you would consider lending it to me for just one night? If I promised to return it in the morning? ...'

The Italian hesitated. He toyed undecidedly with a heavy gold watch chain.

'No, I am sorry ...'

'Ten dollars and back tomorrow unharmed.'

Larla studied his shoe.

'Very well, *Signor*, I will trust you. But please, I ask you, please be sure and return it.'

That night in the quiet of my apartment I opened the book. Immediately my attention was drawn to three lines scrawled in a feminine hand across the inside of the front cover, lines written in a faded red solution that looked more like blood than ink. They read:

'Revelations meant to destroy but only binding without the stake. Read, fool, and enter my field, for we are chained to the spot. Oh, woe unto Larla!'

I mused over these undecipherable sentences for some time without solving their meaning. At last, shrugging my shoulders, I turned to the first page and began the last work of Alessandro Larla, the strangest story I had ever, in my years of browsing through old books, come upon.

'On the evening of the fifteenth of October I turned my steps into the cold and walked until I was tired. The roar of the present was in the distance when I came to twenty-six blue-jays silently contemplating the ruins. Passing in the midst of them I wandered by the skeleton trees and seated myself where I could watch the leering fish. A child worshipped. Glass threw the moon at me. Grass sang a litany at my feet. And the pointed shadow moved slowly to the left.

'I walked along the silver gravel until I came to five unicorns galloping beside water of the past. Here I found a pearl, a magnificent pearl, a pearl beautiful but black. Like a flower it carried a rich perfume, and once I thought the odour was but a mask, but why should such a perfect creation need a mask?

'I sat between the leering fish and the five galloping unicorns, and I fell madly in love with the pearl. The past lost itself in drabness and—'

I laid the book down and sat watching the smoke-curls from my pipe eddy ceilingward. There was much more, but I could make no sense to any of it. All was in that strange style and completely incomprehensible. And yet is seemed the story was more than the mere wanderings of a madman. Behind it all seemed to lie a narrative cloaked in symbolism.

Something about the few sentences – just what I cannot say – had cast an immediate spell of depression over me. The vague lines weighed upon my mind, hung before my eyes like a design, and I felt myself slowly seized by a deep feeling of uneasiness.

The air of the room grew heavy and close. The open casement and the out-of-doors seemed to beckon to me. I walked to the window, thrust the curtain aside, stood there, smoking furiously. Let me say that regular habits have long been a part of my make-up. I am not addicted to nocturnal strolls or late meanderings before seeking my bed; yet now, curiously enough, with the pages of the book still in my mind I suddenly experienced an indefinable urge to leave my apartment and walk the darkened streets.

I paced the room nervously, irritated that the sensation did not pass. The clock on the mantel pushed its ticks slowly through the quiet. And at length with a shrug I threw my pipe to the table, reached for my hat and coat and made for the door.

Ridiculous as it may sound, upon reaching the street I found that urge had increased to a distinct attraction: felt that under no circumstances must I turn any direction but northward, and although this way led into a district quite unknown to me, I was in a moment pacing forward, choosing streets deliberately and heading without knowing why towards the outskirts of the city. It was a brilliant moonlight night in September. Summer had passed and already there was the smell of frosted vegetation in the air. The great chimes in Capitol tower were sounding midnight, and the buildings and shops and later the private houses were dark and silent as I passed.

Try as I would to erase from my memory the queer book which I had just read, the mystery of its pages hammered at me, arousing my curiosity, dampening my spirits. 'Five Unicorns and a Pearl!' What did it all mean?

More and more I realized as I went on that a power other

than my own will was leading my steps. It was absurd, and I tried to resist, to turn back. Yet once when I did momentarily come to a halt that attraction swept upon me as inexorably as the desire for a narcotic.

It was far out on Easterly Street that I came upon a high stone wall flanking the sidewalk. Over its ornamented top I could see the shadows of a dark building set well back in the grounds. A wrought-iron gate in the wall opened upon a view of wild desertion and neglect. Swathed in the light of the moon, an old courtyard strewn with fountains, stone benches and statues lay tangled in rank weeds and under-growth. The windows of the building, which evidently had once been a private dwelling, were boarded up, all except those on a little tower or cupola rising to a point in the front. And here the glass caught the blue-grey light and refracted it into the shadows.

Before that gate my feet stopped like dead things. The psychic power which had been leading me had now become a reality. Directly from the courtyard it emanated, drawing me towards it with an intensity that smothered all reluctance.

Strangely enough, the gate was unlocked; and feeling like a man in a trance I swung the creaking hinges and entered, making my way along a grass-grown path to one of the benches. It seemed that once inside the court the distant sounds of the city died away, leaving a hollow silence broken only by the wind rustling through the tall dead weeds. Rearing up before me, the building with its dark wings, cupola and façade oddly resembled a colossal hound, crouched and ready to spring.

There were several fountains, weather-beaten and orna-mented with curious figures, to which at the time I paid only casual attention. Farther on, half hidden by the underbrush, was the life-size statue of a little child kneeling in position of prayer. Erosion on the soft stone had disfigured the face, and in the half-light the carved features presented an ex-pression strangely grotesque and repelling.

How long I sat there in the quiet, I don't know. The sur-roundings under the moonlight blended harmoniously with my mood. But more than that I seemed physically unable to rouse myself and pass on.

It was with a suddenness that brought me electrified to my feet that I became aware of the real significance of the objects about me. Held motionless, I stood there running my eyes wildly from place to place, refusing to believe. Surely I must be dreaming. In the name of all that was unusual this ... this absolutely couldn't be. And yet—

It was the fountain at my side that had caught my attention first. Across the top of the water basin were *five stone unicorns*, all identically carved, each seeming to follow the other in galloping procession. Looking farther, prompted now by a madly rising recollection, I saw that the cupola, towering high above the house, eclipsed the rays of the moon and threw *a long pointed shadow* across the ground *at my left*. The other fountain some distance away was ornamented with the figure of a stone fish, *a fish* whose empty eye-sockets *were leering* straight in my direction. And the climax of it all – the wall! At intervals of every three feet on top of the street expanse were mounted crude carven stone shapes of birds. And counting them I saw *that those birds were twenty-six blue-jays*.

Unquestionably – startling and impossible as it seemed – I was in the same setting as described in Larla's book! It was a staggering revelation, and my mind reeled at the thought of it. How strange, how odd that I should be drawn to a portion of the city I had never before frequented and thrown into the midst of a narrative written almost a year before!

I saw now that Alessandro Larla, writing as a patient in the institution for the insane, had seized isolated details but neglected to explain them. Here was a problem for the psychologist, the mad, the symbolic, the incredible story of the dead Italian. I was bewildered, confused, and I pondered for an answer.

As if to soothe my perturbation there stole into the court then a faint odour of perfume. Pleasantly it touched my nostrils, seemed to blend with the moonlight. I breathed it in deeply as I stood there by the curious fountain. But slowly that odour became more noticeable, grew stronger, a sickish sweet smell that began to creep down my lungs like smoke. And absently I recognized it. Heliotrope! The honeyed aroma blanketed the garden, thickened the air, seemed to fall upon me like a drug.

And then came my second surprise of the evening. Looking about to discover the source of the irritating fragrance I saw opposite me, seated on another stone bench, a woman. She was dressed entirely in black, and her face was hidden by a veil. She seemed unaware of my presence. Her head was slightly bowed, and her whole position suggested a person deep in contemplation.

I noticed also the thing that crouched by her side. It was a dog, a tremendous brute with a head strangely out of proportion and eyes as large as the ends of big spoons. For several moments I stood staring at the two of them. Although the air was quite chilly, the woman wore no over-jacket, only the black dress relieved solely by the whiteness of her throat.

With a sigh of regret at having my pleasant solitude thus disturbed I moved across the court until I stood at her side. Still she showed no recognition of my presence, and clearing my throat I said hesitatingly:

'I suppose you are the owner here. I ... I really didn't know the place was occupied, and the gate ... well, the gate was unlocked. I'm sorry I trespassed.'

She made no reply to that, and the dog merely gazed at me in dumb silence. No graceful words of polite departure came to my lips, and I moved hesitatingly towards the gate.

'Please don't go,' she said suddenly, looking up. 'I'm lonely. Oh, if you but knew how lonely I am!' She moved to one side of the bench and motioned that I sit beside her. The dog continued to examine me with its big eyes.

Whether it was the nearness of that odour of heliotrope, the suddenness of it all, or perhaps the moonlight, I did not know, but at her words a thrill of pleasure ran through me, and I accepted the proffered seat.

There followed an interval of silence, during which I puzzled my brain for a means to start conversation. But abruptly she turned to the beast and said in German:

'*Fort mit dir, Johann!*'

The dog rose obediently to its feet and stole slowly off into the shadows. I watched it for a moment until it disappeared in the direction of the house. Then the woman said to me in English which was slightly stilted and marked with an accent:

'It has been ages since I have spoken to anyone ... We are strangers. I do not know you, and you do not know me. Yet ... strangers sometimes find in each other a bond of interest. Supposing ... supposing we forget customs and formality of introduction? Shall we?'

For some reason I felt my pulse quicken as she said that. 'Please do,' I replied. 'A spot like this is enough introduction in itself. Tell me, do you live here?'

She made no answer for a moment, and I began to fear I had taken her suggestion too quickly. Then she began slowly:

'My name is Perle von Mauren, and I am really a stranger to your country, though I have been here now more than a year. My home is in Austria near what is now the Czechoslovakian frontier. You see, it was to find my only brother that I came to the United States. During the war he was a lieutenant under General Makensen,* but in 1916, in April I believe it was, he ... he was reported missing.

'War is a cruel thing. It took our money; it took our castle on the Danube, and then – my brother. Those following years were horrible. We lived always in doubt, hoping against hope that he was still living.

'Then after the Armistice a fellow officer claimed to have served next to him on grave-digging detail at a French prison camp near Monpré. And later came a thin rumour that he was in the United States. I gathered together as much money as I could and came here in search of him.'

Her voice dwindled off, and she sat in silence staring at

the brown weeds. When she resumed, her voice was low and wavering.

'I ... found him ... but would to God I hadn't! He ... he was no longer living.'

I stared at her. 'Dead?' I asked.

The veil trembled as though moved by a shudder, as though her thoughts had exhumed some terrible event of the past. Unconscious of my interruption she went on:

'Tonight I came here – I don't know why – merely because the gate was unlocked, and there was a place of quiet within. Now have I bored you with my confidences and personal history?'

'Not at all,' I replied. 'I came here by chance myself. Probably the beauty of the place attracted me. I dabble in amateur photography occasionally and react strongly to unusual scenes. Tonight I went for a midnight stroll to relieve my mind from the bad effect of a book I was reading.'

She made a strange reply to that, a reply away from our line of thought and which seemed an interjection that escaped her involuntarily.

'Books,' she said, 'are powerful things. They can fetter one more than the walls of a prison.'

She caught my puzzled stare at the remark and added hastily: 'It is odd that we should meet here.'

For a moment I didn't answer. I was thinking of her heliotrope perfume, which for a woman of her apparent culture was applied in far too great a quantity to manifest good taste. The impression stole upon me that the perfume cloaked some secret, that if it were removed I should find ... but what? It was ridiculous, and I tried to cast the feeling aside.

The hours passed, and still we sat there talking, enjoying each other's companionship. She did not remove her veil, and though I was burning with a desire to see her features, I had not dared ask her to. A strange nervousness had slowly seized me. The woman was a charming conversationalist, but there was about her an indefinable something which produced in me a distinct feeling of unease.

It was, I should judge, but a few moments before the first streaks of dawn when it happened. As I look back now, even with mundane objects and thoughts on every side, it is not difficult to realize the dire significance, the absolute baseness of that vision. But at the time my brain was too much in a whirl to understand.

A thin shadow moving across the garden attracted my gaze once again into the night about me. I looked up over the spire of the deserted house and started as if struck by a blow. For a moment I thought I had seen a curious cloud formation racing low directly above me, a cloud black and impenetrable with two winglike ends strangely in the shape of a monstrous flying bat.

I blinked my eyes hard and looked again.

'That cloud!' I exclaimed, 'that strange cloud! ... Did you see—'

I stopped and stared dumbly.

The bench at my side was empty. The woman had disappeared.

During the next day I went about my professional duties in the law office with only half interest, and my business partner looked at me queerly several times when he came upon me mumbling to myself. The incidents of the evening before were rushing through my mind in grand turmoil. Questions unanswerable hammered at me. That I should have come upon the very details described by mad Larla in his strange book: the leering fish, the praying child, the twenty-six blue-jays, the pointed shadow of the cupola – it was unexplainable; it was weird.

Five Unicorns and a Pearl. The unicorns were the stone statues ornamenting the old fountain, yes – but the pearl? With a start I suddenly recalled the name of the woman in black: *Perle* von Mauren. The revelation climaxed my train of thought. What did it all mean?

Dinner had little attraction for me that evening. Earlier I had gone to the antique-dealer and begged him to loan me the sequel, the second volume of his brother Alessandro. When he had refused, objected because I had not yet returned the first book, my nerves had suddenly jumped on edge. I felt like a narcotic fiend faced with the realization that he could not procure the desired drug. In desperation, yet hardly knowing why, I offered the man money, more money, until at length I had come away, my powers of persuasion and my pocket book successful.

The second volume was identical in outward respects to its predecessor except that it bore no title. But if I was expecting more disclosures in symbolism I was doomed to disappointment. Vague as *Five Unicorns and a Pearl* had been, the text of the sequel was even more wandering and was obviously only the ramblings of a mad brain. By watching the sentences closely I did gather that Alessandro Larla had made a second trip to his court of the twenty-six blue-jays and met there again his 'pearl'.

There was a paragraph towards the end that puzzled me. It read:

'Can it possibly be? I pray that it is not. And yet I have seen it and heard it snarl. Oh, the loathsome creature! I will not, I will not believe it.'

I closed the book with a snap and tried to divert my attention elsewhere by polishing the lens of my newest portable camera. But again, as before, that same urge stole upon me, that same desire to visit the garden. I confess that I had watched the intervening hours until I would meet the woman in black again; for strangely enough, in spite of her abrupt exit before, I never doubted but that she would be there waiting for me. I wanted her to lift the veil. I wanted to talk with her. I wanted to throw myself once again into the narrative of Larla's book.

Yet the whole thing seemed preposterous, and I fought the sensation with every ounce of willpower I could call to mind. Then it suddenly occurred to me what a remarkable picture she would make, sitting there on the stone bench, clothed in black, with the classic background of the old courtyard. If I could but catch the scene on a photographic plate ...

I halted my polishing and mused a moment. With a new

electric flash-lamp, that handy invention which has supplanted the old mussy flash-powder, I could illuminate the garden and snap the picture with ease. And if the result were satisfactory it would make a worthy contribution to the international Camera Contest at Geneva next month.

The idea appealed to me, and gathering together the necessary equipment I drew on an ulster (for it was a wet, chilly night) and slipped out of my rooms and headed northward. Mad, unseeing fool that I was! If only I had stopped then and there, returned the book to the antique dealer and closed the incident! But the strange magnetic attraction had gripped me in earnest, and I rushed headlong into the horror. A fall rain was drumming the pavement, and the streets were deserted. Off to the east, however, the heavy blanket of clouds glowed with a soft radiance where the moon was trying to break through, and a strong wind from the south gave promise of clearing the skies before long. With my collar turned well up at the throat I passed once again into the older section of the town and down forgotten Easterly Street. I found the gate to the grounds unlocked as before, and the garden a dripping place masked in shadow.

The woman was not there. Still the hour was early, and I did not for a moment doubt that she would appear later. Gripped now with the enthusiasm of my plan, I set the camera carefully on the stone fountain, training the lens as well as I could on the bench where we had sat the previous evening. The flash-lamp with its battery handle I laid within easy reach.

Scarcely had I finished my arrangements when the crunch of gravel on the path caused me to turn. She was approaching the stone bench, heavily veiled as before and with the same sweeping black dress.

'You have come again,' she said as I took my place beside her.

'Yes,' I replied. 'I could not stay away.'

Our conversation that night gradually centred about her dead brother, although I thought several times that the woman tried to avoid the subject. He had been, it seemed, the black sheep of the family, had led more or less of a dissolute life and had been expelled from the University of Vienna not only because of his lack of respect for the pedagogues of the various sciences but also because of his queer unorthodox papers on philosophy. His sufferings in the war prison camp must have been intense. With a kind of grim delight she dwelt on his horrible experiences in the grave-digging detail which had been related to her by the fellow officer. But of the manner in which he had met his death she would say absolutely nothing.

Stronger than on the night before was the sweet smell of heliotrope. And again as the fumes crept nauseatingly down my lungs there came that same sense of nervousness, that same feeling that the perfume was hiding something I should know. The desire to see beneath the veil had become maddening by this time, but still I lacked the boldness to ask her to lift it.

Towards midnight the heavens cleared and the moon in splendid contrast shone high in the sky. The time had come for my picture.

'Sit where you are,' I said. 'I'll be back in a moment.'

Stepping quickly to the fountain I grasped the flash-lamp, held it aloft for an instant and placed my finger on the shutter lever of the camera. The woman remained motionless on the bench, evidently puzzled as to the meaning of my movements. The range was perfect. A click, and a dazzling white light enveloped the courtyard about us. For a brief second she was outlined there against the old wall. Then the blue moonlight returned, and I was smiling in satisfaction.

'It ought to make a beautiful picture,' I said.

She leaped to her feet.

'Fool!' she cried hoarsely. 'Blundering fool! What have you done?'

Even though the veil was there to hide her face I got the instant impression that her eyes were glaring at me, smouldering with hatred. I gazed at her curiously as she stood erect, head thrown back, body apparently taut as wire, and a slow shudder crept down my spine. Then without warning she gathered up her dress and ran down the path towards the deserted house. A moment later she had disappeared somewhere in the shadows of the giant bushes.

I stood there by the fountain, staring after her in a daze. Suddenly, off in the umbra of the house's façade there rose a low animal snarl.

And then before I could move, a huge grey shape came hurtling through the long weeds, bounding in great leaps straight towards me. It was the woman's dog, which I had seen with her the night before. But no longer was it a beast passive and silent. Its face was contorted in diabolic fury, and its jaws were dripping slaver. Even in that moment of terror as I stood frozen before it, the sight of those white nostrils and those black hyalescent eyes emblazoned itself on my mind, never to be forgotten.

Then with a lunge it was upon me. I had only time to thrust the flash-lamp upward in half protection and throw my weight to the side. My arm jumped in recoil. The bulb exploded, and I could feel those teeth clamp down hard on the handle. Backwards I fell, a scream gurgling to my lips, a terrific heaviness surging upon my body.

I struck out frantically, beat my fists into that growling face. My fingers groped blindly for its throat, sank deep into the hairy flesh. I could feel its breath mingling with my own now, but desperately I hung on.

The pressure of my hands told. The dog coughed and fell back. And seizing that instant I struggled to my feet, jumped forward and planted a terrific kick straight into the brute's middle.

'Fort mit dir, Johann!' I cried, remembering the woman's German command.

It leaped back and, fangs bared, glared at me motionless for a moment. Then abruptly it turned and slunk off through the weeds.

Weak and trembling, I drew myself together, picked up my camera and passed through the gate towards home.

Three days passed. Those endless hours I spent confined to my apartment suffering the tortures of the damned.

On the day following the night of my terrible experience with the dog I realized I was in no condition to go to work. I drank two cups of strong black coffee and then forced myself to sit quietly in a chair, hoping to soothe my nerves. But the sight of the camera there on the table excited me to action. Five minutes later I was in the dark room arranged as my studio, developing the picture I had taken the night before. I worked feverishly, urged on by the thought of what an unusual contribution it would make for the amateur contest next month at Geneva, should the result be successful.

An exclamation burst from my lips as I stared at the still-wet print. There was the old garden clear and sharp with the bushes, the statue of the child, the fountain and the wall in the background, but the bench – the stone bench was empty. There was no sign, not even a blur of the woman in black.

My brain in a whirl, I rushed the negative through a saturated solution of mercuric chloride in water, then treated it with ferrous oxalate. But even after this intensifying process the second print was like the first, focused in every detail, the bench standing in the foreground in sharp relief, but no trace of the woman.

I stared incredulously. She had been in plain view when I snapped the shutter. Of that I was positive. And my camera was in perfect condition. What then was wrong? Not until I had looked at the print hard in the daylight would I believe my eyes. No explanation offered itself, none at all; at length, confused unto weakness, I returned to my bed and fell into a heavy sleep.

Straight through the day I slept. Hours later I seemed to wake from a vague nightmare, and had not strength to rise from my pillow. A great physical faintness had overwhelmed me. My arms, my legs, lay like dead things. My heart was fluttering weakly. All was quiet, so still that the clock on my bureau ticked distinctly each passing second. The curtain billowed in the night breeze, though I was positive I had closed the casement when I entered the room.

And then suddenly I threw back my head and screamed from the bottomest depths of my soul! For slowly, slowly creeping down my lungs was that detestable odour of heliotrope.

Morning, and I found all was not a dream. My head was ringing, my hands trembling, and I was so weak I could hardly stand. The doctor I called in looked grave as he felt my pulse.

'You are on the verge of a complete collapse,' he said. 'If you do not allow yourself a rest it may permanently affect your mind. Take things easy for a while. And if you don't mind I'll cauterize those two little cuts on your neck. They're rather raw wounds. What caused them?'

I moved my fingers to my throat and drew them away again tipped with blood.

'I . . . I don't know,' I faltered.

He busied himself with his medicines, and a few minutes later reached for his hat.

'I advise that you don't leave your bed for a week at least,' he said. 'I'll give you a thorough examination then and see if there are any signs of anaemia.' But as he went out the door I thought I saw a puzzled look on his face.

Those subsequent hours allowed my thoughts to run wild once more. I vowed I would forget it all, go back to my work and never look upon the books again. But I knew I could not. The woman in black persisted in my mind, and each minute away from her became a torture. But more than that, if there had been a decided urge to continue my reading in the second book, the desire to see the third book, the last of the trilogy, was slowly increasing to an obsession. It gripped me, etched itself deep into my thoughts.

At length I could stand it no longer, and on the morning of the third day I took a cab to the antique store and tried to persuade Larla to give me the third volume of his brother. But the Italian was firm. I had already taken two books, neither of which I had returned. Until I brought them back he would not listen. Vainly I tried to explain that one was of no value without the sequel and that I wanted to read the entire narrative as a unit. He merely shrugged his shoulders and toyed with his watch chain.

Cold perspiration broke out on my forehead as I heard my desire disregarded. Like the blows of a bludgeon the thought beat upon me that I must have that book. I argued. I pleaded. But to no avail.

At length when Larla had turned the other way I gave in to desperation, seized the third book as I saw it lying on the shelf, slid it into my pocket and walked guiltily out. I make no apologies for my action. In the light of what developed later it may be considered a temptation inspired, for my will at the time was a conquered thing blanketed by that strange lure.

Back in my apartment I dropped into a chair and hastened to open the velvet cover. Here was the last chronicle of that strange series of events which had so completely become a part of my life during the last five days. Larla's volume three. Would all be explained in its pages? If so, what secret would be revealed?

With the light from a reading lamp glaring full over my shoulder I opened the book, thumbed through it slowly, marvelling at the exquisite hand-printing. It seemed then as I sat there that an almost palpable cloud of intense quiet settled over me, a mental miasma muffling the distant sounds of the street. I was vaguely aware of an atmosphere, heavy and dense, in which objects other than the book lost their focus and became blurred in proportion.

For a moment I hesitated. Something psychic, something indefinable seemed to forbid me to read farther. Conscience, curiosity, that queer urge told me to go on. Slowly, like a man in a hypnotic trance wavering between two wills, I began to turn the pages, one at a time, from back to front.

Symbolism again. Vague wanderings with no sane meaning.

But suddenly my fingers stopped! My eyes had caught sight of the last paragraph on the last page, the final pennings of Alessandro Larla. I started downwards as a terrific shock ripped through me from head to foot. I read, re-read, and read again those words, those blasphemous words. I brought the book closer. I traced each word in the lamplight, slowly, carefully, letter for letter. I opened and closed my eyes. Then the horror of it burst like a bomb within me.

In blood-red ink the lines read:

'What shall I do? She has drained my blood and rotted my soul. My pearl is black, black as all evil. The curse be upon her brother, for it is he who made her thus. I pray the truth in these pages will destroy them for ever.

'But my brain is hammering itself apart. Heaven help me, Perle von Mauren and her brother, Johann, are vampires!'

With a scream I leaped to my feet.

'Vampires!' I shrieked. 'Vampires! Oh, my God!'

I clutched at the edge of the table and stood there swaying, the realization of it surging upon me like the blast of a furnace. Vampires! Those horrible creatures with a lust for human blood, fiends of hell, taking the shape of men, of bats, of dogs. I saw it all now, and my brain reeled at the horror of it.

Oh, why had I been such a fool? Why had I not looked beneath the surface, taken away the veil, gone farther than the perfume? That damnable heliotrope was a mask, a mask hiding all the unspeakable foulness of the grave.

My emotions burst out of control then. With a cry I swept the water-glass, the books, the vase from the table, smote my fist down upon the flat surface again and again until a thousand little pains were stabbing the flesh.

'Vampires!' I screamed. 'No, no – oh God, it isn't true!'

But I knew that it was. The events of the past few days rose before me in all their horror now, and I could see the black significance of every detail.

The brother, Johann – some time since the war he had become a vampire. When the woman sought him out years later he had forced this terrible existence upon her too. Yes, that was it.

With the garden as their lair the two of them had entangled poor Alessandro Larla in their serpentine coils a year before. He had loved the woman, had worshipped her madly. And then he had found the truth, the awful truth that had sent him stumbling home, stark, raving mad.

Mad, yes, but not mad enough to keep him from writing the facts in his three velvet-bound books for the world to see. He had hoped the disclosures would dispatch the woman and her brother for ever. But it was not enough.

Following my thoughts, I whipped the first book from the table stand and opened the front cover. There again I saw those scratched lines which had meant nothing to me before.

'Revelations meant to destroy but only binding without the stake. Read, fool, and enter my field, for we are chained to the spot. Oh, woe unto Larla!'

Perle von Mauren had written that. Fool that I was, unseeing fool! The books had not put an end to the evil of her or her brother. No, only one thing could do that. Yet the exposures had not been written in vain. They were recorded for mortal posterity to see.

Those books bound the two vampires, Perle von Mauren and her brother, Johann, to the old garden, kept them from roaming the night streets in search of victims. Only he who had once passed through the gate could they pursue and attack.

It was the old metaphysical law: evil shrinking in the face of truth.

Yet if the books had bound their power in chains they had also opened a new avenue for their attacks. Once immersed in the pages of the trilogy, the reader fell helplessly into their clutches. Those printed lines had become the outer reaches of their web. They were an entrapping net within which the power of the vampires always crouched.

That was why my life had blended so strangely with the story of Larla. The moment I had cast my eyes on the opening paragraph I had fallen into their coils to do with as they had done with Larla a year before. I had been lured, drawn relentlessly into the tentacles of the woman in black. Once I was past the garden gate the binding spell of the books was gone, and they were free to pursue me and to—

A giddy sensation rose within me. Now I saw why the scientific doctor had been puzzled. Now I saw the reason for my physical weakness. Oh, the foulness of it! She had been –feasting on my blood!

With a sobbing cry I flung the book to a far corner, turned and began madly pacing up and down the room. Cold perspiration oozed from every pore. My heart pounded like a runner's. My brain ran wild.

Was I to end as Larla had ended, another victim of this loathsome being's power? Was she to gorge herself further on my life and live on? Were others to be preyed upon and go down into the pits of despair? No, and again no! If Larla had been ignorant of the one and only way in which to dispose of such a creature, I was not. I had not vacationed in southern Europe without learning something of these ancient evils.

Frantically I looked about the room, took in the objects about me. A chair, a table, a taboret, one of my cameras with its long tripod. I stared at the latter as in my terror-stricken mind a plan leaped into action. With a lunge I was across the floor, had seized one of the wooden legs of the tripod in my hands. I snapped it across my knee. Then, grasping the two broken pieces, both now with sharp splintered ends, I rushed hatless out of the door to the street.

A moment later I was racing northward in a cab bound for Easterly Street.

'Hurry!' I cried to the driver as I glanced at the westering sun. 'Faster, do you hear?'

We shot along the cross-streets, into the old suburbs and towards the outskirts of town. Every traffic halt found me fuming at the delay. But at length we drew up before the wall of the garden.

Tossing the driver a bill, I swung the wrought-iron gate open and with the wooden pieces of the tripod still under my arm, rushed in. The courtyard was a place of reality in the daylight, but the mouldering masonry and tangled weeds were steeped in silence as before.

Straight for the house I made, climbing the rotten steps to the front entrance. The door was boarded up and locked. Smothering an impulse to scream, I retraced my steps at a run and began to circle the south wall of the building. It was this direction I had seen the woman take when she had fled after I had tried to snap her picture. The twenty-six blue-jays on the wall leered at me like a flock of harpies.

Well towards the rear of the building I reached a small half-open door leading to the cellar. For a moment I hesitated there, sick with the dread of what I knew lay before me. Then, clenching hard the two wooden tripod stakes, I entered.

Inside, cloaked in gloom, a narrow corridor stretched before me. The floor was littered with rubble and fallen masonry, the ceiling interlaced with a thousand cobwebs.

I stumbled forward, my eyes quickly accustoming themselves to the half-light from the almost opaque windows. A maddening urge to leave it all and flee back to the sunlight was welling up within me now. I fought it back. Failure would mean a continuation of the horrors – a lingering death – would leave the gate open for others.

At the end of the corridor a second door barred my passage. I thrust it open – and stood swaying there on the sill staring inward. A great loathing crept over me, a stifling sense of utter repulsion. Hot blood rushed to my head. The air seemed to move upward in palpable swirls.

Beyond was a small room, barely ten feet square, with a low-raftered ceiling. And by the light of the open door I saw side by side in the centre of the floor – two white wood coffins.

How long I stood there leaning weakly against the stone wall I don't know. There was a silence so profound the beating of my heart pulsed through the passage like the blows of a mallet. And there was a slow penetrating odour drifting from out of that chamber that entered my nostrils and

claimed instant recognition. Heliotrope! But heliotrope defiled by the rotting smell of an ancient grave.

Then suddenly with a determination born of despair I
leaped forward, rushed to the nearest coffin, seized its cover
and ripped it open.

Would to heaven I could forget the sight that met my
eyes. There lay Perle von Mauren, the woman in black – un-
veiled.

That face – how can I describe it? It was divinely beautiful, the hair black as sable, the cheeks a classic white. But
the lips – oh God! those lips! I grew suddenly sick as I
looked upon them. They were scarlet, crimson ... and sticky
with human blood.

I moved like an automaton then. With a low sob I reached
for one of the tripod stakes, seized a flagstone from the floor
and with the pointed end of the wood resting directly over
the woman's heart, struck a crashing blow. The stake
jumped downward. A sickening crunch – and a violent con-
tortion shook the coffin. Up to my face rushed a warm,
nauseating breath of rot and decay.

I wheeled and hurled open the lid of her brother's coffin.
With only a flashing glance at the young masculine Teutonic
face I raised the other stake high in the air and brought
it stabbing down with all the strength in my right arm.
Red blood suddenly began to form a thick pool on the
floor.

For an instant I stood rooted to the spot, the utter ob-
scenity of it all searing its way into my brain like a hot
sword. Even in that moment of stark horror I realized that
not even the most subtle erasures of Time would be able to
remove that blasphemous sight from my inner eye.

It was a scene so abysmally corrupt – I pray heaven my
dreams will never find it and re-vision its unholy tableau.
There before me, focused in the shaft of light that filtered
through the open door like the miasma from a fever swamp,
lay the two white caskets.

And within them now, staring up at me from eyeless

sockets – two grey and mouldering skeletons, each with its hideous leering head of death.

*   *   *

The rest is but a vague dream. I seem to remember rushing madly outside, along the path to the gate and down the street, down Easterly, away from that accursed garden of the jays.

At length, utterly exhausted, I reached my apartment, burst open the door and staggered in. Those mundane surroundings that confronted me were like balm to my burning eyes. But as if in mocking irony there centred into my gaze three objects lying where I had left them, the three volumes of Larla.

I moved across to them, picked them up and stared down vacantly upon their black sides. These were the hellish works that had caused it all. These were the pages that were responsible...

With a low cry I turned to the grate on the other side of the room and flung the three of them on to the still glowing coals.

There was an instant hiss, and a line of yellow flame streaked upward and began eating into the velvet. I watched the fire grow higher ... higher ... and diminish slowly.

And as the last glowing spark died into a blackened ash there swept over me a mighty feeling of quiet and relief.

* Properly Field-Marshal von Makensen. Of the famous Death's Head Hussars in World War I he served under the Kaiser and the Führer with distinction.

THE ROOM IN THE TOWER

by

E. F. Benson

It is probable that everybody who is at all a constant dreamer has had at least one experience of an event or a sequence of circumstances which have come to his mind in sleep being subsequently realized in the material world. But, in my opinion, so far from this being a strange thing, it would be far odder if this fulfilment did not occasionally happen, since our dreams are, as a rule, concerned with people whom we know and places with which we are familiar, such as might very naturally occur in the awake and daylit world. True, these dreams are often broken into by some absurd and fantastic incident, which puts them out of court in regard to their subsequent fulfilment, but on the mere calculation of chances, it does not appear in the least unlikely that a dream imagined by anyone who dreams constantly should occasionally come true. Not long ago, for instance, I experienced such a fulfilment of a dream which seems to me in no way remarkable and to have no kind of physical significance. The manner of it was as follows.

A certain friend of mine, living abroad, is amiable enough to write to me about once in a fortnight. Thus, when fourteen days or thereabouts have elapsed since I last heard from him, my mind, probably, either consciously or subconsciously, is expectant of a letter from him. One night last week I dreamed that as I was going upstairs to dress for dinner I heard, as I often heard, the sound of the postman's knock on my front door, and diverted my direction downstairs instead. There, among other correspondence, was a letter from him. Thereafter the fantastic entered, for on opening it I found inside the ace of diamonds, and scribbled across it in his well-known handwriting, 'I am sending you this for safe custody, as you know it is running an unreasonable risk to keep aces in Italy.' The next evening I was just preparing to go upstairs to dress when I heard the postman's knock, and did precisely as I had done in my dream. There, among other letters, was one from my friend. Only it did not contain the ace of diamonds. Had it done so, I should have attached more weight to the matter, which, as it stands, seems to me a perfectly ordinary coincidence. No doubt I consciously or subconsciously expected a letter from him, and this suggested to me my dream. Similarly, the fact that my friend had not written to me for a fortnight suggested to him that he should do so. But occasionally it is not so easy to find such an explanation, and for the following story I can find no explanation at all. It came out of the dark, and into the dark it has gone again.

All my life I have been a habitual dreamer: the nights are few, that is to say, when I do not find on awaking in the morning that some mental experience has been mine, and sometimes, all night long, apparently, a series of the most dazzling adventures befall me. Almost without exception these adventures are pleasant, though often merely trivial. It is of an exception that I am going to speak.

It was when I was about sixteen that a certain dream first came to me, and this is how it befell. It opened with my being set down at the door of a big red-brick house, where, I understood, I was going to stay. The servant who opened the door told me that tea was going on in the garden, and led me through a low dark-panelled hall, with a large open fireplace, on to a cheerful green lawn set round with flower beds. There were grouped about the tea-table a small party of people, but they were all strangers to me except one, who was a school-fellow called Jack Stone, clearly the son of the house, and he introduced me to his mother and father and a couple of sisters. I was, I remember, somewhat astonished to find myself here, for the boy in question was scarcely known to me, and I rather disliked what I knew of him; moreover, he had left school nearly a year before. The afternoon was very hot, and an intolerable oppression reigned. On the far side of the lawn ran a red-brick wall, with an iron gate in its centre, outside which stood a walnut tree. We sat in the shadow of the house opposite a row of long windows inside which I could see a table with cloth laid, glimmering with glass and silver. This garden front of the house was very long, and at one end of it stood a tower of three storeys, which looked to me much older than the rest of the building.

Before long, Mrs Stone, who, like the rest of the party, had sat in absolute silence, said to me, 'Jack will show you your room: I have given you the room in the tower.'

Quite inexplicably my heart sank at her words. I felt as if I had known that I should have the room in the tower, and that it contained something dreadful and significant. Jack instantly got up, and I understood that I had to follow him. In silence we passed through the hall, and mounted a great oak staircase with many corners, and arrived at a small landing with two doors set in it. He pushed one of these open for me to enter, and without coming in himself, closed it behind me. Then I knew that my conjecture had been right: there was something awful in the room, and with the terror of nightmare growing swiftly and enveloping me, I awoke in a spasm of terror.

Now that dream or variations on it occurred to me inter-mittently for fifteen years. Most often it came in exactly this form, the arrival, the tea laid out on the lawn, the deadly silence succeeded by that one deadly sentence, the mounting with Jack Stone up to the room in the tower where horror dwelt, and it always came to a close in the nightmare of terror at that which was in the room, though I never saw what it was. At other times I experienced variations on this same theme. Occasionally, for instance, we would be sitting at dinner in the dining-room, into the windows of which I had looked on the first night when the dream of this house visited me, but wherever we were, there was the same silence, the same sense of dreadful oppression and fore-boding. And the silence I knew would always be broken by

Mrs Stone saying to me, 'Jack will show you your room: I have given you the room in the tower.' Upon which (this was invariable) I had to follow him up the oak staircase with many corners, and enter the place that I dreaded more and more each time that I visited it in sleep. Or, again, I would find myself playing cards still in silence in a drawing-room lit with immense chandeliers, that gave a blinding illumination. What the game was I have no idea; what I remember, with a sense of miserable anticipation, was that soon Mrs Stone would get up and say to me, 'Jack will show you your room: I have given you the room in the tower.' This drawing-room where we played cards was next to the dining-room, and, as I have said, was always brilliantly illuminated, whereas the rest of the house was full of dusk and shadows. And yet, how often, in spite of those bouquets of lights, have I not pored over the cards that were dealt me, scarcely able for some reason to see them. Their designs, too, were strange: there were no red suits, but all were black, and among them there were certain cards which were black all over. I hated and dreaded those.

As this dream continued to recur, I got to know the greater part of the house. There was a smoking-room beyond the drawing-room, at the end of a passage with a green baize door. It was always very dark there, and as often as I went there I passed somebody whom I could not see in the doorway coming out. Curious developments, too, took place in the characters that peopled the dream as might happen to living persons. Mrs Stone, for instance, who, when I first saw her, had been black haired, became grey, and instead of rising briskly, as she had done when she said, 'Jack will show you your room: I have given you the room in the tower,' got up very feebly, as if the strength was leaving her limbs. Jack also grew up, and became a rather ill-looking young man, with a brown moustache, while one of the sisters ceased to appear, and I understood she was married.

Then it so happened that I was not visited by this dream for six months or more, and I began to hope, in such inexplicable dread did I hold it, that it had passed away for

good. But one night after this interval I again found myself
being shown out on to the lawn for tea, and Mrs Stone was
not there, while the others were all dressed in black. At once
I guessed the reason, and my heart leaped at the thought
that perhaps this time I should not have to sleep in the
room in the tower, and though we usually all sat in silence,
on this occasion the sense of relief made me talk and laugh
as I had never yet done. But even then matters were not
altogether comfortable, for no one else spoke, but they all
looked secretly at each other. And soon the foolish stream
of my talk ran dry, and gradually an apprehension worse
than anything I had previously known gained on me as the
light slowly faded.

Suddenly a voice which I knew well broke the stillness,
the voice of Mrs Stone, saying, 'Jack will show you your
room: I have given you the room in the tower.' It seemed
to come from near the gate in the red-brick wall that
bounded the lawn, and looking up, I saw that the grass outside was sown thick with gravestones. A curious greyish
light shone from them, and I could read the lettering on
the grave nearest me, and it was, 'In evil memory of Julia
Stone.' And as usual Jack got up, and again I followed him
through the hall and up the staircase with many corners.
On this occasion it was darker than usual, and when I passed
into the room in the tower I could only just see the furniture,
the position of which was already familiar to me. Also there
was a dreadful odour of decay in the room, and I woke
screaming.

The dream, with such variations and developments as I
have mentioned, went on at intervals for fifteen years. Sometimes I would dream it two or three nights in succession;
once, as I have said, there was an intermission of six months,
but taking a reasonable average, I should say that I dreamed
it quite as often as once in a month. It had, as is plain, something of nightmare about it, since it always ended in the
same appalling terror, which so far from getting less, seemed
to me to gather fresh fear every time that I experienced it.
There was, too, a strange and dreadful consistency about it.

The characters in it, as I have mentioned, got regularly older, death and marriage visited this silent family, and I never in the dream, after Mrs Stone had died, set eyes on her again. But it was always her voice that told me that the room in the tower was prepared for me, and whether we had tea out on the lawn, or the scene was laid in one of the rooms overlooking it, I could always see her gravestone standing just outside the iron gate. It was the same, too, with the married daughter; usually she was not present, but once or twice she returned again, in company with a man, whom I took to be her husband. He, too, like the rest of them, was always silent. But, owing to the constant repetition of the dream, I had ceased to attach, in my waking hours, any significance to it. I never met Jack Stone again during all those years, nor did I ever see a house that resembled this dark house of my dream. And then something happened.

I had been in London in this year, up till the end of July, and during the first week in August went down to stay with a friend in a house he had taken for the summer months, in the Ashdown Forest district of Sussex. I left London early, for John Clinton was to meet me at Forest Row Station, and we were going to spend the day golfing, and go to his house in the evening. He had his motor with him, and we set off, about five of the afternoon, after a thoroughly delightful day, for the drive, the distance being some ten miles. As it was still so early we did not have tea at the club house, but waited till we should get home. As we drove, the weather, which up till then had been, though hot, deliciously fresh, seemed to me to alter in quality, and become very stagnant and oppressive, and I felt that indefinable sense of ominous apprehension that I am accustomed to before thunder. John, however, did not share my views, attributing my loss of lightness to the fact that I had lost both my matches. Events proved, however, that I was right, thought I do not think that the thunderstorm that broke that night was the sole cause of my depression.

Our way lay through deep high-banked lanes, and before we had gone very far I fell asleep, and was only awakened by the stopping of the motor. And with a sudden thrill, partly of fear but chiefly of curiosity, I found myself standing in the doorway of my house of dream. We went, I half wondering whether or not I was dreaming still, through a low oak-panelled hall, and out on to the lawn, where tea was laid in the shadow of the house. It was set in flower-beds, a red-brick wall, with a gate in it, bounded one side, and out beyond that was a space of rough grass with a walnut tree. The façade of the house was very long, and at one end stood a three-storeyed tower, markedly older than the rest.

Here for the moment all resemblance to the repeated dream ceased. There was no silent and somehow terrible family, but a large assembly of exceedingly cheerful persons, all of whom were known to me. And in spite of the horror with which the dream itself had always filled me, I felt nothing of it now that the scene of it was thus reproduced before me. But I felt the intensest curiosity as to what was going to happen.

Tea pursued its cheerful course, and before long Mrs Clinton got up. And at that moment I think I knew what she was going to say. She spoke to me, and what she said was:

'Jack will show you your room: I have given you the room in the tower.'

At that, for half a second, the horror of the dream took hold of me again. But it quickly passed, and again I felt nothing more than the most intense curiosity. It was not very long before it was amply satisfied.

John turned to me.

'Right up at the top of the house,' he said, 'but I think you'll be comfortable. We're absolutely full up. Would you like to go and see it now? By Jove, I believe that you are right, and that we are going to have a thunderstorm. How dark it has become.'

I got up and followed him. We passed through the hall, and up the perfectly familiar staircase. Then he opened the door, and I went in. And at that moment sheer unreasoning terror again possessed me. I did not know for certain what I feared: I simply feared. Then like a sudden recollection, when one remembers a name which has long escaped the memory, I knew what I feared. I feared Mrs Stone, whose grave with the sinister inscription, 'In evil memory', I had so often seen in my dream, just beyond the lawn which lay below my window. And then once more the fear passed so completely that I wondered what there was to fear, and I found myself, sober and quiet and sane, in the room in the tower, the name of which I had so often heard in my dreams, and the scene of which was so familiar.

I looked round it with a certain sense of proprietorship, and found that nothing had been changed from the dreaming nights in which I knew it so well. Just to the left of the door was the bed, lengthways along the wall, with the head of it in the angle. In a line with it was the fireplace and a small bookcase; opposite the door the outer wall was pierced by two lattice-paned windows, beween which stood the dressing-table, while ranged along the fourth wall was the washing-stand and a big cupboard. My luggage had already been unpacked, for the furniture of dressing and undressing lay orderly on the wash-stand and toilet-table, while my dinner clothes were spread out on the coverlet of the bed. And then, with a sudden start of unexplained dismay, I saw that there were two rather conspicuous objects which I had not seen before in my dreams: one a life-sized oil painting of Mrs Stone, the other a black-and-white sketch of Jack Stone, representing him as he had appeared to me only a week before in the last of the series of these repeated dreams, a rather secret and evil-looking man of about thirty. His picture hung between the windows, looking straight across the room to the other portrait, which hung at the side of the bed. At that I looked next, and as I looked I felt once more the horror of nightmare seize me.

It represented Mrs Stone as I had seen her last in my dreams: old and withered and white haired. But in spite of the evident feebleness of body, a dreadful exuberance and vitality shone through the envelope of flesh, an exuberance wholly malign, a vitality that foamed and frothed with un-imaginable evil. Evil beamed from the narrow, leering eyes; it laughed in the demon-like mouth. The whole face was instinct with some secret and appalling mirth; the hands, clasped together on the knee, seemed shaking with sup-pressed and nameless glee. Then I saw also that it was signed in the left-hand bottom corner, and wondering who the artist could be, I looked more closely, and read the inscrip-tion, 'Julia Stone by Julia Stone'.

There came a tap at the door, and John Clinton entered.

'Got everything you want?' he asked.

'Rather more than I want,' said I, pointing to the picture. He laughed.

'Hard-featured old lady,' he said. 'By herself, too, I re-member. Anyhow, she can't have flattered herself much.'

'But don't you see?' said I. 'It's scarcely a human face at all. It's the face of some witch, of some devil.'

He looked at it more closely.

'Yes; it isn't very pleasant,' he said. 'Scarcely a bedside manner, eh? Yes; I can imagine getting the nightmare if I went to sleep with that close by my bed. I'll have it taken down if you like.'

'I really wish you would,' I said.

He rang the bell, and with the help of a servant we de-tached the picture and carried it out on to the landing, and put it with its face to the wall.

'By Jove, the old lady is a weight,' said John, mopping his forehead. 'I wonder if she had something on her mind.'

The extraordinary weight of the picture had struck me too. I was about to reply when I caught sight of my own hand. There was blood on it, in considerable quantities, covering the whole palm.

'I've cut myself somehow,' said I.

John gave a little startled exclamation.

'Why, I have too,' he said.

Simultaneously the footman took out his handkerchief and wiped his hand with it. I saw that there was blood also on his handkerchief.

John and I went back into the tower room and washed the blood off; but neither on his hand nor on mine was there the slightest trace of a scratch or cut. It seemed to me that, having ascertained this, we both, by a sort of tacit consent, did not allude to it again. Something in my case had dimly occurred to me that I did not wish to think about. It was but a conjecture, but I fancied that I knew the same thing had occurred to him.

The heat and the oppression of the air, for the storm we had expected was still undischarged, increased very much after dinner, and for some time most of the party, among whom were John Clinton and myself, sat outside on the path bounding the lawn, where we had had tea. The night was absolutely dark, and no twinkle of star or moon ray could penetrate the pall of cloud that overset the sky. By degrees our assembly thinned, the women went up to bed, men dispersed to the smoking or billiard room, and by eleven o'clock my host and I were the only two left. All the evening I thought that he had something on his mind, and as soon as we were alone he spoke.

'The man who helped us with the picture had blood on his hand, too, did you notice?' he asked. 'I asked him just now if he had cut himself, and he said he supposed he had, but that he could find no mark of it. Now where did that blood come from?'

By dint of telling myself that I was not going to think about it, I had succeeded in not doing so, and I did not want, especially just at bedtime, to be reminded of it.

'I don't know,' said I, 'and I don't really care so long as the picture of Mrs Julia Stone is not by my bed.'

He got up.

'But it's odd,' he said. 'Ha! Now you'll see another odd thing.'

A dog of his, an Irish terrier by breed, had come out of the house as we talked. The door behind us into the hall was open, and a bright oblong of light shone across the lawn to the iron gate which led on to the rough grass outside, where the walnut tree stood. I saw that the dog had all his hackles up, bristling with rage and fright; his lips were curled back from his teeth, as if he were ready to spring at something, and he was growling to himself. He took not the slightest notice of his master or me, but stiffly and tensely walked across the grass to the iron gate. There he stood for a moment, looking through the bars and still growling. Then all of a sudden his courage seemed to desert him: he gave one long howl, and scuttled back to the house with a curious crouching sort of movement.

'He does that half-a-dozen times a day,' said John. 'He sees something which he both hates and fears.'

I walked to the gate and looked over it. Something was moving on the grass outside, and soon a sound which I could not instantly identify came to my ears. Then I remembered what it was: it was the purring of a cat. I lit a match, and saw the purrer, a big blue Persian, walking round and round in a little circle just outside the gate, stepping high and ecstatically, with tail carried aloft like a banner. Its eyes were bright and shining, and every now and then it put its head down and sniffed at the grass.

I laughed.

'The end of that mystery, I am afraid,' I said. 'Here's a large cat having Walpurgis night all alone.'

'Yes, that's Darius,' said John. 'He spends half the day and all night there. But that's not the end of the dog mystery, for Toby and he are best of friends, but the beginning of the cat mystery. What's the cat doing there? And why is Darius pleased, while Toby is terror-stricken?'

At that moment I remembered the rather horrible detail of my dreams when I saw through the gate, just where the cat was now, the white tombstone with the sinister inscription. But before I could answer the rain began, as suddenly and heavily as if a tap had been turned on, and simultaneously the big cat squeezed through the bars of the gate, and came leaping across the lawn to the house for shelter. Then it sat in the doorway, looking out eagerly into the dark. It spat and struck at John with its paw, as he pushed it in, in order to close the door.

Somehow, with the portrait of Julia Stone in the passage outside, the room in the tower had absolutely no alarm for me, and as I went to bed, feeling very sleepy and heavy, I had nothing more than interest for the curious incident about our bleeding hands, and the conduct of the cat and dog. The last thing I looked at before I put out my light was the square empty space by my bed where the portrait had been. Here the paper was of its original full tint of dark red : over the rest of the walls it had faded. Then I blew out my candle and instantly fell asleep.

My awaking was equally instantaneous, and I sat bolt upright in bed under the impression that some bright light had been flashed in my face, though it was now absolutely pitch dark. I knew exactly where I was, in the room which I had dreamed in dreams, but no horror that I ever felt when asleep approached the fear that now invaded and froze my brain. Immediately after a peal of thunder crackled just above the house, but the probability that it was only a flash of lightning which awoke me gave no reassurance to my galloping heart. Something I knew was in the room with me, and instinctively I put out my right hand, which was nearest the wall, to keep it away. And my hand touched the edge of a picture frame hanging close to me.

I sprang out of bed, upsetting the small table that stood by it, and I heard my watch, candle, and matches clatter on to the floor. But for the moment there was no need of light, for a blinding flash leaped out of the clouds, and showed me that by my bed again hung the picture of Mrs Stone. And instantly the room went into blackness again. But in that flash I saw another thing also, namely a figure that leaned over the end of my bed, watching me. It was dressed in some close-clinging white garment, spotted and stained with mould, and the face was that of the portrait.

Overhead the thunder cracked and roared, and when it ceased and the deathly stillness succeeded, I heard the rustle of movement coming nearer me, and, more horrible yet, perceived an odour of corruption and decay. And then a hand was laid on the side of my neck, and close beside my ear I heard quick-taken eager breathing. Yet I knew that this thing, thought it could be perceived by touch, by smell, by eye and by ear, was still not of this earth, but something that had passed out of the body and had power to make itself manifest. Then a voice, already familiar to me, spoke.

'I knew you would come to the room in the tower,' it said. 'I have been long waiting for you. At last you have come. Tonight I shall feast; before long we will feast together.'

And the quick breathing came closer to me; I could feel it on my neck.

At that the terror, which I think had paralysed me for the moment, gave way to the wild instinct of self-preservation. I hit wildly with both arms, kicking out at the same moment, and heard a little animal-squeal, and something soft dropped with a thud beside me. I took a couple of steps forward, nearly tripping up over whatever it was that lay there, and by the merest good luck found the handle of the door. In another second I ran out on the landing, and had banged the door behind me. Almost at the same moment I heard a door open somewhere below, and John Clinton, candle in hand, came running upstairs.

'What is it?' he said. 'I slept just below you, and heard a noise as if – Good heavens, there's blood on your shoulder.'

I stood there, so he told me afterwards, swaying from side to side, white as a sheet, with the mark on my shoulder as if a hand covered with blood had been laid there.

'It's in there,' I said, pointing. 'She, you know. The portrait is in there too, hanging up on the place we took it from.'

At that he laughed.

'My dear fellow, this is a mere nightmare,' he said.

He pushed by me, and opened the door, I standing there simply inert with terror, unable to stop him, unable to move.

'Phew! What an awful smell!' he said.

Then there was silence; he had passed out of my sight behind the open door. Next moment he came out again, as white as myself, and instantly shut it.

'Yes, the portrait's there,' he said, 'and on the floor is a thing – a thing spotted with earth, like what they bury people in. Come away, quick, come away.'

How I got downstairs I hardly know. An awful shuddering and nausea of the spirit rather than of the flesh had seized me, and more than once he had to place my feet upon the steps, while every now and then he cast glances of terror and apprehension up the stairs. But in time we came to his dressing-room on the floor below, and there I told him what I have here described.

The sequel can be made short; indeed, some of my readers have perhaps already guessed what it was, if they remember that inexplicable affair of the churchyard at West Fawley, some eight years ago, when an attempt was made three times to bury the body of a certain woman who had committed suicide. On each occasion the coffin was found in the course of a few days again protruding from the ground. After the third attempt, in order that the thing should not be talked about, the body was buried elsewhere in unconsecrated ground. Where it was buried was just outside the iron gate of the garden belonging to the house where this woman had lived. She had committed suicide in a room at the top of the tower in that house. Her name was Julia Stone.

Subsequently the body was again secretly dug up, and the coffin was found to be full of blood.

THE DEATH OF HALPIN FRAYSER

by

Ambrose Bierce

For by death is wrought greater change than hath been shown. Whereas in general the spirit that removed cometh back upon occasion, and is sometimes seen of those in flesh (appearing in the form of the body it bore) yet it hath happened that the veritable body without the spirit hath walked. And it is attested of those encountering who have lived to speak thereon that a lich so raised up hath no natural affection, nor remembrance thereof, but only hate. Also, it is known that some spirits which in life were benign become by death evil altogether – HALL.

One dark night in midsummer a man waking from a dreamless sleep in a forest lifted his head from the earth, and staring a few moments into the blackness, said: 'Catherine Larue.' He said nothing more; no reason was known to him why he should have said so much.

The man was Halpin Frayser. He lived in St Helena, but where he lives now is uncertain, for he is dead. One who practises sleeping in the woods with nothing under him but the dry leaves and the damp earth, and nothing over him but the branches from which the leaves have fallen and the sky from which the earth has fallen, cannot hope for great longevity, and Frayser had already attained the age of thirty-two. There are persons in this world, millions of persons, and far and away the best persons, who regard that as a very advanced age. They are the children. To those who view the voyage of life from the port of departure the bark that has accomplished any considerable distance appears already in close approach to the farther shore. However, it is not certain that Halpin Frayser came to his death by exposure.

He had been all day in the hills west of the Napa Valley, looking for doves and such small game as was in season. Late in the afternoon it had come on to be cloudy, and he had lost his bearings; and although he had only to go always downhill – everywhere the way to safety when one is lost – the absence of trails had so impeded him that he was over-taken by night while still in the forest. Unable in the dark-ness to penetrate the thickets of manzanita and other undergrowth, utterly bewildered and overcome with fatigue, he had lain down near the root of a large madrono and fallen into a dreamless sleep. It was hours later, in the very middle of the night, that one of God's mysterious messengers, glid-ing ahead of the incalculable host of his companions sweep-ing westward with the dawn line, pronounced the awakening word in the ear of the sleeper, who sat upright and spoke, he knew not why, a name, he knew not whose.

Halpin Frayser was not much of a philosopher, nor a scientist. The circumstance that, waking from a deep sleep at night in the midst of the forest, he had spoken aloud a name that he had not in memory and hardly had in mind did not arouse an enlightened curiosity to investigate the phenomenon. He thought it odd, and with a little perfunc-tory shiver, as if in deference to a seasonal presumption that the night was chill, he lay down again and went to sleep. But his sleep was no longer dreamless.

He thought he was walking along a dusty road that showed white in the gathering darkness of a summer night. Whence and whither it led, and why he travelled it, he did not know, though all seemed simple and natural, as is the way in dreams; for in the Land Beyond the Bed surprises cease from troubling and the judgement is at rest. Soon he came to a parting of the ways; leading from the highway was a road less travelled, having the appearance, indeed, of hav-ing been long abandoned, because, he thought, it led to something evil; yet he turned into it without hesitation, im-pelled by some imperious necessity.

As he pressed forward he became conscious that his way

was haunted by invisible existences whom he could not definitely figure to his mind. From among the trees on either side he caught broken and incoherant whispers in a strange tongue which yet he partly understood. They seemed to him fragmentary utterances of a monstrous conspiracy against his body and soul.

It was now long after nightfall, yet the interminable forest through which he journeyed was lit with a wan glimmer having no point of diffusion, for in its mysterious lumination nothing cast a shadow. A shallow pool in the guttered depression of an old wheel rut, as from a recent rain, met his eye with a crimson gleam. He stooped and plunged his hand into it. It stained his fingers; it was blood! Blood, he then observed, was about him everywhere. The weeds growing rankly by the roadside, showed it in blots and splashes on their big, broad leaves. Patches of dry dust between the wheelways were pitted and spattered as with a red rain. Defiling the trunks of the trees were broad maculations of crimson, and blood dripped like dew from their foliage.

All this he observed with a terror which seemed not incompatible with the fulfilment of a natural expectation. It seemed to him that it was all in expiation of some crime which, though conscious of his guilt, he could not rightly remember. To the menaces and mysteries of his surroundings the consciousness was an added horror. Vainly he sought, by tracing life backward in memory, to reproduce the moment of his sin; scenes and incidents came crowding tumultuously into his mind, one picture effacing another, or commingling with it in confusion and obscurity, but nowhere could he catch a glimpse of what he sought. The failure augmented his terror; he felt as one who has murdered in the dark, not knowing whom or why. So frightful was the situation – the mysterious light burned with so silent and awful a menace; the noxious plants, the trees that by common consent are invested with a melancholy or baleful character, so openly in his sight conspired against his peace; from overhead and all about came so audible and startling whispers and the sighs of creatures so obviously not of earth – that he could endure it no longer, and with a great effort to break some malign spell that bound his faculties to silence and inaction, he shouted with the full strength of his lungs! His voice, broken, it seemed, into an infinite multitude of unfamiliar sounds, went babbling and stammering away into the distant reaches of the forest, died into silence, and all was as before. But he had made a beginning at resistance and was encouraged. He said:

'I will not submit unheard. There may be powers that are not malignant travelling this accursed road. I shall leave them a record and an appeal. I shall relate my wrongs, the persecutions that I endure – I, a helpless mortal, a penitent, an unoffending poet!' Halpin Frayser was a poet only as he was a penitent: in his dream.

Taking from his clothing a small red-leather pocket book, one half of which was leaved for memoranda, he discovered that he was without a pencil. He broke a twig from a bush, dipped it into a pool of blood and wrote rapidly. He had hardly touched the paper with the point of his twig when a low, wild peal of laughter broke out at a measureless distance away, and growing ever louder, seemed approaching ever nearer; a soulless, heartless, and unjoyous laugh, like that of the loon, solitary by the lakeside at midnight; a laugh which culminated in an unearthly shout close at hand, then died away by slow gradations, as if the accursed being that uttered it had withdrawn over the verge of the world whence it had come. But the man felt that this was not so – that it was near by and had not moved.

A strange sensation began slowly to take possession of his body and his mind. He could not have said which, if any, of his senses was affected; he felt it rather as a consciousness – a mysterious mental assurance of some overpowering presence – some supernatural malevolence different in kind from the invisible existences that swarmed about him, and superior to them in power. He knew that it had uttered that hideous laugh. And now it seemed to be approaching him; from what direction he did not know – dared not conjecture.

All his former fears were forgotten or merged in the gigantic terror that now held him in thrall. Apart from that, he had but one thought: to complete his written appeal to the benign powers who, traversing the haunted wood, might some time rescue him if he should be denied the blessing of annihilation. He wrote with terrible rapidity, the twig in his fingers rilling blood without renewal; but in the middle of a sentence his hands denied their service to his will, his arms fell to his sides, the book to the earth; and powerless to move or cry out, he found himself staring into the sharply drawn face and blank, dead eyes of his own mother, standing white and silent in the garments of the grave!

§ 2

In his youth Halpin Frayser had lived with his parents in Nashville, Tennessee. The Fraysers were well-to-do, having a good position in such society as had survived the wreck wrought by civil war. Their children had the social and educational opportunities of their time and place, and had responded to good associations and instruction with agreeable manners and cultivated minds. Halpin being the youngest and not over robust was perhaps a trifle 'spoiled'. He had the double disadvantage of a mother's assiduity and a father's neglect. Frayser père was what no Southern man of means is not – a politician. His country, or rather his section and State, made demands upon his time and attention so exacting that to those of his family he was compelled to turn an ear partly deafened by the thunder of the political captains and the shouting, his own included.

Young Halpin was of a dreamy, indolent and rather romantic turn, somewhat more addicted to literature than law, the profession to which he was bred. Among those of his relations who professed the modern faith of heredity it was well understood that in him the character of the late Myron Bayne, a maternal great-grandfather, had revisited the glimpses of the moon – by which orb Bayne had in his lifetime been sufficiently affected to be a poet of no small

Colonial distinction. If not specially observed, it was observable that while a Frayser who was not the proud possessor of a sumptuous copy of the ancestral 'poetical works' (printed at the family expense, and long ago withdrawn from an inhospitable market) was a rare Frayser indeed, there was an illogical indisposition to honour the great deceased in the person of his spiritual ancestor. Halpin was pretty generally deprecated as an intellectual black sheep who was likely at any moment to disgrace the flock by bleating in metre. The Tennessee Fraysers were a practical folk – not practical in the popular sense of devotion to sordid pursuits, but having a robust contempt for any qualities unfitting a man for the wholesome vocation of politics.

In justice to young Halpin it should be said that while in him were pretty faithfully reproduced most of the mental and moral characteristics ascribed by history and family tradition to the famous Colonial bard, his succession to the gift and faculty divine was purely inferential. Not only had he never been known to court the Muse, but in truth he could not have written correctly a line of verse to save himself from the Killer of the Wise. Still, there was no knowing when the dormant faculty might wake and smite the lyre.

In the meantime the young man was rather a loose fish, anyhow. Between him and his mother was the most perfect sympathy, for secretly the lady was herself a devout disciple of the late and great Myron Bayne, though with the tact so generally and justly admired in her sex (despite the hardy calumniators who insist that it is essentially the same thing as cunning) she had always taken care to conceal her weakness from all eyes but those of him who shared it. Their common guilt in respect of that was an added tie between them. If in Halpin's youth his mother had 'spoiled' him he had assuredly done his part towards being spoiled. As he grew to such manhood as is attainable by a Southerner who does not care which way elections go, the attachment between him and his beautiful mother – whom from early childhood he had called Katy – became yearly stronger and more tender. In these romantic natures was manifest in a signal way that neglected phenomenon, the dominance of the sexual element in all the relations of life, strengthening, softening, and beautifying even those of consanguinity. The two were nearly inseparable, and by strangers observing their manners were not infrequently mistaken for lovers.

Entering his mother's boudoir one day Halpin Frayser kissed her upon the forehead, toyed for a moment with a lock of her dark hair which had escaped from its confining pins, and said, with an obvious effort at calmness:

'Would you greatly mind, Katy, if I were called away to California for a few weeks?'

It was hardly needful for Katy to answer with her lips a question to which her tell-tale cheeks had made instant reply. Evidently she would greatly mind; and the tears, too, sprang into her large brown eyes as corroborative testimony.

'Ah, my son,' she said, looking up into his face with infinite tenderness, 'I should have known that this was coming. Did I not lie awake a half of the night weeping because, during the other half, Grandfather Bayne had come to me in a dream, and standing by his portrait – young, too, as handsome as that – pointed to yours on the same wall? And when I looked it seemed that I could not see the features; you had been painted with a face cloth, such as we put upon the dead. Your father has laughed at me, but you and I, dear, know that such things are not for nothing. And I saw below the edge of the cloth the marks of hands on your throat – forgive me, but we have not been used to keep such things from each other. Perhaps you have another interpretation. Perhaps it does not mean that you will go to California. Or maybe you will take me with you?'

It must be confessed that this ingenious interpretation of the dream in the light of newly discovered evidence did not wholly commend itself to the son's more logical mind; he had, for the moment at least, a conviction that it foreshadowed a more simple and immediate, if less tragic, disaster than a visit to the Pacific Coast. It was Halpin Frayser's impression that he was to be garrotted on his native heath.

'Are there not medicinal springs in California?' Mrs

Frayser resumed before he had time to give her the true
reading of the dream – 'places where one recovers from
rheumatism and neuralgia? Look – my fingers feel so stiff;
and I am almost sure they have been giving me great pain
while I slept.'

She held out her hands for his inspection. What diagnosis
of her case the young man may have thought it best to
conceal with a smile, the historian is unable to state, but for
himself he feels bound to say that fingers looking less stiff,
and showing fewer evidences of even insensible pain, have
seldom been submitted for medical inspection by even the
fairest patient desiring a prescription of unfamiliar scenes.

The outcome of it was that of these two odd persons having equally odd notions of duty, the one went to California,
as the interest of his client required, and the other remained
at home in compliance with a wish that her husband was
scarcely conscious of entertaining.

While in San Francisco Halpin Frayser was walking one
dark night along the waterfront of the city, when, with a
suddenness that surprised and disconcerted him, he became
a sailor. He was in fact 'shanghaied' aboard a gallant, gallant
ship, and sailed for a far country. Nor did his misfortunes
end with the voyage; for the ship was cast ashore on an
island of the South Pacific, and it was six years afterward
when the survivors were taken off by a venturesome trading
schooner and brought back to San Francisco.

Though poor in purse, Frayser was no less proud in spirit
than he had been in the years that seemed ages and ages
ago. He would accept no assistance from strangers, and it
was while living with a fellow survivor near the town of St
Helena, awaiting news and remittances from home, that he
had gone gunning and dreaming.

§ 3

The apparition confronting the dreamer in the haunted
wood – the thing so like, yet so unlike, his mother – was
horrible! It stirred no love nor longing in his heart; it came

unattended with pleasant memories of a golden past – inspired no sentiment of any kind; all the finer emotions were swallowed up in fear. He tried to turn and run from before it, but his legs were as lead; he was unable to lift his feet from the ground. His arms hung helpless at his sides; of his eyes only he retained control, and these he dared not remove from the lustreless orbs of the apparition, which he knew was not a soul without a body, but that most dreadful of all existences infesting that haunted wood – a body without a soul! In its blank stare was neither love, nor pity, nor intelligence – nothing to which to address an appeal for mercy. 'An appeal will not lie,' he thought, with an absurd reversion to professional slang, making the situation more horrible, as the fire of a cigar might light up a tomb.

For a time, which seemed so long that the world grew grey with age and sin, and the haunted forest, having fulfilled its purpose in this monstrous culmination of its terrors, vanished out of his consciousness with all its sights and sounds, the apparition stood within a pace, regarding him with the mindless malevolence of a wild brute; then thrust its hands forward and sprang upon him with appalling ferocity! The act released his physical energies without unfettering his will, his mind was still spellbound, but his powerful body and agile limbs, endowed with a blind insensate life of their own, resisted stoutly and well. For an instant he seemed to see this unnatural contest between a dead intelligence and a breathing mechanism only as a spectator – such fancies are in dreams; then he regained his identity almost as if by a leap forward into his body, and the straining automaton had a directing will as alert and fierce as that of its hideous antagonist.

But what mortal can cope with a creature of his dream? The imagination creating the enemy is already vanquished; the combat's result is the combat's cause. Despite his struggles – despite his strength and activity, which seemed wasted in a void, he felt the cold fingers close upon his throat. Borne backward to the earth, he saw above him the dead and drawn face within a hand's-breadth of his own,

and then all was black. A sound as of the beating of distant
drums – a murmur of swarming voices, a sharp, far cry
signing all to silence, and Halpin Frayser dreamed that he
was dead.

§ 4

A warm, clear night had been followed by a morning of
drenching fog. At about the middle of the afternoon of the
preceding day a little whiff of light vapour – a mere thickening of the atmosphere, the ghost of a cloud – had been observed clinging to the western side of Mount St Helena,
away up along the barren altitudes near the summit. It was
so thin, so diaphanous, so like a fancy made visible, that
one would have said: 'Look quickly! in a moment it will be
gone.'

In a moment it was visibly larger and denser. While with
one edge it clung to the mountain, with the other it reached
farther and farther out into the air above the lower slopes.
At the same time it extended itself to north and south, joining small patches of mist that appeared to come out of the
mountainside on exactly the same level, with an intelligent
design to be absorbed. And so it grew and grew until the
summit was shut out of view from the valley, and over the
valley itself was an ever-extending canopy, opaque and
grey. At Calistoga, which lies near the head of the valley and
the foot of the mountain, there were a starless night and a
sunless morning. The fog, sinking into the valley, had
reached southward, swallowing up ranch after ranch, until
it had blotted out the town of St Helena, nine miles away.
The dust in the road was laid; trees were adrip with moisture; birds sat silent in their coverts; the morning light was
wan and ghastly, with neither colour nor fire.

Two men left the town of St Helena at the first glimmer
of dawn, and walked along the road northward up the valley
towards Calistoga. They carried guns on their shoulders, yet
no one having knowledge of such matters could have mistaken them for hunters of bird or beast. They were a deputy
sheriff from Napa and a detective from San Francisco –

Holker and Jaralson, respectively. Their business was man-hunting.

'How far is it?' inquired Holker, as they strode along, their feet stirring white the dust beneath the damp surface of the road.

'The White Church? Only a half mile farther,' the other answered. 'By the way,' he added, 'it is neither white nor a church; it is an abandoned schoolhouse, grey with age and neglect. Religious services were once held in it – when it was white, and there is a graveyard that would delight a poet. Can you guess why I sent for you, and told you to come armed?'

'Oh, I never have bothered you about things of that kind. I've always found you communicative when the time came. But if I may hazard a guess, you want me to help you arrest one of the corpses in the graveyard.'

'You remember Branscom?' said Jaralson, treating his companion's wit with the inattention that it deserved.

'The chap who cut his wife's throat? I ought; I wasted a week's work on him and had my expenses for my trouble. There is a reward of five hundred dollars, but none of us ever got a sight of him. You don't mean to say—'

'Yes, I do. He has been under the noses of you fellows all the time. He comes by night to the old graveyard at the White Church.'

'The devil! That's where they buried his wife.'

'Well, you fellows might have had sense enough to suspect that he would return to her grave some time?'

'The very last place that anyone would have expected him to return to.'

'But you had exhausted all the other places. Learning your failure at them, I "laid for him" there.'

'And you found him?'

'Damn it! he found *me*. The rascal got the drop on me – regularly held me up and made me travel. It's God's mercy that he didn't go through me. Oh, he's a good one, and I fancy the half of that reward is enough for me if you're needy.'

Holker laughed good-humouredly, and explained that his creditors were never more importunate.

'I wanted merely to show you the ground, and arrange a plan with you,' the detective explained. 'I thought it as well for us to be armed, even in daylight.'

'The man must be insane,' said the deputy sheriff. 'The reward is for his capture and conviction. If he's mad he won't be convicted.'

Mr Holker was so profoundly affected by that possible failure of justice that he involuntarily stopped in the middle of the road, then resumed his walk with abated zeal.

'Well, he looks it,' assented Jaralson. 'I'm bound to admit that a more unshaven, unshorn, unkempt, and uneverything wretch I never saw outside the ancient and honourable order of tramps. But I've gone in for him, and can't make up my mind to let go. There's glory in it for us, anyhow. Not another soul knows that he is this side of the Mountains of the Moon.'

'All right,' Holker said; 'we will go and view the ground,' and he added, in the words of a once favourite inscription for tombstones: ' "where you must shortly lie" – I mean if old Branscom ever gets tired of you and your impertinent intrusion. By the way, I heard the other day that "Branscom" was not his real name.'

'What is?'

'I can't recall it. I had lost all interest in the wretch, and it did not fix itself in my memory – something like Pardee. The woman whose throat he had the bad taste to cut was a widow when he met her. She had come to California to look up some relatives – there are persons who will do that sometimes. But you know all that.'

'Naturally.'

'But not knowing the right name, by what happy inspiration did you find the right grave? The man who told me what the name was said it had been cut on the headboard.'

'I don't know the right grave.' Jaralson was apparently a trifle reluctant to admit his ignorance of so important a

point of his plan. 'I have been watching about the place generally. A part of our work this morning will be to identify
that grave. Here is the White Church.'

For a long distance the road had been bordered by fields
on both sides, but now on the left there was a forest of oaks,
madronos, and gigantic spruces whose lower parts only
could be seen, dim and ghostly in the fog. The undergrowth
was, in places, thick, but nowhere impenetrable. For some
moments Holker saw nothing of the building, but as they
turned into the woods it revealed itself in faint grey outline
through the fog, looking huge and far away. A few steps
more, and it was within an arm's length, distinct, dark with
moisture, and insignificant in size. It had the usual country-
schoolhouse form – belonged to the packing-box order of
architecture; had an underpinning of stones, a moss-grown
roof, and blank window spaces, whence both glass and sash
had long departed. It was ruined, but not a ruin – a typical
Californian substitute for what are known to the guide-
bookers abroad as 'monuments of the past'. With scarcely
a glance at this uninteresting structure Jaralson moved on
into the dripping undergrowth beyond.

'I will show you where he held me up,' he said. 'This is
the graveyard.'

Here and there among the bushes were small enclosures
containing graves, sometimes no more than one. They were
recognized as graves by the discoloured stones or rotting
boards at head and foot, leaning at all angles, some prostrate;
by the ruined picket fences surrounding them; or, infrequently, by the mound itself showing its gravel through
the fallen leaves. In many instances nothing marked the
spot where lay the vestiges of some poor mortal – who,
leaving 'a large circle of sorrowing friends', had been left
by them in turn – except a depression in the earth, more
lasting than that in the spirits of the mourners. The paths,
if any paths had been, were long obliterated; trees of a considerable size had been permitted to grow up from the
graves and thrust aside with root or branch the enclosing
fences. Over all was that air of abandonment and decay

which seems nowhere so fit and significant as in a village of the forgotten dead.

As the two men, Jaralson leading, pushed their way through the growth of young trees, that enterprising man suddenly stopped and brought up his shotgun to the height of his breast, uttered a low note of warning, and stood motionless, his eyes fixed upon something ahead. As well as he could, obstructed by brush, his companion, though seeing nothing, imitated the posture and so stood, prepared for what might ensue. A moment later Jaralson moved cautiously forward, the other following.

Under the branches of an enormous spruce lay the dead body of a man. Standing silent above it they noted such particulars as first strike the attention – the face, the attitude, the clothing; whatever most promptly and plainly answers the unspoken question of a sympathetic curiosity.

The body lay upon its back, the legs wide apart. One arm was thrust upward, the other outward; but the latter was bent acutely, and the hand was near the throat. Both hands were tightly clenched. The whole attitude was that of desperate but ineffectual resistance to – what?

Nearby lay a shotgun and a game bag through the meshes of which was seen the plumage of shot birds. All about were evidences of a furious struggle; small sprouts of poison-oak were bent and denuded of leaf and bark; dead and rotting leaves had been pushed into heaps and ridges on both sides of the legs by the action of other feet than theirs; alongside the hips were unmistakable impressions of human knees.

The nature of the struggle was made clear by a glance at the dead man's throat and face. While breast and hands were white, those were purple – almost black. The shoulders lay upon a low mound, and the head was turned back at an angle otherwise impossible, the expanded eyes staring blankly backward in a direction opposite to that of the feet. From the froth filling the open mouth the tongue protruded, black and swollen. The throat showed horrible contusions; not mere finger-marks, but bruises and lacerations wrought by two strong hands that must have buried themselves in the yielding flesh, maintaining their terrible grasp until long after death. Breast, throat, face, were wet; the clothing was saturated; drops of water, condensed from the fog, studded the hair and moustache.

All this the two men observed without speaking – almost at a glance. Then Holker said:

'Poor devil! he had a rough deal.'

Jaralson was making a vigilant circumspection of the forest, his shotgun held in both hands and at full cock, his finger upon the trigger.

'The work of a maniac,' he said, without withdrawing his eyes from the enclosing wood. 'It was done by Branscom – Pardee.'

Something half hidden by the disturbed leaves on the earth caught Holker's attention. It was a red-leather pocket book. He picked it up and opened it. It contained leaves of white paper for memoranda, and upon the first leaf was the name 'Halpin Frayser'. Written in red on several succeeding leaves – scrawled as if in haste and barely legible – were the following lines, which Holker read aloud, while his companion continued scanning the dim grey confines of their narrow world and hearing matter of apprehension in the drip of water from every burdened branch:

'Enthralled by some mysterious spell, I stood
In the lit gloom of an enchanted wood.
The cypress there and myrtle twined their boughs,
Significant, in baleful brotherhood.

'The brooding willow whispered to the yew;
Beneath, the deadly nightshade and the rue,
With immortelles self-woven into strange
Funeral shapes, and horrid nettles grew.

'No song of bird nor any drone of bees,
Nor light leaf lifted by the wholesome breeze:
The air was stagnant all, and Silence was
A living thing that breathed among the trees.

'Conspiring spirits whispered in the gloom,
Half-heard, the stilly secrets of the tomb.
With blood the trees were all adrip; the leaves
Shone in the witch-light with a ruddy bloom.

'I cried aloud! – the spell, unbroken still,
Rested upon my spirit and my will.
Unsouled, unhearted, hopeless and forlorn,
I strove with monstrous presages of ill!

'At last the viewless—'

Holker ceased reading; there was no more to read. The manuscript broke off in the middle of a line.

'That sounds like Bayne,' said Jaralson, who was something of a scholar in his way. He had abated his vigilance and stood looking down at the body.

'Who's Bayne?' Holker asked rather incuriously.

'Myron Bayne, a chap who flourished in the early years of the nation – more than a century ago. Wrote mighty dismal stuff; I have his collected works. That poem is not among them, but it must have been omitted by mistake.'

'It is cold,' said Holker; 'let us leave here; we must have up the coroner from Napa.'

Jaralson said nothing, but made a movement in compliance. Passing the end of the slight elevation of earth upon which the dead man's head and shoulders lay, his foot struck some hard substance under the rotting forest leaves, and he took the trouble to kick it into view. It was a fallen headboard, and painted on it were the hardly decipherable words, 'Catharine Larue'.

'Larue, Larue!' exclaimed Holker, with sudden animation. 'Why, that is the real name of Branscom – not Pardee. And – bless my soul! how it all comes to me – the murdered woman's name had been Frayser!'

'There is some rascally mystery here,' said Detective Jaralson. 'I hate anything of that kind.'

There came to them out of the fog – seemingly from a

great distance – the sound of a laugh, a low, deliberate soulless laugh which had no more of joy than that of a hyena night-prowling in the desert; a laugh that rose by slow gradation, louder and louder, clearer, more distinct and terrible, until it seemed barely outside the narrow circle of their vision; a laugh so unnatural, so unhuman, so devilish, that it filled those hardy man-hunters with a sense of dread unspeakable! They did not move their weapons nor think of them; the menace of that horrible sound was not of the kind to be met with arms. As it had grown out of silence, so now it died away; from a culminating shout which had seemed almost in their ears, it drew itself away in the distance, until its failing notes, joyless and mechanical to the last, sank to silence at a measureless remove.

THE TRUE STORY OF A VAMPIRE

by

Eric, Count Stenbock

Vampire stories are generally located in Styria; mine is also. Styria is by no means the romantic kind of place described by those who have certainly never been there. It is a flat, uninteresting country, only celebrated for its turkeys, its capons, and the stupidity of its inhabitants. Vampires generally arrive at night, in carriages drawn by two black horses.

Our Vampire arrived by the commonplace means of the railway train, and in the afternoon. You must think I am joking, or perhaps that by the word 'Vampire' I mean a financial vampire. No, I am quite serious. The Vampire of whom I am speaking, who laid waste our hearth and home, was a *real* vampire.

Vampires are generally described as dark, sinister-looking, and singularly handsome. Our Vampire was, on the contrary, rather fair, and certainly was not at first sight sinister-looking, and though decidedly attractive in appearance, not what one would call singularly handsome.

Yes, he desolated our home, killed my brother – the one object of my adoration – also my dear father. Yet, at the same time, I must say that I myself came under the spell of his fascination, and, in spite of all, have no ill-will towards him now.

Doubtless you have read in the papers *passim* of 'the Baroness and her beasts'. It is to tell how I came to spend most of my useless wealth on an asylum for stray animals that I am writing this.

I am old now; what happened then was when I was a little girl of about thirteen. I will begin by describing our household. We were Poles; our name was Wronski: we lived in Styria, where we had a castle. Our household was very limited. It consisted, with the exclusion of domestics, of only my father, our governess – a worthy Belgian named Mademoiselle Vonnaert – my brother, and myself. Let me begin with my father: he was old and both my brother and I were children of his old age. Of my mother I remember nothing: she died in giving birth to my brother, who was only one year, or not as much, younger than myself. Our father was studious, continually occupied in reading books, chiefly on recondite subjects and in all kinds of unknown languages. He had a long white beard, and wore habitually a black velvet skull-cap.

How kind he was to us! It was more than I could tell. Still it was not I who was the favourite. His whole heart went out to Gabriel – Gabryel as we spelt it in Polish. He was always called by the Russian abbreviation Gavril – I mean, of course, my brother, who had a resemblance to the only portrait of my mother, a slight chalk sketch which hung in my father's study. But I was by no means jealous: my brother was and has been the only love of my life. It is for his sake that I am now keeping in Westbourne Park a home for stray cats and dogs.

I was at that time, as I said before, a little girl; my name was Carmela. My long tangled hair was always all over the place, and never would be combed straight. I was not pretty – at least, looking at a photograph of me at that time, I do not think I could describe myself as such. Yet at the same time, when I look at the photograph, I think my expression may have been pleasing to some people: irregular features, large mouth, and large wild eyes.

I was by way of being naughty – not so naughty as Gabriel in the opinion of Mlle Vonnaert. Mlle Vonnaert, I may intercalate, was a wholly excellent person, middle-aged, who really did speak good French, although she was a Belgian, and could also make herself understood in German, which, as you may or may not know, is the current language of Styria.

I find it difficult to describe my brother Gabriel; there

was something about him strange and superhuman, or perhaps I should rather say praeterhuman, something between the animal and the divine. Perhaps the Greek idea of the Faun might illustrate what I mean; but that will not do either. He had large, wild, gazelle-like eyes: his hair, like mine, was in a perpetual tangle – that point he had in common with me, and indeed, as I afterwards heard, our mother having been of gipsy race, it will account for much of the innate wildness there was in our natures. I was wild enough, but Gabriel was much wilder. Nothing would induce him to put on shoes and stockings, except on Sundays – when he also allowed his hair to be combed, but only by me. How shall I describe the grace of that lovely mouth, shaped verily 'en arc d'amour'. I always think of the text in the Psalm, 'Grace is shed forth on thy lips, therefore has God blessed thee eternally' – lips that seemed to exhale the very breath of life. Then that beautiful, lithe, living, elastic form!

He could run faster than any deer: spring like a squirrel to the topmost branch of a tree: he might have stood for the sign and symbol of vitality itself. But seldom could he be induced by Mlle Vonnaert to learn lessons; but when he did so, he learnt with extraordinary quickness. He would play upon every conceivable instrument, holding a violin here, there, and everywhere except the right place: manufacturing instruments for himself out of reeds – even sticks. Mlle Vonnaert made futile efforts to induce him to learn to play the piano. I suppose he was what was called spoilt, though merely in the superficial sense of the word. Our father allowed him to indulge in every caprice.

One of his peculiarities, when quite a little child, was horror at the sight of meat. Nothing on earth would induce him to taste it. Another thing which was particularly remarkable about him was his extraordinary power over animals. Everything seemed to come tame to his hand. Birds would sit on his shoulder. Then sometimes Mlle Vonnaert and I would lose him in the woods – he would suddenly dart away. Then we would find him singing softly or whistling to himself, with all manner of woodland creatures around him – hedgehogs, little foxes, wild rabbits, marmots, squirrels, and such like. He would frequently bring these things home with him and insist on keeping them. This strange menagerie was the terror of poor Mlle Vonnaert's heart. He chose to live in a little room at the top of a turret; but which, instead of going upstairs, he chose to reach by means of a very tall chestnut-tree, through the window. But in contradiction of all this, it was his custom to serve every Sunday Mass in the parish church, with hair nicely combed and with white surplice and red cassock. He looked as demure and tamed as possible. Then came the element of the divine. What an expression of ecstasy there was in those glorious eyes!

Thus far I have not been speaking about the Vampire. However, let me begin with my narrative at last. One day my father had to go to the neighbouring town – as he frequently had. This time he returned accompanied by a guest. The gentleman, he said, had missed his train, through the late arrival of another at our station, which was a junction, and he would therefore, as trains were not frequent in our parts, have had to wait there all night. He had joined in conversation with my father in the too-late-arriving train from the town: and had consequently accepted my father's invitation to stay the night at our house. But of course, you know, in those out-of-the-way parts we are almost patriarchal in our hospitality.

He was announced under the name of Count Vardalek – the name being Hungarian. But he spoke German well enough: not with the monotonous accentuation of Hungarians, but rather, if anything, with a slight Slavonic intonation. His voice was peculiarly soft and insinuating. We soon afterwards found that he could talk Polish, and Mlle Vonnaert vouched for his good French. Indeed he seemed to know all languages. But let me give my first impressions. He was rather tall with fair wavy hair, rather long, which accentuated a certain effeminacy about his smooth face. His figure had something – I cannot say what – serpentine about it. The features were refined; and he had long, slender, subtle, magnetic-looking hands, a somewhat long sinuous

nose, a graceful mouth, and an attractive smile, which be-
lied the intense sadness of the expression of the eyes. When
he arrived his eyes were half closed – indeed they were
habitually so – so that I could not decide their colour. He
looked worn and wearied. I could not possibly guess his
age.

Suddenly Gabriel burst into the room: a yellow butterfly
was clinging to his hair. He was carrying in his arms a little
squirrel. Of course he was bare-legged as usual. The stranger
looked up at his approach; then I noticed his eyes. They
were green: they seemed to dilate and grow larger. Gabriel
stood stock-still, with a startled look, like that of a bird fascinated by a serpent. But nevertheless he held out his hand
to the newcomer. Vardalek, taking his hand – I don't know
why I noticed this trivial thing – pressed the pulse with his
forefinger. Suddenly Gabriel darted from the room and
rushed upstairs, going to his turret-room this time by the
staircase instead of the tree. I was in terror what the Count
might think of him. Great was my relief when he came down
in his velvet Sunday suit, and shoes and stockings. I combed
his hair, and set him generally right.

When the stranger came down to dinner his appearance
had somewhat altered; he looked much younger. There was
an elasticity of the skin, combined with a delicate complex-
ion, rarely to be found in a man. Before, he had struck me
as being very pale.

Well, at dinner we were all charmed with him, especially
my father. He seemed to be thoroughly acquainted with all
my father's particular hobbies. Once, when my father was
relating some of his military experiences, he said something
about a drummer-boy who was wounded in battle. His eyes
opened completely again and dilated: this time with a particularly disagreeable expression, dull and dead, yet at the
same time animated by some horrible excitement. But this
was only momentary.

The chief subject of his conversation with my father was
about certain curious mystical books which my father had
just lately picked up, and which he could not make out, but

Vardalek seemed completely to understand. At dessert-time
my father asked him if he were in a great hurry to reach his
destination: if not, would he not stay with us a little while:
though our place was out of the way, he would find much
that would interest him in his library.

He answered, 'I am in no hurry. I have no particular reason for going to that place at all, and if I can be of service
to you in deciphering these books, I shall be only too glad.'
He added with a smile which was bitter, very very bitter:
'You see I am a cosmopolitan, a wanderer on the face of
the earth.'

After dinner my father asked him if he played the piano.
He said, 'Yes, I can a little,' and he sat down at the piano.
Then he played a Hungarian csardas – wild, rhapsodic, won-
derful.

That is the music which makes men mad. He went on in
the same strain.

Gabriel stood stock-still by the piano, his eyes dilated and
fixed, his form quivering. At last he said very slowly, at
one particular motive – for want of a better word you may
call it the relâche of a csardas, by which I mean that point
where the original quasi-slow movement begins again – 'Yes,
I think I could play that.'

Then he quickly fetched his fiddle and self-made xylo-
phone, and did, actually alternating the instruments, render
the same very well indeed.

Vardalek looked at him, and said in a very sad voice,
'Poor child! you have the soul of music within you.'

I could not understand why he should seem to commiser-
ate instead of congratulate Gabriel on what certainly showed
an extraordinary talent.

Gabriel was shy even as the wild animals who were tame
to him. Never before had he taken to a stranger. Indeed, as
a rule, if any stranger came to the house by any chance, he
would hide himself, and I had to bring him up his food to
the turret chamber. You may imagine what was my surprise
when I saw him walking about hand in hand with Vardalek

the next morning, in the garden, talking livelily with him, and showing his collection of pet animals, which he had gathered from the woods, and for which we had had to fit up a regular zoological gardens. He seemed utterly under the domination of Vardalek. What surprised us was (for otherwise we liked the stranger, especially for being kind to him) that he seemed, though not noticeably at first – except perhaps to me, who noticed everything with regard to him – to be gradually losing his general health and vitality. He did not become pale as yet; but there was a certain languor about his movements which certainly there was by no means before.

My father got more and more devoted to Count Vardalek. He helped him in his studies: and my father would hardly allow him to go away, which he did sometimes – to Trieste, he said: he always came back, bringing us presents of strange Oriental jewellery or textures.

I knew all kinds of people came to Trieste, Orientals included. Still, there was a strangeness and magnificence about these things which I was sure even then could not possibly have come from such a place as Trieste, memorable to me chiefly for its necktie shops.

When Vardalek was away, Gabriel was continually asking for him and talking about him. Then at the same time he seemed to regain his old vitality and spirits. Vardalek always returned looking much older, wan, and weary. Gabriel would rush to meet him, and kiss him on the mouth. Then he gave a slight shiver: and after a little while began to look quite young again.

Things continued like this for some time. My father would not hear of Vardalek's going away permanently. He came to be an inmate of our house. I indeed, and Mlle Vonnaert also, could not help noticing what a difference there was altogether about Gabriel. But my father seemed totally blind to it.

One night I had gone downstairs to fetch something which I had left in the drawing-room. As I was going up again I passed Vardalek's room. He was playing on a piano, which had been specially put there for him, one of Chopin's nocturnes, very beautifully: I stopped, leaning on the banisters to listen.

Something white appeared on the dark staircase. We believed in ghosts in our part. I was transfixed with terror, and clung to the banisters. What was my astonishment to see Gabriel walking slowly down the staircase, his eyes fixed as though in a trance! This terrified me even more than a ghost would. Could I believe my senses? Could that be Gabriel?

I simply could not move. Gabriel, clad in his long white night-shirt, came downstairs and opened the door. He left it open. Vardalek still continued playing, but talked as he played.

He said – this time speaking in Polish – *Nie umiem wyrazic jak ciechi kocham* – 'My darling, I fain would spare thee; but thy life is my life, and I must live, I who would rather die. Will God not have any mercy on me? Oh! Oh! life; oh, the torture of life!' Here he struck one agonized and strange chord, then continued playing softly, 'O Gabriel, my beloved! my life, yes *life* – oh, why life? I am sure this is but a little that I demand of thee. Surely thy superabundance of life can spare a little to one who is already dead. No, stay,' he said now almost harshly, 'what must be, must be!'

Gabriel stood there quite still, with the same fixed vacant expression, in the room. He was evidently walking in his sleep. Vardalek played on: then said, 'Ah!' with a sign of terrible agony. Then very gently, 'Go now, Gabriel; it is enough.' And Gabriel went out of the room and ascended the staircase at the same slow pace, with the same unconscious stare. Vardalek struck the piano, and although he did not play loudly, it seemed as though the strings would break. You never heard music so strange and so heart-rending!

I only know I was found by Mlle Vonnaert in the morning, in an unconscious state, at the foot of the stairs. Was it a dream after all? I am sure now that it was not. I thought then it might be, and said nothing to anyone about it. Indeed, what could I say?

Well, to let me cut a long story short, Gabriel, who had never known a moment's sickness in his life, grew ill: and we had to send to Gratz for a doctor, who could give no explanation of Gabriel's strange illness. Gradual wasting away, he said: absolutely no organic complaint. What could this mean?

My father at last became conscious of the fact that Gabriel was ill. His anxiety was fearful. The last trace of grey faded from his hair, and it became quite white. We sent to Vienna for doctors. But all with the same result.

Gabriel was generally unconscious, and when conscious, only seemed to recognize Vardalek, who sat continually by his bedside, nursing him with the utmost tenderness.

One day I was alone in the room: and Vardalek cried suddenly, almost fiercely, 'Send for a priest at once, at once,' he repeated. 'It is now almost too late!'

Gabriel stretched out his arms spasmodically, and put them round Vardalek's neck. This was the only movement he had made, for some time. Vardalek bent down and kissed him on the lips. I rushed downstairs: and the priest was sent for. When I came back Vardalek was not there. The priest administered extreme unction. I think Gabriel was already dead, although we did not think so at the time.

Vardalek had utterly disappeared; and when we looked for him he was nowhere to be found; nor have I seen or heard of him since.

My father died very soon afterwards: suddenly aged, and bent down with grief. And so the whole of the Wronski property came into my sole possession. And here I am, an old woman, generally laughed at for keeping, in memory of Gabriel, an asylum for stray animals – and – people do not, as a rule, believe in Vampires!

THE HOUND

by

H. P. Lovecraft

In my tortured ears there sounds unceasingly a nightmare whirring and flapping, and a faint, distant baying as of some gigantic hound. It is not dream – it is not, I fear, even madness – for too much has already happened to give me these merciful doubts.

St John is a mangled corpse; I alone know why, and such is my knowledge that I am about to blow out my brains for fear I shall be mangled in the same way. Down unlit and illimitable corridors of eldritch phantasy sweeps the black, shapeless Nemesis that drives me to self-annihilation.

May heaven forgive the folly and morbidity which led us both to so monstrous a fate! Wearied with the commonplaces of a prosaic world, where even the joys of romance and adventure soon grow stale, St John and I had followed enthusiastically every aesthetic and intellectual movement which promised respite from our devastating ennui. The enigmas of the symbolists and the ecstasies of the pre-Raphaelites all were ours in their time, but each new moon was drained too soon of its diverting novelty and appeal.

Only the sombre philosophy of the decadents could help us, and this we found potent only by increasing gradually the depth and diabolism of our penetrations. Baudelaire and Huysmans were soon exhausted of thrills, till finally there remained for us only the more direct stimuli of unnatural personal experiences and adventures. It was this frightful emotional need which led us eventually to that detestable course which even in my present fear I mention with shame and timidity – that hideous extremity of human outrage, and abhorred practice of grave-robbing.

I cannot reveal the details of our shocking expeditions, or catalogue even partly the worst of the trophies adorning the nameless museum we prepared in the great stone house where we jointly dwelt, alone and servantless. Our museum was a blasphemous, unthinkable place, where with the satanic taste of neurotic virtuosi we had assembled a universe of terror and decay to excite our jaded sensibilities. It was a secret room, far, far, underground; where huge winged daemons carven of basalt and onyx vomited from wide grinning mouths weird green and orange light, and hidden pneumatic pipes ruffled into kaleidoscopic dances of death the lines of red charnel things hand in hand woven in voluminous black hangings. Through these pipes came at will the odours our moods most craved; sometimes the scent of pale funereal lilies, sometimes the narcotic incense of imagined Eastern shrines of the kingly dead and sometimes – how I shudder to recall it! – the frightful, soul-upheaving stenches of the uncovered grave.

Around the walls of this repellent chamber were cases of antique mummies alternating with comely, lifelike bodies perfectly stuffed and cured by the taxidermist's art, and with head-stones snatched from the oldest churchyards of the world. Niches here and there contained skulls of all shapes, and heads preserved in various stages of dissolution. There one might find the rotting, bald pates of famous noblemen, and the fresh and radiantly golden heads of new-buried children.

Statues and paintings there were, all of fiendish subjects and some executed by St John and myself. A locked portfolio, bound in tanned human skin, held certain unknown and unnameable drawings which it was rumoured Goya had perpetrated but dared not acknowledge. There were nauseous musical instruments, stringed, brass, and wood-wind, on which St John and I sometimes produced dissonances of exquisite morbidity and cacodaemoniacal ghastliness; whilst in a multitude of inlaid ebony cabinets reposed the most incredible and unimaginable variety of tomb-loot ever assembled by human madness and perversity. It is of this loot in particular that I must not speak – thank God I had the courage to destroy it long before I thought of destroying myself!

The predatory excursions on which we collected our unmentionable treasures were always artistically memorable events. We were no vulgar ghouls, but worked only under certain conditions of mood, landscape, environment, weather, season and moonlight. These pastimes were to us the most exquisite form of aesthetic expression, and we gave their details a fastidious technical care. An inappropriate hour, a jarring lighting effect, or a clumsy manipulation of the damp sod, would almost totally destroy for us that titillation which followed the exhumation of some ominous, grinning secret of the earth. Our quest for novel scenes and piquant conditions was feverish and insatiate – St John was always the leader, and he it was who led the way at last to that mocking, accursed spot which brought us our hideous and inevitable doom.

By what malign fatality were we lured to that terrible Holland churchyard? I think it was the dark rumour and legendry, the tales of one buried for five centuries, who had himself been a ghoul in his time and had stolen a potent thing from a mighty sepulchre. I can recall the scene in these final moments – the pale autumnal moon over the graves, casting long horrible shadows; the grotesque trees, drooping sullenly to meet the neglected grass and the crumbling slabs; the vast legions of strangely colossal bats that flew against the moon; the antique ivied church pointing a huge spectral finger at the livid sky; the phosphorescent insects that danced like death-fires under the yews in a distant corner – the odours of mould, vegetation, and less explicable things that mingled feebly with the night wind from over far swamps and seas; and, worst of all, the faint deep-toned baying of some gigantic hound which we could neither see nor definitely place. As we heard this suggestion of baying we shuddered, remembering the tales of the peasantry; for he whom we sought had centuries before been found in this self-same spot, torn and mangled by the claws and teeth of some unspeakable beast.

I remember how we delved in the ghoul's grave with our spades, and how we thrilled at the picture of ourselves, the grave, the pale watching moon, the horrible shadows, the grotesque trees, the titanic bats, the antique church, the dancing death-fires, the sickening odours, the gentle moaning night wind, and the strange, half-heard directionless baying of whose objective existence we could scarcely be sure.

Then we struck a substance harder than the damp mould, and beheld a rotting oblong box crusted with mineral deposits from the long undisturbed ground. It was incredibly tough and thick, but so old that we finally pried it open and feasted our eyes on what it held.

Much – amazingly much – was left of the object despite the lapse of five hundred years. The skeleton, though crushed in places by the jaws of the thing that had killed it, held together with surprising firmness, and we gloated over the clean white skull and its long, firm teeth and its eyeless sockets that once had glowed with a charnel fever like our own. In the coffin lay an amulet of curious and exotic design, which had apparently been worn around the sleeper's neck. It was the oddly conventionalized figure of a crouching winged hound, or sphinx with a semi-canine face, and was exquisitely carved in antique Oriental fashion from a small piece of green jade. The expression of its features was repellent in the extreme, savouring at once of death, bestiality, and malevolence. Around the base was an inscription in characters which neither St John nor I could identify; and on the bottom, like a maker's seal, was given a grotesque and formidable skull.

Immediately upon beholding this amulet we knew that we must possess it; that this treasure alone was our logical pelt from the centuried grave. Even had its outlines been unfamiliar we would have desired it, but as we looked more closely we saw that it was not wholly unfamiliar. Alien it indeed was to all art and literature which sane and balanced readers know, but we recognized it as the thing hinted at in the forbidden *Necronomicon* of the mad Arab Abdul Alhazred; the ghastly soul-symbol of the corpse-eating cult of inaccessible Leng, in Central Asia. All too well did we trace the sinister lineaments described by the old Arab daemonologist; lineaments, he wrote, drawn from some obscure supernatural manifestation of the souls of those who vexed and gnawed at the dead.

Seizing the green jade object, we gave a last glance at the bleached and cavern-eyed face of its owner and closed up the grave as we found it. As we hastened from the abhorrent spot, the stolen amulet in St John's pocket, we thought we saw the bats descend in a body to the earth we had so lately rifled, as if seeking for some cursed and unholy nourishment. But the autumn moon shone weak and pale, and we could not be sure.

So, too, as we sailed the next day away from Holland to our home, we thought we heard the faint distant baying of some gigantic hound in the background. But the autumn wind moaned sad and wan, and we could not be sure.

Less than a week after our return to England, strange things began to happen. We lived as recluses; devoid of friends, alone, and without servants in a few rooms of an ancient manorhouse on a bleak and unfrequented moor; so that our doors were seldom disturbed by the knock of the visitor.

Now, however, we were troubled by what seemed to be a frequent fumbling in the night, not only around the doors but around the windows also, upper as well as lower. Once we fancied that a large opaque body darkened the library window when the moon was shining against it, and another time we thought we heard a whirring or flapping sound not far off. On each occasion investigation revealed nothing, and we began to ascribe the occurrences to imagination which still prolonged in our ears the faint far baying we thought we had heard in the Holland churchyard. The jade amulet now reposed in a niche in our museum, and sometimes we burned a strangely scented candle before it. We read much in Al-hazred's *Necronomicon* about its properties, and about the relation of ghosts' souls to the objects it symbolized; and were disturbed by what we read.

Then terror came.

On the night of 24 September 19—, I heard a knock at my chamber door. Fancying it St John's, I bade the knocker enter, but was answered only by a shrill laugh. There was no one in the corridor. When I aroused St John from his sleep, he professed entire ignorance of the event, and became as worried as I. It was the night that the faint, distant baying over the moor became to us a certain and dreaded reality.

Four days later, whilst we were both in the hidden museum, there came a low, cautious scratching at the single door which led to the secret library staircase. Our alarm was now divided, for, besides our fear of the unknown, we had always entertained a dread that our grisly collection might be discovered. Extinguishing all lights, we proceeded to the door and threw it suddenly open; whereupon we felt an un-accountable rush of air, and heard, as if receding far away, a queer combination of rustling, tittering, and articulate chatter. Whether we were mad, dreaming, or in our senses, we did not try to determine. We only realized, with the blackest of apprehensions, that the apparently disembodied chatter was beyond a doubt in the Dutch language.

After that we lived in growing horror and fascination. Mostly we held to the theory that we were jointly going mad from our life of unnatural excitements, but sometimes it pleased us more to dramatize ourselves as the victims of some creeping and appalling doom. Bizarre manifestations were now too frequent to count. Our lonely house was seem-ingly alive with the presence of some malign being whose nature we could not guess, and every night that daemoniac baying rolled over the windswept moor, always louder and louder. On 29 October we found in the soft earth under-neath the library window a series of footprints utterly im-possible to describe. They were as baffling as the hordes of great bats which haunted the old manorhouse in unprecedented and increasing numbers.

The horror reached a culmination on 18 November, when St John, walking home after dark from the dismal railway station, was seized by some frightful carnivorous thing and torn to ribbons. His screams had reached the house, and I had hastened to the terrible scene in time to hear a whirr of wings and see a vague black cloudy thing silhouetted against the rising moon.

My friend was dying when I spoke to him, and he could not answer coherently. All he could do was to whisper, 'The amulet – that damned thing—'

Then he collapsed, an inert mass of mangled flesh.

I buried him the next midnight in one of our neglected gardens, and mumbled over his body one of the devilish rituals he had loved in life. And as I pronounced the last daemoniac sentence I heard afar on the moor the faint baying of some gigantic hound. The moon was up, but I dared not look at it. And when I saw on the dim-lighted moor a wide nebulous shadow sweeping from mound to mound, I shut my eyes and threw myself face down upon the ground. When I arose, trembling, I know not how much later, I staggered into the house and made shocking obeisances before the enshrined amulet of green jade.

Being now afraid to live alone in the ancient house on the moor, I departed on the following day for London, taking with me the amulet after destroying by fire and burial the rest of the impious collection in the museum. But after three nights I heard the baying again, and before a week was over felt strange eyes upon me whenever it was dark. One evening as I strolled on Victoria Embankment for some needed air, I saw a black shape obscure one of the reflections of the lamps in the water. A wind, stronger than the night wind, rushed by, and I know that what had befallen St John must soon befall me.

The next day I carefully wrapped the green jade amulet and sailed for Holland. What mercy I might gain by returning the thing to its silent, sleeping owner I knew not; but I felt that I must try any step conceivably logical. What the hound was, and why it had pursued me, were questions still vague; but I had first heard the baying in that ancient churchyard, and every subsequent event including St John's dying whisper had served to connect the curse with the stealing of the amulet. Accordingly I sank into the nethermost abysses of despair when, at an inn in Rotterdam, I discovered that thieves had despoiled me of this sole means of salvation.

The baying was loud that evening, and in the morning I read of a nameless deed in the vilest quarter of the city. The rabble were in terror, for upon an evil tenement had fallen a red death beyond the foulest previous crime of the neighbourhood. In a squalid thieves' den an entire family had been torn to shreds by an unknown thing which left no trace, and those around had heard all night a faint, deep insistent note as of a gigantic hound.

So at last I stood again in the unwholesome churchyard where a pale winter moon cast hideous shadows, and leafless trees dropped sullenly to meet the withered, frosty grass and cracking slabs, and the ivied church pointed a jeering finger at the unfriendly sky, and the night wind howled maniacally from over frozen swamps and frigid seas. The baying was very faint now, and it ceased altogether as I approached the ancient grave I had once violated, and frightened away an abnormally large horde of bats which had been hovering curiously around it.

I know not why I went thither unless to pray, or gibber out insane pleas and apologies to the calm white thing that lay within; but, whatever my reason, I attacked the halffrozen sod with a desperation partly mine and partly that of a dominating will outside myself. Excavation was much easier than I expected, though at one point I encountered a queer interruption; when a lean vulture darted down out of the cold sky and pecked frantically at the grave-earth until I killed him with a blow of my spade. Finally I reached the rotting oblong box and removed the damp nitrous cover. This is the last rational act I ever performed.

For crouched within that centuried coffin, embraced by a close-packed nightmare retinue of high, sinewy, sleeping bats, was the bony thing my friend and I had robbed; not clean and placid as we had seen it then, but covered with caked blood and shreds of alien flesh and hair, and leering sentiently at me with phosphorescent sockets and sharp ensanguined fangs yawning twistedly in mockery of my inevitable doom. And when it gave from those grinning jaws a deep, sardonic bay as of some gigantic hound, and I saw that it held in its gory filthy claw the lost and fateful amulet of green jade, I merely screamed and ran away idiotically, my screams soon dissolving into peals or hysterical laughter.

Madness rides the star-wind ... claws and teeth sharpened on centuries of corpses ... dripping death astride a bacchanal of bats from night-black ruins of buried temples of Belial ... Now, as the baying of that dead fleshless monstrosity grows louder and louder, and the stealthy whirring and flapping of those accursed web-wings circles closer and closer, I shall seek with my revolver the oblivion which is my only refuge from the unnamed and unnameable.

WHEN IT WAS MOONLIGHT

by

Manly Wade Wellman

Let my heart be still a moment, and this mystery explore.
                                                    The Raven

His hand, as slim as a white claw, dipped a quillful of ink and wrote in one corner of the page the date – 3 March 1842. Then:

THE PREMATURE BURIAL
by Edgar A. Poe

He hated his middle name, the name of his miserly and spiteful stepfather. For a moment he considered crossing out even the initial; then he told himself that he was only wool-gathering, putting off the drudgery of writing. And write he must, or starve – the Philadelphia *Dollar Newspaper* was clamouring for the story he had promised. Well, today he had heard a tag of gossip – his mother-in-law had it from a neighbour – that revived in his mind a subject always fascinating.

He began rapidly to write, in a fine copperplate hand:

There are certain themes of which the interest is all-absorbing, but which are entirely too horrible for the purposes of legitimate fiction ...

This would really be an essay, not a tale, and he could do it justice. Often he thought of the whole world as a vast fat cemetery, close set with tombs in which not all the occupants were at rest – too many struggled unavailingly against their smothering shrouds, their locked and weighted coffin lids.

What were his own literary labours, he mused, but a struggle against being shut down and throttled by a society as heavy and grim and senseless as clods heaped by a sexton's spade?

He paused, and went to the slate mantelshelf for a candle. His kerosene lamp had long ago been pawned, and it was dark for mid-afternoon, even in March. Elsewhere in the house his mother-in-law swept busily, and in the room next to his sounded the quiet breathing of his invalid wife. Poor Virginia slept, and for the moment knew no pain. Returning with his light, he dipped more ink and continued down the sheet:

To be buried while alive is, beyond question, the most terrific of these extremes which has ever fallen to the lot of mere mortality. That it has frequently, very frequently, fallen will scarcely be denied ...

Again his dark imagination savoured the tale he had heard that day. It had happened here in Philadelphia, in this very quarter, less than a month ago. A widower had gone, after weeks of mourning, to his wife's tomb, with flowers. Stooping to place them on the marble slab, he had heard noise beneath. At once joyful and aghast, he fetched men and crowbars, and recovered the body, all untouched by decay. At home that night, the woman returned to consciousness.

So said the gossip, perhaps exaggerated, perhaps not. And the house was only six blocks away from Spring Garden Street, where he sat.

Poe fetched out his notebooks and began to marshal bits of narrative for his composition – a gloomy tale of resurrection in Baltimore, another from France, a genuinely creepy citation from the *Chirurgical Journal* of Leipzig; a sworn case of revival, by electrical impulses, of a dead man in London. Then he added an experience of his own, romantically embellished, a dream adventure of his boyhood in Virginia. Just as he thought to make an end, he had a new inspiration.

Why not learn more about that reputed Philadelphia

burial and the one who rose from seeming death? It would point up his piece, give it a timely local climax, ensure acceptance – he could hardly risk a rejection. Too, it would satisfy his own curiosity. Laying down the pen, Poe got up. From a peg he took his wide black hat, his old military cloak that he had worn since his ill-fated cadet days at West Point. Huddling it round his slim little body, he opened the front door and went out.

March had come in like a lion and, lion-like, roared and rampaged over Philadelphia. Dry, cold dust blew up into Poe's full grey eyes, and he hardened his mouth under the gay dark moustache. His shins felt goosefleshy; his striped trousers were unseasonably thin and his shoes badly needed mending. Which way lay his journey?

He remembered the name of the street, and something about a ruined garden. Eventually he came to the place, or what must be the place – the garden was certainly ruined, full of dry, hardy weeds that still stood in great ragged clumps after the hard winter. Poe forced open the creaky gate, went up the rough-flagged path to the stoop. He saw a bronzed nameplate – 'Gauber', it said. Yes, that was the name he had heard. He swung the knocker loudly, and thought he caught a whisper of movement inside. But the door did not open.

'Nobody lives there, Mr Poe,' said someone from the street. It was a grocery boy, with a heavy basket on his arm. Poe left the doorstep. He knew the lad; indeed he owed the grocer eleven dollars.

'Are you sure?' Poe prompted.

'Well' – and the boy shifted the weight of his burden – 'if anybody lived there, they'd buy from our shop, wouldn't they? And I'd deliver, wouldn't I? But I've had this job for six months, and never set foot inside that door.'

Poe thanked him and walked down the street, but did not take the turn that would lead home. Instead he sought the shop of one Pemberton, a printer and friend, to pass the time of day and ask for a loan.

Pemberton could not lend even one dollar – times were

hard – but offered a drink of Monogahela whiskey, which Poe forced himself to refuse; then a supper of crackers, cheese and garlic sausage, which Poe thankfully shared. At home, unless his mother-in-law had begged or borrowed from the neighbours, would be only bread and molasses. It was past sundown when the writer shook hands with Pemberton, thanked him with warm courtesy for his hospitality, and ventured into the evening.

Thank Heaven, it did not rain. Poe was saddened by storms. The wind had abated and the March sky was clear save for a tiny fluff of scudding cloud and a banked dark line at the horizon, while up rose a full moon the colour of frozen cream. Poe squinted from under his hat brim at the shadow-pattern on the disc. Might he not write another story of a lunar voyage – like the one about Hans Pfaal, but dead serious this time? Musing thus, he walked along the dusk-filling street until he came again opposite the ruined garden, the creaky gate, and the house with the doorplate marked: 'Gauber.'

Hello, the grocery boy had been wrong. There was light inside the front window, water-blue light – or was there? Anyway, motion – yes, a figure stooped there, as if to peer out at him.

Poe turned in at the gate, and knocked at the door once again.

Four or five moments of silence; then he heard the old lock grating. The door moved inwards, slowly and noisily. Poe fancied that he had been wrong about the blue light; for he saw only darkness inside. A voice spoke:

'Well, sir.'

The two words came huskily but softly, as though the door-opener scarcely breathed. Poe swept off his broad black hat and made one of his graceful bows.

'If you will pardon me . . .' He paused, not knowing whether he addressed man or woman. 'This is the Gauber residence?'

'It is,' was the reply, soft, hoarse and sexless. 'Your business, sir?'

Poe spoke with official crispness; he had been a sergeant-major of artillery before he was twenty-one, and knew how to inject the proper note. 'I am here on public duty,' he announced. 'I am a journalist, tracing a strange report.'

'Journalist?' repeated his interrogator. 'Strange report? Come in, sir.'

Poe complied, and the door closed abruptly behind him, with a rusty snick of the lock. He remembered being in jail once, and how the door of his cell had slammed just so. It was not a pleasant memory. But he saw more clearly, now he was inside – his eyes got used to the tiny trickle of moonlight.

He stood in a dark hallway, all panelled in wood, with no furniture, drapes or pictures. With him was a woman, in full skirt and down-drawn lace cap, a woman as tall as he and with intent eyes that glowed as from within. She neither moved nor spoke, but waited for him to tell her more of his errand.

Poe did so, giving his name and, stretching a point, claiming to be a sub-editor of the *Dollar Newspaper*, definitely assigned to the interview. 'And now, madam, concerning this story that is rife concerning a premature burial ...'

She had moved very close, but as his face turned towards her she drew back. Poe fancied that his breath had blown her away like a feather; then, remembering Pemberton's garlic sausage, he was chagrined. To confirm his new thought, the woman was offering him wine – to sweeten his breath.

'Would you take a glass of canary, Mr Poe,' she invited, and opened a side door. He followed her into a room papered in pale blue. Moonglow, drenching it, reflected from that paper and seemed an artificial light. That was what he had seen from outside. From an undraped table his hostess lifted a bottle, poured wine into a metal goblet and offered it.

Poe wanted that wine, but he had recently promised his sick wife, solemnly and honestly, to abstain from even a sip of the drink that so easily upset him. Through thirsty lips he said: 'I thank you kindly, but I am a temperance man.'

'Oh,' and she smiled. Poe saw white teeth. Then: 'I am Elva Gauber – Mrs John Gauber. The matter of which you ask I cannot explain clearly, but it is true. My husband was buried, in the Eastman Lutheran Churchyard ...'

'I had heard, Mrs Gauber, that the burial concerned a woman.'

'No, my husband. He had been ill. He felt cold and quiet. A physician, a Dr Mechem, pronounced him dead, and he was interred beneath a marble slab in his family vault.' She sounded weary, but her voice was calm. 'This happened shortly after the New Year. On Valentine's Day, I brought flowers. Beneath his slab he stirred and struggled. I had him brought forth. And he lives – after a fashion – today.'

'Lives today?' repeated Poe. 'In this house?'

'Would you care to see him? Interview him?'

Poe's heart raced, his spine chilled. It was his peculiarity that such sensations gave him pleasure. 'I would like nothing better,' he assured her, and she went to another door, an inner one.

Opening it, she paused on the threshold, as though summoning her resolution for a plunge into cold, swift water. Then she started down a flight of steps.

Poe followed, unconsciously drawing the door shut behind him.

The gloom of midnight, of prison – yes, of the tomb – fell at once upon those stairs. He heard Elva Gauber gasp:

'No – the moonlight – let it in ...' And then she fell, heavily and limply, rolling downstairs.

Aghast, Poe quickly groped his way after her. She lay against a door at the foot of the flight, wedged against the panel. He touched her – she was cold and rigid, without motion or elasticity of life. His thin hand groped for and found the knob of the lower door, flung it open. More dim reflected moonlight, and he made shift to drag the woman into it.

Almost at once she sighed heavily, lifted her head, and rose. 'How stupid of me,' she apologized hoarsely.

'The fault was mine,' protested Poe. 'Your nerves, your health, have naturally suffered. The sudden dark – the closeness – overcame you.' He fumbled in his pocket for a tinderbox. 'Suffer me to strike a light.'

But she held out a hand to stop him. 'No, no. The moon is sufficient.' She walked to a small oblong pane set in the wall. Her hands, thin as Poe's own, with long grubby nails, hooked on the sill. Her face, bathed in the full light of the moon, strengthened and grew calm. She breathed deeply, almost voluptuously. 'I am quite recovered,' she said. 'Do not fear for me. You need not stand so near, sir.'

He had forgotten that garlic odour, and drew back contritely. She must be as sensitive to the smell as ... as ... what was it that was sickened and driven by garlic? Poe could not remember, and he took time to note that they were in a basement, stone-walled and with a floor of dirt. In one corner water seemed to drip, forming a dank pool of mud. Close to this, set into the wall, showed a latched trap door of planks, thick and wide, cleated crosswise, as though to cover a window. But no window would be set so low. Everything smelt earthy and close, as though fresh air had been shut out for decades.

'Your husband is here?' he inquired.

'Yes.' She walked to the shutter-like trap, unlatched it and drew it open.

The recess beyond was as black as ink, and from it came a feeble mutter. Poe followed Elva Gauber, and strained his eyes. In a little stone-flagged nook a bed had been made up. Upon it lay a man, stripped almost naked. His skin was as white as dead bone, and only his eyes, now opening, had life. He gazed at Elva Gauber and past her at Poe.

'Go away,' he mumbled.

'Sir,' ventured Poe formally, 'I have come to hear of how you came to life in the grave ...'

'It's a lie,' broke in the man on the pallet. He writhed halfway to a sitting posture, labouring upwards as against a crushing weight. The wash of moonlight showed how wasted and fragile he was. His face stared and snarled bare-toothed, like a skull. 'A lie, I say!' he cried, with a sudden strength that might well have been his last. 'Told by this monster who is not – my wife . . .'

The shutter-trap slammed upon his cries. Elva Gauber faced Poe, withdrawing a pace to avoid his garlic breath.

'You have seen my husband,' she said. 'Was it a pretty sight, sir?'

He did not answer, and she moved across the dirt to the stair doorway. 'Will you go up first?' she asked. 'At the top, hold the door open, that I may have' – she said 'life,' or, perhaps, 'light'. Poe could not be sure which.

Plainly she, who had almost welcomed his intrusion at first, now sought to lead him away. Her eyes, compelling as shouted commands, were fixed upon him. He felt their power, and bowed to it.

Obediently he mounted the stairs, and stood with the upper door wide open. Elva Gauber came up after him. At the top her eyes again seized his. Suddenly Poe knew more than ever before about the mesmeric impulses he loved to write about. 'I hope,' she said measuredly, 'that you have not found your mission fruitless. I live here alone – seeing nobody, caring for the poor thing that was once my husband, John Gauber. My mind is not clear. Perhaps my manners are not good. Forgive me, and goodnight.'

Poe found himself ushered from the house and outside the wind was howling again. The front door closed behind him, and the lock grated.

The fresh air, the whip of gale in his face, and the absence of Elva Gauber's impelling gaze suddenly brought him back, as though from sleep, to a realization of what had happened – or what had not happened.

He had come out, on this uncomfortable March evening, to investigate the report of a premature burial. He had seen a ghastly thing, that had called the gossip a lie. Somehow, then, he had been drawn abruptly away – stopped from full study of what might be one of the strangest adventures it was ever a writer's good fortune to know. Why was he letting things drop at this stage?

He decided not to let them drop. That would be worse than staying away altogether.

He made up his mind, formed quickly a plan. Leaving the doorstep, he turned from the gate, slipped quickly around the house. He knelt by the foundation at the side, just where a small oblong pane was set flush with the ground.

Bending his head, he found that he could see plainly inside, by reason of the flood of moonlight – a phenomenon, he realized, for generally an apartment was disclosed only by light within. The open doorway to the stairs, the swamp mess of mud in the corner, the out-flung trapdoor, were discernible. And something stood or huddled at the exposed niche – something that bent itself upon and above the frail white body of John Gauber.

Full skirt, white cap – it was Elva Gauber. She bent herself down, her face was touching the face or shoulder of her husband.

Poe's heart, never the healthiest of organs, began to drum and race. He pressed closer to the pane, for a better glimpse of what went on in the cellar. His shadow cut away some of the light. Elva Gauber turned to look.

Her face was as pale as the moon itself. Like the moon, it was shadowed in irregular patches. She came quickly, almost running, towards the pane where Poe crouched. He saw her, plainly and at close hand.

Dark, wet, sticky stains lay upon her mouth and cheeks. Her tongue roved out, licking at the stains—

Blood!

Poe sprang up and ran to the front of the house. He forced his thin, trembling fingers to seize the knocker, to swing it heavily again and again. When there was no answer, he pushed heavily against the door itself – it did not give. He moved to a window, rapped on it, pried at the sill, lifted his fist to smash the glass.

A silhouette moved beyond the pane, and threw it up. Something shot out at him like a pale snake striking – before he could move back, fingers had twisted in the front of his coat. Elva Gauber's eyes glared into his.

Her cap was off, her dark hair fallen in disorder. Blood still smeared and dewed her mouth and jowls.

'You have pried too far,' she said, in a voice as measured and cold as the drip from icicles. 'I was going to spare you, because of the odour about you that repelled me – the garlic. I showed you a little, enough to warn any wise person, and let you go. Now . . .'

Poe struggled to free himself. Her grip was immovable, like the clutch of a steel trap. She grimaced in triumph, yet she could not quite face him – the garlic still clung to his breath.

'Look in my eyes,' she bade him. 'Look – you cannot refuse, you cannot escape. You will die, with John – and the two of you, dying, shall rise again like me. I'll have two fountains of life while you remain – two companions after you die.'

'Woman,' said Poe, fighting against her stabbing gaze, 'you are mad.'

She snickered gustily. 'I am sane, and so are you. We both know that I speak the truth. We both know the futility of your struggle.' Her voice rose a little. 'Through a chink in the tomb, as I lay dead, a ray of moonlight streamed and struck my eyes. I woke. I struggled. I was set free. Now at night, when the moon shines – Ugh! Don't breathe that herb in my face!'

She turned her head away. At that instant it seemed to Poe that a curtain of utter darkness fell and with it sank down the form of Elva Gauber.

He peered into the sudden gloom. She was collapsed across the window sill, like a discarded puppet in its booth. Her hand still twisted in the bosom of his coat, and he pried himself loose from it, finger by steely, cold finger. Then he turned to flee from this place of shadowed peril to body and soul.

As he turned, he saw whence had come the dark. A cloud had come up from its place on the horizon – the fat, sooty bank he had noted there at sundown – and now it obscured the moon. Poe paused, in mid-retreat, gazing.

His thoughtful eye gauged the speed and size of tne cloud. It curtained the moon, would continue to curtain it for – well, ten minutes. And for that ten minutes Elva Gauber would lie motionless, lifeless. She had told the truth about the moon giving her life. Hadn't she fallen like one slain on the stairs when they were darkened? Poe began grimly to string the evidence together.

It was Elva Gauber, not her husband, who had died and gone to the family vault. She had come back to life, or a mockery of life, by touch of the moon's rays. Such light was an unpredictable force – it made dogs howl, it flogged madmen to violence, it brought fear, or black sorrow, or ecstasy. Old legends said that it was the birth of fairies, the transformation of werewolves, the motive power of broom-riding witches. It was surely the source of the strength and evil animating what had been the corpse of Elva Gauber – and he, Poe, must not stand there dreaming.

He summoned all the courage that was his, and scrambled in at the window through which clumped the woman's form. He groped across the room to the cellar door, opened it and went down the stairs, through the door at the bottom, and into the stone-walled basement.

It was dark, moonless still. Poe paused only to bring forth his tinder-box, strike a light and kindle the end of a tightly twisted linen rag. It gave a feeble steady light, and he found his way to the shutter, opened it and touched the naked, wasted shoulder of John Gauber.

'Get up,' he said. 'I've come to save you.'

The skull-face feebly shifted its position to meet his gaze. The man managed to speak, moaningly:

'Useless. I can't move – unless she lets me. Her eyes keep me here – half-alive. I'd have died long ago, but some-how ...'

Poe thought of a wretched spider, paralysed by the sting of a mud-wasp, lying helpless in its captive's close den until the hour of feeding comes. He bent down, holding his blazing tinder close. He could see Gauber's neck, and it was a mass of tiny puncture wounds, some of them still beaded with blood drops fresh or dried. He winced but bode firm in his purpose.

'Let me guess the truth,' he said quickly. 'Your wife was brought home from the grave, came back to a seeming of life. She put a spell on you, or played a trick – made you a helpless prisoner. That isn't contrary to nature, that last. I've studied mesmerism.'

'It's true,' John Gauber mumbled.

'And nightly she comes to drink your blood?'

Gauber weakly nodded. 'Yes. She was beginning just now, but ran upstairs. She will be coming back.'

'Good,' said Poe bleakly. 'Perhaps she will come back to more than she expects. Have you ever heard of vampires? Probably not, but I have studied them, too. I began to guess, I think, when first she was so repelled by the odour of garlic. Vampires lie motionless by day and walk and feed at night. They are creatures of the moon – their food is blood. Come.'

Poe broke off, put out his light, and lifted the man in his arms. Gauber was as light as a child. The writer carried him to the slanting shelter of the closed-in staircase, and there set him against the wall stones. The poor fellow would be well hidden.

Next Poe flung off his coat, waistcoat and shirt. Heaping his clothing in a deeper shadow of the stairway, he stood up, stripped to the waist. His skin was almost as bloodlessly pale as Gauber's, his chest and arms almost as gaunt. He dared believe that he might pass momentarily for the unfortunate man.

The cellar sprang full of light again. The cloud must be passing from the moon. Poe listened. There was a dragging sound above, then footsteps.

Elva Gauber, the blood drinker by night, had revived.

Now for it. Poe hurried to the niche, thrust himself in and pulled the trapdoor shut after him.

He grinned, sharing a horrid paradox with the blackness around him. He had heard all the fabled ways of destroying vampires – transfixing stakes, holy water, prayer, fire. But

he, Edgar Allan Poe, had evolved a new way. Myriads of
tales whispered frighteningly of fiends lying in wait for normal men, but who had ever heard of a normal man lying in
wait for a fiend? Well, he had never considered himself
normal, in spirit, or brain, or taste.

He stretched out, feet together, hands crossed on his bare
midriff. Thus it would be in the tomb, he found himself
thinking. To his mind came a snatch of poetry by a man
named Bryant, published long ago in a New England re-
view – 'Breathless darkness, and the narrow house.' It was
breathless and dark enough in this hole, Heaven knew, and
narrow as well. He rejected, almost hysterically, the impli-
cation of being buried. To break the ugly spell, that daunted
him where thought of Elva Gauber failed, he turned side-
ways to face the wall, his naked arm lying across his cheek
and temple.

As his ear touched the musty bedding, it brought to him
once again the echo of footsteps, footsteps descending stairs.
They were rhythmic, confident. They were eager.

Elva Gauber was coming to seek again her interrupted
repast.

Now she was crossing the floor. She did not pause or turn
aside – she had not noticed her husband, lying under the
cadet cloak in the shadow of the stairs. The noise came
straight to the trapdoor, and he heard her fumbling for the
latch.

Light, blue as skimmed milk, poured into his nook. A
shadow fell in the midst of it, full upon him. His imagination, ever out-stripping reality, whispered that the shadow
had weight, like lead – oppressive, baleful.

'John,' said the voice of Elva Gauber in his ear, 'I've
come back. You know why – you know what for.' Her voice
sounded greedy, as though it came through loose, trembling
lips. 'You're my only source of strength now. I thought tonight, that a stranger – but he got away. He had a cursed
odour about him, anyway.'

Her hand touched the skin of his neck. She was prodding
him, like a butcher fingering a doomed beast.

'Don't hold yourself away from me, John,' she was commanding, in a voice of harsh mockery. 'You know it won't do any good. This is the night of the full moon, and I have power for anything, anything!' She was trying to drag his arm away from his face. 'You won't gain by—' She broke off, aghast. Then, in a wild-dry-throated scream:

'You're not John!'

Poe whipped over on his back, and his bird-claw hands shot out and seized her – one hand clinching upon her snaky disorder of dark hair, the other digging its fingertips into the chill flesh of her arm.

The scream quivered away into a horrible breathless rattle. Poe dragged his captive violently inwards, throwing all his collected strength into the effort. Her feet were jerked from the floor and she flew into the recess, hurtling above and beyond Poe's recumbent body. She struck the inner stones with a crashing force that might break bones, and would have collapsed upon Poe; but, at the same moment, he had released her and slid swiftly out upon the floor of the cellar.

With frantic haste he seized the edge of the back-flung trapdoor. Elva Gauber struggled upon hands and knees, among the tumbled bedclothes in the niche; then Poe had slammed the panel shut.

She threw herself against it from within, yammering and wailing like an animal in a trap. She was almost as strong as he, and for a moment he thought that she would burst out of the niche. But, sweating and wheezing, he bore against the planks with his shoulder, bracing his feet against the earth. His fingers found the latch, lifted it, forced it into place.

'Dark,' moaned Elva Gauber from inside. 'Dark – no moon—' Her voice trailed off.

Poe went to the muddy pool in the corner, thrust in his hands. The mud was slimy but workable. He pushed a double handful of it against the trapdoor, sealing cracks and edges. Another handful, another. Using his palms like trowels, he coated the boards with thick mud.

'Gauber,' he said breathlessly, 'how are you?'

'All right – I think.' The voice was strangely strong and clear. Looking over his shoulder, Poe saw that Gauber had come upright of himself, still pale but apparently steady. 'What are you doing?' Gauber asked.

'Walling her up,' jerked out Poe, scooping still more mud. 'Walling her up forever, with her evil.'

He had a momentary flash of inspiration, a symbolic germ of a story; in it a man sealed a woman into such a nook of the wall, and with her an embodiment of active evil – perhaps in the form of a black cat.

Pausing at last to breathe deeply, he smiled to himself. Even in the direst of danger, the most heart-breaking moment of toil and fear, he must ever be coining up new plots for stories.

'I cannot thank you enough,' Gauber was saying to him. 'I feel that all will be well – if only she stays there.'

Poe put his ear to the wall. 'Not a whisper of motion, sir. She's shut off from moonlight – from life and power. Can you help me with my clothes? I feel terribly chilled.'

His mother-in-law met him on the threshold when he returned to the house in Spring Garden Street. Under the white widow's cap, her strong-boned face was drawn with worry.

'Eddie, are you ill?' She was really asking if he had been drinking. A look reassured her. 'No,' she answered herself, 'but you've been away from home so long. And you're dirty, Eddie – filthy. You must wash.'

He let her lead him in, pour hot water into a basin. As he scrubbed himself, he formed excuses, a banal lie about a long walk for inspiration, a moment of dizzy weariness, a stumble into a mud puddle.

'I'll make you some nice hot coffee, Eddie,' his mother-in-law offered.

'Please,' he responded and went back to his own room with the slate mantelpiece. Again he lighted the candle, sat down and took up his pen.

His mind was embellishing the story inspiration that had

come to him at such a black moment, in the cellar of the Gauber house. He'd work on that tomorrow. The *United States Saturday Post* would take it, he hoped. Title? He would call it simply 'The Black Cat.'

But to finish the present task! He dipped his pen in ink. How to begin? How to end? How, after writing and publishing such an account, to defend himself against the growing whisper of his insanity?

He decided to forget it, if he could – at least to seek healthy company, comfort, quiet – perhaps even to write some light verse, some humorous articles and stories. For the first time in his life, he had had enough of the macabre.

Quickly he wrote a final paragraph:

There are moments when, even to the sober eye of Reason, the world of our sad Humanity may assume the semblance of a Hell – but the imagination of man is no Carathis, to explore with impunity its every cavern. Alas! The grim legion of sepulchral terrors cannot be regarded as altogether fanciful – but, like the Demons in whose company Afrasiab made his voyage down the Oxus, they must sleep, or they will devour us – they must be suffered to slumber, or we will perish.

That would do for the public, decided Edgar Allan Poe. In any case, it would do for the Philadelphia *Dollar Newspaper*. His mother-in-law brought in the coffee.

THE CANAL

by

Everil Worrell

Past the sleeping city the river sweeps; along its left bank the old canal creeps.

I did not intend that to be poetry, although the scene is poetic – sombrely, gruesomely poetic, like the poems of Poe. I know it too well – I have walked too often over the grass-grown path beside the reflections of black trees and tumble-down shacks and distant factory chimneys in the sluggish waters that moved so slowly, and ceased to move at all.

I have always had a taste for nocturnal prowling. As a race we have grown too intelligent to take seriously any of the old, instinctive fears that preserved us through preceding generations. Our sole remaining salvation, then, has come to be our tendency to travel in herds. We wander at night – but our objective is somewhere on the brightly lighted streets, or still somewhere where men do not go alone. When we travel far afield, it is in company. Few of my acquaintances, few in the whole city here, would care to ramble at midnight over the grass-grown path I have spoken of – not because they would fear to do so, but because such things are not being done.

Well, it is dangerous to differ individually from one's fellows. It is dangerous to wander from the beaten road. And the fears that guarded the race in the dawn of time and through the centuries were founded on reality.

A month ago, I was a stranger here. I had just taken my first position – I was graduated from college only three months before, in the spring. I was lonely, and likely to remain so for some time, for I have always been of a solitary nature, making friends slowly.

I had received one invitation out, to visit the camp of a fellow employee in the firm for which I worked, a camp which was located on the farther side of the wide river, the side across from the city and the canal, where the bank was high and steep and heavily wooded, and little tents blossomed all along the water's edge. At night these camps were a string of sparkling lights and tiny, leaping camp fires, and the tinkle of music carried faintly across the calmly flowing water. That far bank of the river was no place for an eccentric, solitary man to love. But the near bank, which would have been an eyesore to the campers had not the river been so wide – the near bank attracted me from my first glimpse of it.

We embarked in a motor-boat at some distance downstream, and swept up along the near bank, and then out and across the current. I turned my eyes backward. The murk of stagnant water that was the canal, the jumble of low buildings beyond it, the lonely, low-lying waste of the narrow strip of land between canal and river, the dark, scattered trees growing there – I intended to see more of these things.

That weekend bored me, but I repaid myself no later than Monday evening, the first evening when I was back in the city, alone and free. I ate a solitary dinner immediately after leaving the office. I went to my room and slept from seven until nearly midnight. I wakened naturally, then, for my whole heart was set on exploring the alluring solitude I had discovered. I dressed, slipped out of the house and into the street, started the motor in my roadster and drove through the lighted streets.

When I parked my car on a rough, cobbled street that ran directly down into the inky waters of the canal, and crossed a narrow bridge, I was repaid. In a few minutes I set my feet on the old towpath where mules had drawn riverboats up and down only a year or so ago. As I walked upstream at a swinging pace, the miserable shacks where miserable people lived across the canal seemed to march with me, and then fell behind.

The bridge I had crossed was near the end of the city

going north, as the canal marked its western extremity. Ten minutes of walking, and the dismal shacks were quite a distance behind, the river was farther away and the strip of waste land much wider and more wooded, and tall trees across the canal marched with me as the evil-looking houses had done before. Far and faint, the sound of a bell in the city reached my ears. It was midnight.

I stopped, enjoying the desolation around me. It had the savour I had expected and hoped for. I stood for some time looking up at the sky, watching the low drift of heavy clouds, which were visible in the dull reflected glow from distant lights in the heart of the city, so that they appeared to have a lurid phosphorescence of their own. The ground under my feet, on the contrary, was utterly devoid of light. I had felt my way carefully, knowing the edge of the canal partly by instinct, partly by the even more perfect blackness of the water in it, and even holding fairly well to the path, because it was perceptibly sunken below the ground beside it.

Now as I stood motionless in this spot, my eyes upcast, my mind adrift with strange fancies, suddenly my feelings of satisfaction and well-being gave way to something different. Fear was an emotion unknown to me – for I had always been drawn to those things which make men fear. But now along all the length of my spine I was conscious of a prickling, tingling sensation – such as my forefathers may have felt in the jungle when the hair on their backs stood up. I knew that there were eyes upon me, and that that was why I was afraid to move. I stood perfectly still, my face uptilted towards the sky. But with effort, mastered myself.

Slowly, slowly, with an attempt to propitiate the owner of the unseen eyes by my casual manner, I lowered my own. I looked straight ahead – at the softly swaying silhouette of the tree-tops across the canal as they moved gently in the cool night wind, at the mass of blackness that was those trees, and the opposite shore, at the shiny blackness that was the canal, where the reflections of the clouds glinted vaguely and disappeared. As I grew accustomed to the greater blackness and my pupils expanded, I dimly discerned the contours of an old boat or barge, half sunken in the water. An old, abandoned canal-boat. But was I dreaming or was there a white-clad figure seated on the roof of the low cabin aft, a pale, heart-shaped face gleaming strangely at me from the darkness, the glow of two eyes seeming to light up the face, and to detach it from the darkness?

Surely, there could be no doubt as to the eyes. They shone as the eyes of animals shine in the dark, with a phosphorescent gleam, and a glimmer of red! Well, I had heard that some human eyes have that quality at night.

But what a place for a human being to be – a girl, too, I was sure. That daintily heart-shaped face was the face of a girl, surely; I was seeing it clearer and clearer, either because my eyes were growing more accustomed to peering into the deeper shadows, or because of that phosphorescence in the eyes that shared back at me.

I raised my voice softly, not to break too much of the stillness of night.

'Hello! who's there? Are you lost, or marooned, and can I help?'

There was a little pause. I was conscious of a soft lapping at my feet. A stronger night wind had sprung up, was ruffling the dark water. I had been overwarm, and where it struck me the perspiration turned cold on my body, so that I shivered uncontrollably.

'You can stay and talk awhile, if you will. I am lonely, but not lost. I – live here.'

The voice was little more than a whisper, but it had carried clearly – a girl's voice. And she lived *there*, in an old, abandoned canal-boat, half submerged in the stagnant water.

'You are not *alone* there?'

'No, not alone. My father lives here with me, but he is deaf, and he sleeps soundly.'

Did the night wind blow still colder, as though it came to us from some unseen, frozen sea – or was there something in her tone that chilled me, even as a strange attraction drew me towards her? I wanted to draw near to her, to see closely

the pale, heart-shaped face, to lose myself in the bright eyes
that I had seen shining in the darkness. I wanted – I wanted
to hold her in my arms, to find her mouth with mine, to kiss
it . . .

I took a reckless step nearer the edge of the bank.

'Could I come over to you?' I asked. 'It's warm and I
don't mind a wetting. It's late, I know, but I'd like to sit and
talk, if only for a few minutes before I go back to town. It's
a lonely place here for a girl like you to live.'

Was it the unconventionality of my request that made her
next words sound like a long-drawn shudder of protest?
There was a strangeness in the tones of her voice that held
me wondering, every time she spoke.

'No, no. Oh, no! You must not come across.'

'Then could I come tomorrow, or some day soon, in the
daytime; and would you let me come on board then – or
would you come on shore and talk to me, perhaps?'

'Not in the daytime – *never* in the daytime!'

Again the intensity of her low-toned negation held me
spell-bound.

It was not her sense of the impropriety of the hour, then,
that had dictated her manner. For surely, any girl with the
slightest sense of the fitness of things would rather have a
tryst by daytime than after midnight – yet there was an in-
ference in her last words that if I came again it should be
at night.

Still feeling the spell that had enthralled me, as one does
not forget the presence of a drug in the air that is stealing
one's senses, even when those senses begin to wander and to
busy themselves with other things, I yet spoke shortly.

'Why do you say, "Never in the daytime"? Do you mean
that I may come more than this once at night, though now
you won't let me cross the canal to you at the expense of my
own clothes, and you won't put down your plank or draw-
bridge or whatever you come on shore with, and talk to me
here for only a moment? I'll come again, if you'll let me talk
to you instead of calling across the water. If I came in the
daytime and met your father, wouldn't that be the best thing

to do? Then we could be really acquainted; we could be friends.'

'In the night-time, my father sleeps. In the daytime, *I* sleep. How could I talk to you, or introduce you to my father then? If you came on board this boat in the daytime, you would find my father – and you would be sorry. As for me, I would be sleeping. I could never introduce you to my father, do you see?'

'You sleep soundly, you and your father.' Again there was pique in my voice.

'Yes, we sleep soundly.'

'And always at different times?'

'Always at different times. We are on guard – one of us is always on guard. We have been hardly used, down there in your city. And we have taken refuge here. And we are always – always – on guard.'

My resentment vanished, and I felt my heart go out to her anew. She was so pale, so pitiful in the night. My eyes were learning better and better how to pierce the darkness; they were giving me a more definite picture of my companion – if I could think of her as a companion, between myself and whom stretched the black waters.

The sadness of the lonely scene, the perfection of the solitude itself, these things contributed to her pitifulness. Then there was that strangeness of atmosphere of which, even yet, I had only partly taken note. There was the strange, shivering chill, which yet did not seem like the healthful chill of a cool evening. In fact, it did not prevent me from feeling the oppression of the night, which was unusually sultry. It was like a litle breath of deadly cold that came and went, and yet did not alter the temperature of the air itself, as the small ripples on the surface of the water do not concern the water even a foot down.

And even that was not all. There was an unwholesome smell about the night – a dank, mouldy smell that might have been the very breath of death and decay. Even I, a connoisseur in all things dismal and unwholesome, tried to keep my mind from dwelling overmuch upon that smell.

What it must be to live breathing it constantly, I could not think. But no doubt the girl and her father were used to it; and no doubt it came from the stagnant water of the canal and from the rotting wood of the old, half-sunken boat that was their refuge.

My clearer vision of the girl showed me that she was pitifully thin, even though possessed of a strangely attractive face that drew me to her. Her clothes hung around her like old rags, but hers was no scarecrow aspect. I was sure the little, pale, heart-shaped face would be more beautiful still, if I could only see it closely. I must see it closely – I must establish some claim to consideration as a friend of the strange, lonely crew of the half-sunken wreck.

'This is a poor place to call a refuge,' I said finally. 'One might have very little money, and yet do somewhat better. Perhaps I might help you; I am sure I could. If your ill-treatment in the city was because of poverty – I am not rich, but I could help that. I could help you a little with money, if you would let me; or, in any case, I could find a position for you. I'm sure I could do that.'

The eyes that shone fitfully toward me like two small pools of water intermittently lit by a cloud-swept sky seemed to glow more brightly. She had been half-crouching, half sitting on top of the cabin; now she leaped to her feet with one quick, sinuous, abrupt motion, and took a few rapid, restless steps to and fro before she answered.

'Do you think you would be helping me, to tie me to a desk, to shut me behind doors, away from freedom, away from the delight of doing my own will, of seeking my own way? Rather this old boat, rather a deserted grave under the stars for my home!'

A positive feeling of kinship with this strange being, whose face I had hardly seen, possessed me. So I myself might have spoken, so I had often felt, though I had never dreamed of putting my thoughts so forcibly. My regularized daytime life was a thing I thought little of; I really lived only in my nocturnal prowlings. This girl was right! All life should be free.

'I understand much better than you think,' I answered. 'I want to see you again, to come to know you. Surely, there must be some way in which I can be of use to you. All you have to do from tonight on for ever, is to command me, I swear it!'

'You swear *that* – do you swear it?'

Delighted at the eagerness of her words I lifted my hand towards the dark heavens.

'I swear it. From this night on, for ever – I swear it.'

'Then listen. Tonight you may not come to me, or I to you. I do not want you to board this boat – not tonight, not any night. And most of all, not any day. But do not look so sad. I will come to you. No, not tonight, perhaps not for many nights, yet before very long. I will come to you there, on the bank of the canal, when the water in the canal ceases to flow.'

I must have made a gesture of impatience, or of despair. It sounded like a way of saying 'never' – for why should the water in the canal cease to flow? She read my thoughts in some way, for she answered them.

'You do not understand. I am speaking seriously; I am promising to meet you there on the bank, soon. The water is moving always slower. Higher up, the canal has been drained. Between these lower locks, the water still seeps in and drops slowly downstream. But there will come a night when it will be stagnant – and on that night I will come to you. And when I come, I will ask of you a favour.'

It was all the assurance I could get that night. She had come back to the side of the cabin where she had sat crouched before, and she resumed again that posture and sat still and silent, watching me. Sometimes I could see her eyes upon me, and sometimes not. But I felt that their gaze was unwavering. The little cold breeze, which I had finally forgotten while I was talking with her, was blowing again, and the unwholesome smell of decay grew heavier before the dawn.

I went away, and in the first faint light of dawn I slipped up the stairs of my rooming-house, and into my room.

I was deadly tired at the office next day. And day after day slipped away and I grew more and more weary, for a man cannot wake day and night without suffering. I haunted the old towpath and waited, night after night, on the bank opposite the sunken boat. Sometimes I saw my lady of the darkness, and sometimes not. When I saw her, she spoke little; but sometimes she sat there on the top of the cabin and let me watch her till the dawn, or until the strange uneasiness that was like fright drove me from her and back to my room, where I tossed restlessly in the heat and dreamed strange dreams, half waking, till the sun shone in on my forehead and I tumbled into my clothes and down to the office again.

Once I asked her why she had made the fanciful condition that she would not come ashore to meet me until the waters of the canal had ceased to run. (How eagerly I studied those waters! How I stole away at noontime more than once, not to approach the old boat, but to watch the almost imperceptible downdrift of bubbles, bits of straw, twigs, rubbish!) But my questioning displeased her, and I asked her that no more. It was enough that she chose to be whimsical. My part was to wait.

It was more than a week later that I questioned her again, this time on a different subject. And after that, I curbed my curiosity relentlessly.

'Never speak to me of things you do not understand about me, or you will not see me again.'

I had asked her what form of persecution she and her father had suffered in the city, that had driven them out to this lonely place, and where in the city they had lived.

Frightened lest I lose the ground I was sure I had gained with her, I was about to speak of something else. But before I could find the words, her low voice came to me again.

'It was horrible, horrible! Those little houses below the bridge, those houses along the canal – tell me, are not they worse than my boat? Life there was shut in and furtive. I wasn't free as I am now, and the freedom I will soon have will make me forget the things I have not yet forgotten. The screaming, the reviling and cursing! Think how you would like to be shut up in one of those houses, and in fear of your life!'

I dared not answer her. I was surprised that she had vouchsafed me so much. But surely her words meant that before she had come to live on the decaying, water-rotted old boat, she had lived in one of those horrible houses I passed by on my way to her. Those houses, each of which looked like the predestined scene of dark crime!

As I left her that night, I felt that I was very daring.

And yet, the next day, for the first time my thoughts were definitely troubled. I had been living in a dream – I began to speculate concerning the end of the path on which my feet were set. I had conceived, from the first, such a horror of those old houses by the canal! Much as I loved all that was weird and eerie about the girl I was wooing so strangely, it was a little too much for my fancy that she had come from them.

By this time, I had become decidedly unpopular in my place of business. Not that I had made enemies, but my peculiar ways had caused too much adverse comment. It would have taken very little, I think, to have made the entire office force decide that I was mad. However, they were punctiliously polite to me, and merely let me alone as much as possible – which suited me perfectly. I dragged wearily through day after day, exhausted from lack of sleep, conscious of their speculative glances, living only for the night to come.

One day, I approached the man who had invited me to the camp across the river. 'Have you ever noticed the row of tumbledown houses along the canal on the city side?' I asked.

He gave me an odd look. I suppose he sensed the significance of my breaking silence after so long to speak of them.

'You have odd tastes, Morton,' he said after a moment. 'I suppose you wander into strange places sometimes. But my advice to you is to keep away from those houses. They're unsavoury, and their reputation is pretty bad. You might very well be in danger of your life, if you go poking around there. They have been the scene of several murders, and a dope den or two has been cleaned out of them. Why in the world you should want to investigate them—'

'I don't expect to investigate them,' I said. 'I was merely interested in them – from the outside. To tell you the truth, I'd heard a story, a rumour – never mind where. But you say there have been murders there – I suppose this rumour I heard may have had to do with an attempted one. There was a girl who lived there with her father once, and they were set upon there, or something of the sort, and had to run away. Did you ever hear *that* story?'

Barrett gave me an odd look such as one gives in speaking of a past horror so dreadful that the mere speaking of it makes it live terribly again.

'What you say reminds me of something that was said to have happened down there once,' he answered. 'It was in all the papers. A little child disappeared in one of those houses, and a girl and her father were accused of having made away with it. They were accused of – oh, well, I don't like to talk about such things. It was pretty disagreeable. The child's body was found – or, rather, *part* of it was found. It was mutilated, and the people seemed to believe it had been mutilated in order to conceal the manner of its death; there was an ugly wound in the throat, it finally came out, and it seemed as if this child might have been bled to death. It was found in the girl's room, hidden away. The old man and his daughter escaped before the police were called. The countryside was scoured, but they were never found. Why, you must have read it in the papers several years ago.'

I *had* read it in the papers, I remembered now. And again, a terrible doubt came over me. Who was this girl, *what* was this girl, who seemed to have my heart in her keeping?

Befogged with exhaustion, bemused in a dire enchantment, my mind was incapable of thought. And yet, some soul-process akin to that which saves the sleepwalker poised at perilous heights sounded its warning now.

My mind was filled with doleful images. There were

women, I had heard and read, who slew to satisfy a blood-lust. There were ghosts, spectres – call them what you will; their names have been legion in the dark pages of that lore which dates back to the infancy of the races of the earth – who retained even in death this blood-lust. Vampires – they had been called that. Corpses by day, spirits of evil by night, roaming abroad in their own forms or in the forms of bats or unclean beasts, killing body and soul of their victims – for whoever dies of the repeated 'kiss' of the vampire, which leaves its mark on the throat and draws the blood from the body, becomes a vampire also – of such beings I had read.

And, in that last day at the office, I remembered reading of these undead, that in their nocturnal flights they had one limitation – *they could not cross running water*.

That night I went my usual way, recognizing fully the misery of being the victim of an enchantment stronger than my feeble will. I approached the neighbourhood of the canal-boat as the distant city clock chimed the first stroke of twelve. It was the dark of the moon and the sky was over-cast. Heat-lightning flickered low in the sky, seeming to come from every point of the compass and circumscribe the horizon, as if unseen fires burned behind the rim of the world. By its fitful glimmer, I saw a new thing: between the old boat and the canal bank stretched a long, slim, solid-looking shadow – a plank had been let down! In that mo-ment, I realized that I had been playing with powers of evil which had no intention now to let me go, which were indeed about to lay hold upon me with an inexorable grasp. Why had I come tonight? Why, but that the spell of the enchant-ment laid upon me was a thing more potent and far more unbreakable, than any wholesome spell of love?

Behind me in the darkness there was a crackle of a twig, and something brushed against my arm.

This, then, was the fulfilment of my dream. I knew, with-out turning my head, that the pale, dainty face with its glow-ing eyes was near my own – that I had only to stretch out my arm to touch the slender grace of the girl I had so longed to draw near. I knew, and should have felt the rapture I had anticipated. Instead, the miasmic odours of the night, heavy and oppressive with heat and unrelieved by a breath of air, all but overcame me. The little waves of coldness I had felt often in this spot were possessing all my body, yet they were not from any breeze; the leaves on the trees hung down motionless, as though they were actually wilting on their branches.

With an effort, I turned my head.

Two hands caught me at my neck. The pale face was so near that I felt the warm breath from its nostrils fanning my cheek.

And, suddenly, all that was wholesome in my perverted nature rose uppermost. I longed for the touch of the red mouth, like a dark flower opening before me in the night, I longed for it – and yet more I dreaded it. I shrank back, catching in a powerful grip the fragile wrists of the hands that strove to hold me.

I was facing down the path towards the city. A low rumble of thunder broke the torrid hush of the summer night. A glare of lightning seemed to tear the night asunder, to light up the universe. Overhead, the clouds were careering madly in fantastic shapes, driven by a wind that swept the upper heavens without causing even a trembling in the air lower down. And far down the canal, that baleful glare seemed to play around and hover over the little row of shanties – murder-cursed and haunted by the ghost of a dead child.

My gaze was fixed on them, while I held away from me the pallid face and fought off the embrace that sought to overcome my resisting will. And so a long moment passed. The glare faded out of the sky, and a greater darkness took the world. But there was a near, more menacing light fastened upon my face – the light of two eyes that watched mine, that had watched me as I, unthinking, stared down at the dark houses.

This girl – this woman who had come to me at my own importunate requests, did not love me, since I had shrunk from her. She did not love me – but it was not only that. She had watched me as I gazed down at the houses that held her dark past, and I was sure that she divined my thoughts. She knew my horror of those houses – she knew my new-born horror of *her*. And she hated me for it, hated me more malignantly than I had believed a human being could hate.

Could a *human* being cherish such hatred as I read, trembling more and more, in those glowing fires lit with what seemed to me more like the fires of hell than any light that ought to shine in a woman's eyes?

At this point in the happenings of that night, my calmness deserted me; at this point I felt that I had been drawn into the midst of a horrible nightmare from which there was no escape, no waking! As I write, this feeling again overwhelms me, until I can hardly write at all – until, were it not for the thing which I must do, I would rush out into the street and run, screaming, until I was caught and dragged away, to be put behind strong bars. Perhaps I would feel safe there – perhaps!

I know that, terrified at the hate I saw confronting me in those red gleaming eyes, I would have slunk away. But the two thin hands that caught my arm again were strong enough to prevent that. I had been spared her kiss, but I was not to escape from the oath I had taken to serve her.

'You promised, you swore,' she whispered at my ear. 'And tonight you are to keep your oath.'

My oath – yes, I had an oath to keep. I had lifted my hand towards the dark heavens, and sworn to serve her in any way she chose. Freely, and of my own volition, I had sworn.

I sought to evade her.

'Let me help you back to your boat,' I begged. 'You have no kindly feeling for me, and – you have seen it – I love you no longer. I will go back to the city – you can go back to your father, and forget that I broke your peace.'

The laughter that greeted my speech I shall never forget.

'So you do not love me, and I hate you! Have I waited these weary months for the water to stop, only to go back now? When the water was turned into the canal while I slept, so that I could never escape until its flow should cease, *because of the thing that I am* – when the imprisonment we shared ceased to matter to my father – come on board the deserted boat tomorrow, and see why, if you dare! – I dreamed of tonight! I have been lonely, desolate, starving – now the whole world shall be mine! And by *your* help!'

I asked her what she wanted of me. I knew that there was that on the opposite shore of the great river where the summer camps were, that she wanted to find. In the madness of my terror, she made me understand and obey her. I must carry her in my arms across the long bridge over the river, deserted in the small hours of the night.

The way back to the city was long tonight – long. She walked behind me, and I turned my eyes neither to right nor left. Only as I passed the tumbledown houses, I saw their reflection in the canal and trembled at the thought of the little child this woman had been accused of slaying there, and at the certainty I felt that she was reading my thoughts.

I know that we set our feet on the long, wide bridge that spanned the river. I know the storm broke there, so that I battled for my footing, almost for my life, it seemed, against the pelting deluge. And the horror I had invoked was in my arms, clinging to me, burying its head upon my shoulder. So increasingly dreadful had my pale-faced companion become to me, that I hardly thought of her now as a woman at all.

The tempest raged still when she leaped down out of my arms on the other side. And again I walked with her against my will, while the trees lashed their branches around me, showing the pale undersides of their leaves in the vivid frequent flashes that rent the heavens.

On and on we went, branches flying through the air and missing us by a miracle of ill fortune. Such as she and I are not slain by falling branches. The river was a welter of whitecaps, flattened down into strange shapes by the pounding rain. The clouds as we glimpsed them were like devils flying through the sky.

Past dark tent after dark tent we stole, and past a few where lights burned dimly behind their canvas walls.

Outside a lighted tent she stopped, motioning me back. I saw her dark form silhouetted against the tent; saw it move stealthily toward the door-flap – saw it stand once more against the canvas wall and then grow in size and blur in outline as she moved away inside the tent. I heard her voice speak in those low, thrilling tones that had enchanted my soul at our first meeting:

'I'm so sorry. I lost my way in the storm. Please let me stay awhile; I'm so very tired, and cold.'

I knew the nature of the woman I had carried across the river in my arms. I knew what was to follow. She would kiss him and then—

She had spared *me* the vampire kiss. She was so eager to use me as a tool, to get her away into the world of living men and women. And so now I might go free. Within this tent, tonight, she would satisfy the long-denied blood-lust. There had been that urgent hunger in her voice which told me so.

The two voices in the tent fell so low I lost their words; yet those low tones spoke for themselves. And there was nothing in the world that I could do in the way of giving an alarm. You can't bolt into a man's tent and warn him against a beautiful woman to whom he is about to make love, because she is a vampire. Having myself locked up in an asylum would save no one from the evil I had unwittingly loosed.

Head bent under the rain that fell more quietly now, I climbed down to the water's edge. The wind had fallen. Reeds sighed along the river bank. The crash of waves subsided to a sombre lapping against the rocks. The clouds parted and drifted away horizonward as I stood long in thought, and the gibbous moon shone far and dim behind a mist-veil.

And I knew what I must do. I know, as I write these last words, that it is what I *want* to do. If love and hate are akin, so, too, are enchantment and horror. When my terrible love crept into the tent of that other man, I knew that, abhor her as I might, I could not live without her.

She has spared me the vampire kiss. But I will have that from her, even as I save others from her curse. I have earned it with my soul. I will know that dark ecstasy, and I will insure that no other knows it after me.

It is strange how life leads one through the happy paths of childhood and of youth to an ordained destiny. I had a young uncle who loved tales of old knighthood, as I have loved the macabre. He made me a sword out of oak, on a happy day in my boyhood. And when he went to volunteer in a war of one of the 'little peoples', he tipped the sword with a point. He fell in his first action, far on foreign soil. The sword hangs on my wall. I have never taken it down since he went away.

The dawn broke at last, sick and storm-washed. I did not see them go; but I know that her victim lover will have carried her back across the bridge over the rushing water. For since she is what she is, she *must* go back to the old canal-boat. There she must sleep until tonight.

And there I will come to her then. I will take the tipped sword, and I will hold it behind me in the shadows.

'I have come back to be with you forever,' I will say. 'There can be no other woman's face before my eyes; only yours, heart-shaped and pale and beautiful. I would leave Heaven and go to Hell for your kiss, and be glad. Kiss me now—'

And then I will take the wooden sword, for wood is fatal to all vampires of whatever age, I will take the wooden sword and I will ...

THE OLD MAN'S STORY

by

Walter Starkie

It was now dark, and I determined to spend the night in the open, for the air was balmy and the moon made the country look like fairyland. In the daytime the meadows looked parched, the roads were dusty and the heat was exhausting, but at night on the Hungarian plain there was a delightful, cool breeze and everything in nature seemed to awaken to life. The moonlight shining through the trees carved everything into queer, fantastic shapes. In some places the white light made the foliage look like silver filigree work; in other places the branches became shadowy, ghostly forms. It is difficult to explain in definite words the sensation of mystery and romance that the wayside traveller finds in Hungary. The scenery seen by the light of day is uninteresting, for the whole country is just a huge plain. But at night in the moonlight the fields of corn, the clumps of trees, the little knolls here and there become meeting-places of fairies. It is the mixture of races that has given to this countryside its poetical charm. To the Magyar mind all that country is inhabited by invisible beings that spring to life when the sun goes down, and I have met peasants who were afraid to wander in the light of the moon for, as they said, the fevers descend on the earth when the moon rides in the sky. The primitive Magyar is pantheistic in his attitude towards nature and translates this sentiment into the little folk-poems he improvises to the sound of his rustic flute or the Gipsy's fiddle. The Hungarian projects his personality on to his external surroundings. The forest is in mourning because his love lies on her deathbed; Sari has sowed violets and awaits their growing because they symbolize the home-coming of her lover; the shepherd tending his flocks by the Tiza river looks up at the starry sky and thinks of his mother far away in Transylvania or his sister sweeping her room with rosemary boughs. In the northern countries of Europe the scenery is more majestic than the Hungarian plain, but the peasants do not look on their country through the veil of their own folk-lore or folk-music, nor do they associate each legend and melody with definite events in their country's history to the same extent as the Magyar does. Every step that the lonely traveller makes through the plain is accompanied by songs, dirges and dances until his mind echoes and re-echoes to a mighty symphony composed of countless fragmentary tunes.

I halted for the night at the foot of a knoll where there was a small rustic graveyard nestling peacefully in the moonlight. At the back of a big sheltering tombstone I made a fire of twigs and prepared to bivouac in Gipsy style in this desolate spot, feeling sure that no one would come to disturb me in a cemetery. I had some cheese and bread in my rucksack and my wine-skin was full. As the night continued and the fire burnt low I began to feel acute melancholy and loneliness. I was sorry that I had chosen a graveyard for a bivouacking ground, for graveyards brought thoughts of vampires and werewolves to the mind. I tried to dispel this attack of the shivers by music, but my violin sounded harsh and discordant like a *danse macabre*. I nearly dropped the bow in terror, for all of a sudden there was a soft whirr of wings and something brushed past my face: it was a bat. Round and round the bat circled like a spirit of evil omen and I thought of 'Dracula' and shuddered.

When I settled down I found that sleeping out of doors, even on the torrid plain of Hungary, is not an unmixed enjoyment for the traveller whose skin is not as weather-beaten as that of a gipsy. The night became for me a series of hopeless struggles with mosquitoes and every other species of stinging insect. As long as the fire was burning merrily the insects gave me a wide berth, but later on in the shadows of the night I heard the ominous high note like the tuning of countless violins by a phantom orchestra and the hordes began their descent upon my unarmed flesh. Soon I felt my face swell under their attacks and sleep became an impossibility. At night, too, in Hungary, in contrast to the day, there were spells of cold and the sleeper in the open would feel his limbs stiffen. When I lie awake in the country all my senses become extraordinarily keen and sensitive to sounds. On that night I understood how the Hungarian peasants people their country graveyards with vampires: I heard the crackling of twigs and I imagined I saw two fiery eyes gleaming at me from behind some bushes. Then something dark darted beside my leg and I fancied it was a rat. Even in normal life at home the proximity of a rat would fill me with a sickening anguish, but here I felt inclined to shriek my helplessness. Another distressing feature of outdoor sleeping was the prevalence of such crawling beasts as earwigs and woodlice, not to mention the sprightly flea. When I started to doze in a short period of respite from the mosquito orchestra, I felt an ominous tickling sensation on my neck. I found that a legion of ants was advancing in extended order over my body.

After a dreamless sleep I woke suddenly at the sound of a dog yelping near by. When I looked up above my tombstone I saw at the other side of the cemetery a light burning over one of the graves. For a moment I thought that I was still wandering through the halls of sleep, but then the horrible thought struck me that I might have been unlucky enough to enter a vampire-haunted graveyard. The yelping of dogs and the flickering lights over graves were sure signs of the dreaded vampire. My first thought was to take to my heels, but the whole scene seemed so eerie and unreal that my feelings of curiosity overmastered my fear and I stood my ground. The flickering light came nearer and nearer: I then saw that it was a small lantern carried by an old man who was hobbling on a stick and tugging after him at the end of a rope the dog I had heard yelping. He was a strange little old man like one of the goblins in Grimm's fairy stories. He walked with bent shoulders and his long white beard nearly touched the ground. His clothes were ragged and grimy, but here and there they were patched up with pieces of gaudy colours. So loosely did this ragged raiment hang on his cadaverous form that he seemed to be clothed in a garment of reeds mixed with the plumage of birds. So emaciated was his face that he looked like the figure of death in the mediaeval masquerade. He hobbled over to me and rasped out some unintelligible words in Magyar. I then answered in German and he continued in the latter language. 'What are you doing in this graveyard?' said he. 'Don't you know that the tomb you are resting on is haunted by a nach-toeher? When I saw you in the distance I took you for one of them and I made the sign of the Cross to drive you away. Look here, *mein Herr*, look on that tombstone and you will see two holes: that is the sign that the tomb is inhabited by a vampire: at any moment before dawn it might fly forth and attack you. Have you no garlic upon you to stop up those holes and prevent the foul demon from coming out?' The little old man's voice rose to a shriek as he spoke and his eyes were those of a madman. 'I tell you no one can escape those vampires once they begin to go after you: I have striven for years to escape their visitation, but they have taken everything I have in the world and they would take me were it not for my prayers.' So saying he pulled out of his coat a crucifix of black wood and blessed himself, muttering prayers in a low voice all the while. As he prayed, the dog kept up an accompaniment of snarling and growling, as though it was terrified of something. The old man then called out to the dog trying to soothe it, but the beast slunk behind him and began to tremble violently. 'Look at my dog,' said the old man; 'he knows the werewolves are about and he won't approach that grave.'

For a long time we stood motionless by the tomb, while the old man continued to ramble on in his rasping voice and told me his story. From time to time I had to interrupt him to say that the fire had burnt low and that it was necessary to add sticks. I was terrified to stay listening to stories of vampires without the protection of a fire, for the old man's superstitious nature had already infected me and I felt that all this experience had something supernatural about it. We sat by the fire and the old man's voice gradually droned me into a state of drowsiness and my eyes would close involuntarily. Then he would whine out in a shriller tone and I would awake with a start.

'You wonder why I talk about vampires. My story will show you that I have good cause to fear their terrible vengeance.

'I was born in a village near Budapest, of peasant stock. As a young man I left my homestead and wandered afar, taking the rough with the smooth. I fought in the Turkish War of 1878, and as a legacy was left a wound which crippled my left leg, as you see. The soldier's life in those far-off days was a cruel one, and more than once I thought my greatcoat was to be my shroud. From being a soldier I became a commercial traveller and wandered from village to village in Turkey and Bulgaria. It was at the town of Rustchuk that I met a very beautiful Bulgarian farmer's daughter and paid court to her. I married her and we came to settle down in Hungary in the town of Szeged. Three children we had, a boy and two girls. The boy, who was called Sándor, grew into as fine and strapping a youth as you would see any day: why, he was as reckless and dare-devil as a young colt on the Hortobágy. Aye, it was horses ruined him, for he would wander off with dealers and the copers and there was no holding him at all. I was glad the day came when he put on the grey uniform and I thought army discipline would tame his spirit. After his service he returned home, bringing with him a stranger whom he introduced to the family as his benefactor. He confided to me that the stranger had helped him on more occasions than one when he was in difficulties through gaming debts and had lavished money on him. Naturally we all welcomed the stranger as the friend of Sándor, and he soon looked upon our house as a home. At first I was astonished at Sándor's infatuation for the stranger, seeing that he was at least twenty years older, but then I saw that it was the older man who pursued the younger. He monopolized my son's attention: not a thought would come into the latter's head which was not inspired by the stranger, and from being a wild, irresponsible youth he turned into a silent and thoughtful man, always day-dreaming. The stranger had something Mephistophelian about his appearance; he was tall and thin, with acquiline features and a small pointed beard. His eyes were strained and had a wild look in them like those of a cigány: his mouth coarse and brutal, with very red lips, and when he spoke he would frequently lick them and show his teeth, which were brilliantly white and sharply pointed like those of a dog or wolf.

He was the life and soul of our family, for he had a soft, caressing manner, in spite of his sudden fits of passion when his eyes would blaze and he would show his canine teeth. He would come and visit us in the afternoon and delight us by his many accomplishments. He was the man of the world and we were the humble village folk whom he was pleased to honour. There was something fantastic about the stranger who had travelled all over the world enduring exciting adventures, and Julcsa, my eldest daughter, would call him the fairy prince, and she said that he was sent to our house by the Délibáb or Fata Morgana. We never knew when he would come, for he gave us no warning of his arrival in the town. He seemed to glide in unperceived, and after some days of consecutive visits he would suddenly depart on the pretext of urgent business. I could never find out what his business was, for he contented himself with telling me that he had to travel far and wide. As time went on Julcsa became more and more attracted towards him. She would sit for hours listening to his stories of travels and he seemed to hypnotize her by his cold, piercing grey eyes. Everything about the mysterious stranger thrilled her: his brown, close-fitting squire's costume, his polished top-boots, his purple necktie, which gave him the air of an Oriental prince, his long white fingers like those of a woman, with sharp nails cut to a point. Poor Julcsa, she was distracted with love for her cavalier, and she would confess to me with tears in her eyes that she loved him madly, but she was always terrified lest he might one day vanish away into the distance like Lohengrin on his fairy swan.

'My wife had always looked with misgivings on the stranger in spite of all his charm. "He is an adventurer," she cried, "and he will seduce our Julcsa and then depart in the night like a thief." In my mind I agreed with her, but I sympathized with Julcsa. When we tried to reason with Julcsa there were tears and lamentations. I could see she was hopelessly infatuated and I was afraid she might do something desperate. The best course seemed to me to say farewell to the stranger and forbid him to visit our house any more. Our leave-taking was stormy, and I saw a look of demoniacal hate in his grey eyes and his mouth was twisted into a grimace of sardonic triumph. In order to distract Julcsa's thoughts from her sufferings we closed our house and went to live for a while in the country near Temesvár.

'One night when all the household had retired to rest and all was as still as the grave, I heard the sound of horses' hoofs clattering on the road. The night was dark and misty, but when I looked out of the window I saw dimly in the distance a carriage drawn by four black horses galloping away in a cloud of dust. I was naturally superstitious and the sight of those four black horses paralysed me with horror, for I knew they were of evil omen. My first impulse was to rush into Julcsa's room. She was not there. The bed was tossed and one of the sheets twisted into a rope hung from the window. On the table I found a note saying: "Dearest Father and Mother. Forgive me for what I am doing and pray for my soul. Julcsa."

'I cannot describe for you the grief of all of us. We searched high and low, we informed the police, we searched the country for miles round, but no definite news did we get of Julcsa. As so often happens in such cases of disappearance, many came forward to say that they had seen her here or there, accompanied by an elderly man, but the clues led to nothing. As for my wife, she was convinced that Julcsa had been carried away by a vampire and what agonized her more than the loss of her eldest daughter was the terrifying thought that Julcsa if she once came into the power of a vampire would turn into one herself. "The stranger was a vampire," she cried. "Did you notice his pointed teeth, his red lips? The four black horses were his and he now possesses her body and soul. When he has sucked her blood she will become as he is and haunt us to our ruin." She spent her whole day in prayer. Each moment she thought she heard poor Julcsa crying out and she fancied that Julcsa would appear in the night in the form of a bat to haunt her remaining daughter Sari or else Sándor. She hung crucifixes in every room and at night she would insist on hanging garlic leaves over Sari's and Sándor's bed to protect them. Her mind gave way and she would wander aimlessly round the house with a vacant stare on her face calling out Julcsa's name and blessing herself as though to exorcise her. Some months after that I followed her hearse to the cemetery.

'As for Sándor, he left home after his mother's death and I was left alone with Sari in our house of mourning. From time to time Sándor wrote to me telling me of his life. He had obtained employment as a clerk in an office in Budapest and from his letters I inferred that he was satisfied with his humdrum life. Then for a long time I had no news of him until one day a letter came telling me to go at once to him as he was seriously ill. When I arrived at Budapest I went straight to his lodgings and I found him lying in a filthy room looking as if he would die any minute. He was as white as a sheet and he could just open his eyes and give me a sad, weary smile. The doctor, who was standing by his bedside, told me that Sándor had not many days to live for he was in the last stages of galloping consumption. All the life seemed to be ebbing fast from my son. At times he would cry out faintly for Julcsa and he told me of a strange dream he had had. He dreamt he met her outside the arched gate of a city and she stood within the arch and beckoned to him to enter. She was dressed in dazzling white and looked radiantly beautiful and happy, but her face was as white as her dress and her lips were like a scarlet wound. She beckoned again and again to him, but though he strove hard he was unable

to cross the threshold of the gate. Then he awoke in a state
of terrible anguish, and he felt so weak that he thought he
was going to die. He could not understand the reason why
he had felt so sad, for the dream had been a happy one and
Julcsa had seemed so radiant. Night after night the dream
repeated itself and on each awakening he would feel the
sense of overwhelming weakness. Then one night in the
dream she had drawn him through the arch and he had
followed her through the town and along a road until they
came to a clump of trees where he saw grey tombstones
dotted about. Sándor used to rave for hours incoherently,
trying to recall the place where he had seen the tombstones.
"If I could only remember the name I should know where
to find Julcsa," he cried. Each day he became weaker in
spite of the doctor's treatment and the drugs that he con-
sumed. But I knew that all the medicine in the world would
be of no avail, for it was Julcsa's spirit which was consuming him. Just as my dear wife had done, I placed garlic
plants about his bed and a crucifix over his head. At night
I never left him alone and I would watch him tossing about
in the bed trying in vain to find peace. There was a look
of wild yearning in his face and he would mutter the name
of Julcsa again and again. I knew that he was hypnotized
by her spirit as a humming-bird is by the snake's eye. Every
prayer that came into my mind I said over him and every
incantation I had learnt from old gipsy women, but it was
in vain. At a certain moment of the night I would feel
drowsy, and a mist would gather before my eyes. After doz-
ing off momentarily I would awake. Sándor would be sleeping peacefully, but his face would look still more deathly
than before and from the corners of his mouth I saw a thin
stream of blood trickle down his white neck. Each hour I
watched by his deathbed became more terrifying than the
last, for I watched him gradually change from my poor,
dying son into the deathless vampire, ready to work evil on
others. Then one night in the midst of a troubled sleep he
suddenly shrieked out: "The tombstones, the tombstones:
I know where they are: I can see the trees and the low

wall. The name of the town is Lepsény. Go through the town and then along the long road mile after mile until you come to the graveyard." When he awoke he was so exhausted that he would not speak and he did not remember his dream. But my mind was made up. I determined to seek out the graveyard and discover Julcsa's tomb and rid the world of the terrible vampire. After handing over the care of Sándor to a trusted relative I set out from Budapest accompanied by an old gipsy woman I had known for many years. She was to be my confederate in the grim task which lay before me. She was one of the *cohalyi*, as the Gipsies call the witches in Hungary, and as we tramped along the road she muttered incantations in the intervals of giving me advice how to rid myself of the vampire pest. When we reached Lepsény we turned back along the road and after a weary search we came to this cemetery where you and I are seated now, and I discovered that it tallied with the description my son had given in his dream. Tomb after tomb we examined and after a long search we came to one in a corner on whose stone the name Julcsa was engraved in big letters. She had died the year before. How had she died? Who had closed her eyes? Did she die in poverty and if so who had raised the tombstone over her grave? Who knows?

'The night after I had discovered the grave I returned with the old woman to carry out my grim task of liberation. It was a stormy night, the wind was whistling through the trees, and rain and sleet lashed our faces. No moon was shining and I thanked God for that. A moon would have exposed our sinister work and perhaps drawn the suspicious peasantry after us. At midnight I started to dig down into the grave while the old woman stood by and muttered incantations. After digging for some time I knocked with my spade against the coffin. The sound of the spade striking the coffin filled me with such horror that I nearly fainted, but the old woman called sternly to me to break open the lid with the spade. With difficulty I did as she commanded, and when I had wrenched open the lid I gazed on all that remained of my poor Julcsa. For a moment I thought I was the victim of an hallucination, for Julcsa looked as if she were sleeping peacefully. Over her eyes there was spread a filmy substance and her lips were bright red as though she had recently fed on a loathsome repast in the land of the living. Again I hesitated, for my eyes were riveted on the corpse in the coffin. Again the old woman's sharp voice broke in upon my meditation: "Make haste and use this knife. You must cut her head off and bury it in another part of the cemetery. If you do that her spirit will trouble you and your family no more." The old hag with these words handed me a sharp knife she had brought with her and straightaway began to gather twigs to make a fire near by. Hardening my heart I tried to do her bidding, but my strength failed me. The witch then seized the knife from my hands and with one slash severed the head from the trunk. I shut my eyes, but it seemed to me as if the corpse moaned and the blood spurted over me. After fastening down the coffin lid and piling the earth over it we buried the head in the opposite side of the cemetery, and we departed on our way towards Budapest. Before she took leave of me the old woman said: "Be sure to go back to that cemetery and pour wine on the grave of your daughter, for there is nothing like wine for laying the ghost to rest." When I reached my son's bedside I found him at death's door, but he had no longer the wild look in his eye, only a serene peace, and he was just able to beg my prayers before he died. I buried him in the same cemetery as his sister, and once every month I come to visit the two graves. Tonight when I came in here I was frightened when I saw the fire, and I was afraid someone might have discovered my secret.'

The old man, after finishing his story, led me over to the opposite side of the graveyard, where he pointed to a recently erected tombstone, and on it I read the name Sándor.

Dawn was now breaking and the air was grey and misty. The old man, pulling his dog after him, and I made our way out of the cemetery. At the top of the hill I saw a woman coming towards us. The old man said to me when he saw her: 'There is my daughter Sari: she always comes to fetch me after my long night's vigil.' The woman when she came near us ran up to the old man and kissed him. I then saw them depart on their way towards Lepsény.

サラリーマンは、二度会社を辞める。

楠木 新